Lestrade and the Brother of Death

Volume VII in the Lestrade Mystery Series

M.J. Trow

A Gateway Mystery

REGNERY
PUBLISHING, INC.

Since 1947 • An Eagle Publishing Company

Library of Congress Cataloging-in-Publication Data

Trow, M.J.
      Lestrade and the brother of death / M.J. Trow
         p.   cm. — (Lestrade mystery series ; v. 7)
      ISBN 0-89526-268-1
      I. Title. II. Series: Trow, M.J. Sholto Lestrade mystery series ; v. 7.
PR6070.R598L46 1999
823'.914—dc21   99-41316
                                                        CIP

Published in the United States by
Regnery Publishing, Inc.
An Eagle Publishing Company
One Massachusetts Avenue, NW
Washington, DC 20001

Originally published in Great Britain

Distributed to the trade by
National Book Network
4720-A Boston Way
Lanham, MD 20706

Printed on acid-free paper
Manufactured in the United States of America

10 9 8 7 6 5 4 3 2 1

Books are available in quantity for promotional or premium use. Write to Director of Special Sales, Regnery Publishing, Inc., One Massachusetts Avenue, NW, Washington, DC 20001, for information on discounts and terms or call (202) 216-0600.

The character of Inspector Lestrade was created by the late Sir Arthur Conan Doyle and appears in the Sherlock Holmes stories and novels by him, as do some other characters in this book.

Care-charming sleep, thou easer of all woes,
Brother to Death
JOHN FLETCHER (1579–1625)

Contents

Death of a Butler

The superintendent stood on the promenade deck, whence all but he had fled to the side. He had checked his berth, though there were those at Scotland Yard who doubted that he'd had one, believing merely that he had been created in Plod's own image, Donegalled and bowler-hatted ready for the race against crime. He fought his way through the happy laughing first-class travellers, feeling decidedly steerage about the whole thing, and saw the sun glinting on Southampton Water.

'I'm going to my cabin, Lestrade,' Stead told him, and the journalist disappeared below the water-line.

Sholto Lestrade, superintendent, reached the rail and looked down. In the mass of boaters and bonnets, below the streaming bunting, he made out his nearest and dearest – and Sergeant Blevvins. There was Emma, his daughter, a picture as always in velvet and satin, her golden hair swaying with the breeze, her eyes, he knew, a little hot and wet. There was Harry Bandicoot, his faithful friend, stolid, still golden after all these years, still the Old Etonian; and Letitia, his wife, who had mothered Emma since she was a baby. There was Chief Inspector Dew, bowler-hatted and Donegalled in the time-honoured tradition. He had his instructions from Lestrade. Carry on with the book on Crippen and pass all major cases to Inspector John Kane. Dew understood. He followed orders to the letter. 'Initiative' was not written on his heart, nor could the upright Remington at the Yard hammer out the word. And then there was Fanny. Fanny Berkeley, whom Lestrade had known since she was a girl.

He smiled broadly, between the bowler and the Donegal.
Minutes ago the girl had proposed to him – it *was* a Leap Year,
this Year of Our Lord 1912 – and he had accepted, though the
ship's siren had drowned his answer and he wasn't sure she had
heard.

In the mean time there was duty. The great engines, which
had been throbbing for some time, roared into life and the band
struck up 'Rule, Britannia' as the White Star's *Titanic* slipped her
moorings and rolled for the sea. Lestrade had told them all this
was a holiday, a much needed break. William Stead knew better.
He was bound for a peace conference in New York, one of the
few men in England who might hold the bickering chancelleries
of Europe together before they blew each other into a million
pieces. There had been one attempt on Stead's life already, and
Lestrade was there to see there were no more. He wouldn't have
wanted Walter Dew to know, but he had never been further
west than the Lizard in his life and he wasn't exactly relishing the
prospect now.

Cheers rose from the quay, and Lestrade leaned out to wave,
when something – was it the weight of his moustache? the cut of
his bowler? – *something* had caused the crosswinds to catch him
and he plummeted over the side in mid-wave. As the decks
flashed by him, one by one, he thought to himself: so far, so
good. Then the water hit him like a brick wall, and he felt a
numbing pain in his leg.

His life flashed before him – a book now closed, now open.
Briefly, he saw panic ripple the watchers on the quayside and
figures running in all directions. He noticed as he surfaced for
the third time that Sergeant Blevvins was running *away* from the
water. He wouldn't forget that. Then the undertow of *Titanic*
caught him and he was carried down, his legs pinned by the
weight of the water. He struggled to wriggle out of the clinging
shroud of his Donegal, but his breath had been knocked out of
him by the fall and he knew he didn't have long.

Then he felt something strong and safe lifting him up, and the
grey-blue of the sky broke again on his eyes. He craned his neck

to see the effortlessly swimming Harry Bandicoot, his left arm crooked under Lestrade's, striking out for the shore.

'I thought it would be you, Harry,' Lestrade spluttered.

'One life to the sea is enough, Sholto,' Bandicoot answered, remembering his son, who had drowned off another coast, falling from another ship.

'I meant, what with your boxing and shooting talents, I knew you wouldn't neglect a little thing like swimming.'

'Well, when you've sculled for Eton . . . ,' Bandicoot explained, dragging Lestrade behind him.

'It's not supposed to be *my* body between your knees, is it?' Lestrade asked.

'Oh, sorry, Sholto.' Bandicoot relaxed his grip.

For a moment, Lestrade was under the impression that Bandicoot was actually trying to catch *Titanic* and perhaps hurl the saturated superintendent the hundred feet or so up on to the deck. But the moment passed as moments do, and Lestrade passed out.

He spent as little time as possible in the draughty hospital ward they put him in. Because his ieg was broken and staff reminded him they couldn't be too careful with a man at that funny age, he was strapped on to a medieval rack and wheeled into the cheerless porticoes of St Bledsoe's. He was even more disconcerted by the apparitions in black and white who attended him night and day. They were Ursulines apparently, but Lestrade thought they were actually women, deep down. Time passed slowly. His days were spent staring at the yellow face of the old man opposite and praying it wasn't his turn for the blanket bath again. Surely Sister had been a strong man in a circus? Miss Nightingale must be turning in her grave.

Lestrade never thought he would actually welcome visits from Sergeant Blevvins of H Division, but they and those of Fanny Berkeley were the only things that kept him sane. She fussed around him, arranging his flowers, plumping his pillows and talking of the arrangements for their forthcoming nuptials.

Lestrade began to have secret doubts as to how serviceable he would be on the honeymoon, and it was as well for Blevvins that Lestrade had not heard the sergeant's comments on Miss Berkeley's intention to marry in white.

She had arrived one evening, late in May, to find the superintendent of her dreams arching his back and jerking around on the ropes which held his leg skyward.

'My dearest' – she flung the flowers at a passing vase and knelt by his side – 'is the pain terrible?'

'Pain be damned,' snarled Lestrade. 'It's the itch, Fanny.'

Blevvins would have made something of that, but Fanny Berkeley looked bemused. Lestrade suddenly tautened, his eyes fixing on a point above Fanny's head.

'What a charming hat,' he hissed.

'Why, thank you, Sholto. You do say the nicest things.'

'I particularly like the hatpin,' Lestrade went on. 'And I'd particularly like it down here.' He motioned to his thigh, encased in plaster.

'Sholto,' Fanny blushed, 'I'm not that sort of girl.'

'Fanny,' Lestrade grimaced, 'this is no time to be coy. If you love me at all, give me that pin.'

She sat on his bed. She looked at him, at the earnest pleading face. She glanced to left and to right. And then, in one fluid movement, whipped out the lethal pin, reversed it and plunged the mother-of-pearl under Lestrade's nightshirt and down his plaster. The yellow man across the ward blinked in disbelief at the sight of Fanny's arm under the bedclothes and the glazed look on Lestrade's face. He felt his heart flutter and turned his face to the wall, just in case.

Lestrade snatched Fanny's arm.

'What is it?' she asked.

'It's come off.'

'What?'

'Pull the pin out,' Lestrade said.

She did. The mother-of-pearl top was not with it. Instead, it was lodged securely somewhere between Lestrade's leg and Lestrade's plaster. Another of life's little ups and downs.

* * *

He crossed off the days on a mental calendar until they let him out. Flanked by Fanny on one side and her father on the other, Lestrade hobbled to the waiting landau.

'Nonsense, Sholto.' Tom Berkeley was adamant. 'Fanny has made all the arrangements. You're staying with us. It'll be a marvellous chance to relive old times.'

'But the Yard. . . .'

'Tut, tut,' Berkeley clucked like a mother hen, 'it won't go away. None of us is indispensable, you know.'

'I've never believed that, Tom.' Lestrade surfaced from the giant eiderdown that Fanny was attempting to smother him with. 'We're talking about Sir Edward Henry, don't forget.'

'Frank Froest's in charge of the Serious Crimes Squad. He will keep an eye on the Assistant Commissioner, and you've got as good a bunch of inspectors as you're likely to get.'

'Pa's right, Sholto. You need the rest. One hot-water bottle or two?'

'None, thank you. I may have a broken leg, Fanny Berkeley, but I'm not ready for my grave just yet.'

Berkeley signalled to his driver, and the state landau of the chief constable of Surrey jolted forward, causing Lestrade to yelp with less than the decorum befitting a superintendent of Scotland Yard. He spent the rest of the journey chewing the rim of his bowler.

'I thought this would be a smoother ride than the Southern Railway,' Berkeley yelled above the wind and the jingle of harness.

Lestrade attempted to turn his grimace of agony into a smile. Fanny wrapped her arm around his and patted his encased leg. By the time they reached Petersfield both Berkeleys were sleeping peacefully. Only Lestrade and arguably the driver remained wakeful, both watching the road for slightly different reasons.

The evening was cheerier. Fanny had obtained a Bath chair, and Lestrade found its mechanics straightforward. Straight backwards was a little trickier. Such was his mastery of the machine that by midnight he had only smashed three vases, half-crippled the butler and the tweenie – they were in the same broom-cupboard at the time – and carried out unspeakable privations on the family cat. The superintendent was profuse in his apologies, but the cat in particular was an unforgiving beast and sat for the duration of his stay fixing Lestrade with its smouldering eye.

Fanny sat on the sofa, curled up as far as the plaster housings would allow against Lestrade's lap. Her father had retired early, whether by design or by exhaustion, and Lestrade breathed in the fragrance of the girl's hair.

'You know,' he said, 'there are those who will point a finger at us.'

'Oh?' She sat up to face him. 'Why?'

'Because I'm old enough to be your father.'

She tapped him playfully with a crochet-hook. 'Stuff and nonsense, Sholto. I am thirty years old and, according to dear Pa, not merely on the shelf but a positive bracket holding it up.'

Lestrade chuckled. 'Did he say that? Same rotten old bastard he always was. Begging your pardon of course, my love. I wonder he ever became Chief Constable at all.'

'Why?'

'Oh, he's a damned good copper, is Tom Berkeley. But I've always presumed chief constables have a certain suavity, a certain glibness of tongue. The Tom Berkeley I knew always called a spade a spade – or a shelf-bracket.'

She turned again to the dying embers. 'How does he seem to you?'

'Seem?' He craned his arm round to reach his brandy-glass.

'He's worried, Sholto. I can always tell. He's been calling me Hannah a lot recently. Whenever he's worried he uses Mamma's name.'

'What do you think it is?'

Fanny shook her head. 'I don't know. The job, I'm sure. But exactly what . . . I don't know.'

'Would you like me to talk to him?'

She tucked herself further into the hollow of his arm. 'Bless you, darling,' she said. 'You know, I'm a lucky woman. The two men I love most in all the world, here, tight around me. I feel . . . safe.' She sat up again. 'Do *you* feel safe, Sholto?'

He smiled, squinted sideways at the cat, and the smile froze.

The news that screamed from the banner headlines next morning knocked the legs from under him. Or it would have, were he not strapped to the Bath chair.

'Fanny!' he roared.

The door crashed back to reveal Mrs M'Travers, armed with brass spray-container. 'Where is the little terror, sir?' she asked.

Lestrade looked around him. 'Who, Mrs M'Travers?'

'The fly, sir. I naturally assumed from the urgency of your cry that you were being bothered by one.'

'Thank you, no.' Lestrade thought it best to humour her. 'I was looking for Miss Berkeley.'

'Oh, she's not as good as I am in these matters, sir' – and began to squirt a fine spray into Lestrade's face.

'Thank you, Mrs M'Travers.' Fanny came to the rescue in the nick of time as Lestrade's eyes crossed and swirled. She shooed the domestic away. 'What is it, Sholto? Was that woman badgering you?'

'Yes' – Lestrade wiped his streaming cheeks – 'but that wasn't why I called. Have you seen *The Times* this morning?'

'No, I haven't.' She kissed him tenderly. 'Stalker fetches it from the village. He shouldn't be long.'

Lestrade was exasperated. 'No, I mean, have you read what's in *The Times* this morning?'

Fanny looked at him.

'Look.' He snatched the paper up. 'It's the *Titanic,* Fanny. She's gone down.'

'Gone down?' Fanny scanned the headlines. 'But that's impossible, Sholto. She was unsinkable.'

'So they claimed. Fanny . . . William Stead?' He had not read the smaller print.

She let the paper fall. 'Fifteen hundred souls lost, Sholto; his among them.'

'So he was right,' Lestrade murmured. 'There'll be no stopping it now.'

'Stopping what, Sholto?'

'It says an iceberg, doesn't it?'

'Yes. The ship hit an iceberg. Stopping what?'

'A war, Fanny. Stead was one of the few men with the ability to keep the peace in Europe. Now he's gone. . . .'

'Oh, Sholto. . . .' She flung herself into his lap. 'It could have been you,' she sobbed. 'If you hadn't fallen . . . I could be reading your name in those lists.'

He stroked her hair and kissed away her tears. 'I really *am* unsinkable,' he said.

M'Travers couldn't remember a hotter May. He blamed the comet that had lit the sky a couple of years ago. Mrs M'Travers blamed that rash expedition led by that brave Captain Scott. Chrissie, the downstairs maid, blamed Mrs M'Travers for the close watch she kept on her and M'Travers. The Berkeleys' cat no doubt blamed Lestrade.

And on Lestrade's first day with the Berkeleys M'Travers pushed the Bath chair on to the terrace and Lestrade took over from there, the butler walking dutifully in the rear with a flask of lemonade. Tom Berkeley had brought his Westley-Richards to bag a pheasant for supper. The day was leaden grey, taunting with its promise of rain. The buds seemed to have burst forth, rejoicing in the heat.

'Come on, Sholto. Last one to the coppice is a cottage loaf.'

'You wouldn't say that if I had two good legs,' Lestrade chaffed him.

'There, there, my dear chap' – Berkeley patted the superintendent's shoulder – 'I never believed the rumours. M'Travers, load up, there's a good fellow.'

Berkeley threw the twelve-bore to his butler, who deftly caught it while pocketing the flask – a manoeuvre born of years of handling downstairs maids in broom-cupboards and fruit-cellars.

'Feel up to a few pots, Sholto?' Berkeley asked.

But before Lestrade could answer there was a roar behind

them which rocked Berkeley on his feet. As he turned, M'Travers's blood slashed in a crimson arc across his Norfolk jacket and Lestrade's Bath chair hurtled forward over the tussocks. The superintendent wrestled manfully with the controls, but the chair bucked and slewed its way over the turf, to bounce and crunch into a clump of yews near the lake, its left wheel spinning sonorously under the startled screeching of the mallards.

Tom Berkeley arrived at a run. 'Sholto, Sholto, are you all right?'

Lestrade's withering eye shot his old friend a deadly look from under the battered bowler and the shawl which had somehow wrapped itself around his head. Berkeley hauled superintendent and machine upright and wheeled them both back up the hill.

'No damage done,' said Lestrade, checking the wheels as they went.

'That's not exactly true,' said Berkeley, motioning ahead. The butler lay sprawled in the morning dew, the shattered Westley-Richards smoking beside him. There was a large bloody cavity where his chest had been.

'What happened?' Lestrade wheeled his chair around to draw level with the body.

'Damnedest thing,' said Berkeley, visibly shocked. 'The gun must have gone off as he was loading it. God, where will I get a new butler at this time of year?'

Lestrade knew Tom Berkeley well enough to know he wasn't that callous, but he *was* a copper. He thought with a copper's mind. To Lestrade something didn't sit right.

'Used to guns, was he, M'Travers?' he asked, poking the remains gingerly with his stick.

'Tolerably,' muttered Berkeley.

'Tom,' Lestrade growled a warning, 'was he used to guns?'

Berkeley set off at a trot for the house, calling back over his shoulder. 'I'll get help,' he shouted. 'Fanny will have to cope with Mrs M'Travers. God knows, I can't.'

Lestrade craned over to compensate for the leg, leaned too far and fell nose-to-nose with the deceased. He was used to the Sights – the rotting corpse in Shanklin Chine, the Ripper's rituals in Whitechapel – but in all his long and grisly career he had never actually lain down with the dead. It unnerved him somewhat, but not as much as it unnerved Fanny Berkeley, who now appeared on the terrace. She saw the bodies, the overturned Bath chair.

'Pa,' she screamed, 'you lied to me. It's Sholto!' – and she raced off across the grass, hitching up her skirts as she ran, the chief constable rushing in the opposite direction in search of the Amazon that was the Widow M'Travers. As Fanny reached the prone policeman and the blasted butler, Lestrade thrust out an arm for her to pull him up. The shock proved too great, and Fanny, unusually perhaps for a policeman's daughter, fainted gracefully away. When Berkeley arrived with his housekeeper in hot pursuit, the orchard below the house looked like a battlefield. The chief constable was at a loss to explain it. Mrs M'Travers howled like a demented she-wolf, collapsing on to her knees.

'Stalker!' he bellowed back into the house. The constable of that name emerged from the breakfast room, tugging on his helmet. When Berkeley saw his daughter move, he mellowed a little. 'Dear Stalker' – he turned to the constable again – 'get Mrs M'Travers away from here, will you? I asked her not to come out.'

The constable wrestled with the sobbing woman for a while, and when she had given up the struggle she allowed him to escort her back indoors. Berkeley supervised as his gardeners carried first Fanny, then Lestrade, then M'Travers into the house. The daughter was wrapped in her bed, the guest was propped back in his chair. The ex-butler was laid out on the billiard-table.

'What's going on, Tom?' Lestrade was still brushing the dew from his jacket and wondering where his bowler was.

'An accident.' Tom Berkeley was pouring himself a large brandy. 'A tragic accident.'

Lestrade held up the broken shotgun he had been trying to

reach when he had fallen beside the deceased. 'I've been a policeman for more years than I care to remember, Tom. So have you. You know more about these guns than I do. I'll wager M'Travers did, too. A little early, isn't it?' He motioned to Berkeley's balloon.

'Dammit, Sholto. My butler has just been blown in half, and you're complaining about my drinking!'

The silence hung between them like a shroud.

'Indulge me for a moment.' Lestrade turned the ratchet, and his lethal machine squeaked towards Berkeley. He held up the barrels of the Westley-Richards. 'Isn't the idea that the lead comes out of this end?'

Berkeley nodded hurriedly, swigging at the brandy.

'Then, why is the end blocked up?' Lestrade looked along the blued steel into blackness.

'The damned thing had a hair trigger,' Berkeley blustered.

'And M'Travers knew that, so he'd have been careful. What he couldn't have known was that the barrels were blocked.'

'What do you want from me, Sholto?' Berkeley grated through clenched teeth.

Lestrade smashed the barrels down hard on the sideboard, making the decanters jump. 'An honest answer, dammit! An acceptance from you that what happened out there just now was not an accident.'

Berkeley's glass hesitated in his hand. 'Not?' he muttered.

Lestrade sighed and wheeled the chair away, taking the pretty little Ming vase with it. He turned back to Berkeley. 'This is me, Tom. Sholto Lestrade. Superintendent Lestrade.'

Nothing.

'Lestrade of the Yard.'

Still nothing.

'Your future son-in-law.'

'All right!' Berkeley threw the goblet at the empty grate. 'So someone wanted M'Travers dead.'

Lestrade looked up in surprise. 'Who?' he asked.

'Good God' – Berkeley poured himself another drink – 'you

were only fished out of the Solent a few weeks ago. You're lucky to be alive. M'Travers is still bloody warm. And you're starting an investigation. It's beyond belief!'

'We never sleep.' Lestrade shrugged. 'You know, Tom, they say doctors make the worst patients. Well, policemen make the worst witnesses. You knew M'Travers. Who would want him dead?'

Berkeley ran exasperated hands through what was left of his hair. 'I don't know,' he said.

'Mrs M'Travers?' Lestrade probed.

'Mrs . . .? Listen.' They did. From the bowels of the house, heart-rending sobs echoed and re-echoed.

'Does that sound like a murderess to you?'

'Who, then? The downstairs maid?'

'Chrissie? Oh, I know M'Travers had something of a reputation where the ladies were concerned, but why should Chrissie want to kill him? They were . . . close.'

'Jealousy?' Lestrade suggested. 'What if Chrissie was one of many? What if there were others, closer to him? What if she were pregnant?'

'Pregnant? This is 1912. Women don't kill men because they're pregnant. Oh, really, Superintendent.' Berkeley dismissed it as too fatuous.

'What about your driver?'

'Stalker? Innocent as the driven snow. He always got on well with M'Travers. With everybody.'

Lestrade changed tack. 'Who has access to your guns?'

'Gun,' Berkeley corrected him. 'Gun. I only have the one.' He was in control again, the professional policeman. 'Myself, of course. And M'Travers. He kept it oiled and ready. No one else.'

'Where was it kept?' Lestrade pirouetted in the chair, and the Dresden flower-girl shattered on the hearth.

'Here, in the cabinet.' Berkeley opened it.

'Was it kept locked?' Lestrade asked.

'Never. I'm not even sure if there's a key.'

'When did you use the gun last?'

'Er. . . .' Berkeley was trying to fight off the effects of the drink and the shock. 'Last week? No, no, the week before. I bagged a widgeon. Penhaligon was coming to dinner.'

'Penhaligon?'

'The vicar.' Berkeley was grateful for the interjection of a new thought. 'He'll be marrying you one day soon. You must meet him.'

'Yes, I must,' Lestrade nodded. 'Of course, Fanny'll take it hard. She thinks I'm marrying *her*.'

Both men did their best to laugh. Then Lestrade caught sight of the cat and decided against it.

'Sholto, we'll get to the bottom of this mess, I promise you. But at the moment there are the formalities. And with M'Travers's wandering hands there'll be an estate full of hysterical women to cope with. I'll see to Mrs M'Travers, Chrissie, Helen Winterbottom, the Adcock girls, Prudence Heycock and the Thomas triplets. Stalker will have to see the others. You'd better get up to Fanny before she wakes. She probably thinks you're dead. Stalker will help you with the stairs.'

It was afternoon when Fanny Berkeley came to. Lestrade had not used the smelling salts her father had recommended. He had merely sat in the armchair and looked at her. She was a woman half his age, and when she slept she looked younger still. He stroked her golden hair and ran his fingers over her cheek. As she woke, he diced with death by balancing over her, kissed her lips tenderly and, with an agility rare in a man with one good leg, spun back into the chair. Her eyes flickered, registering the familiar ceiling of her room, the walls, the curtains. In front of her swirling vision sat a ferret-faced man with a sallow complexion and the spring sunlight playing on the heavy moustache.

'Sholto. . . .' He quietened her cry with a kiss. She sat bolt upright, squeezing him to her, her heart thumping and the tears running down her cheeks. She checked herself and pulled herself away to stare into his steady eyes.

'What . . . happened out there?' she whispered.

He took her hands in his. 'Fanny,' he said, 'there was an accident. M'Travers was loading Tom's gun and it blew up. It killed him, I'm afraid.'

Fanny shuddered at remembrance of the bloodied corpse. Then something made her look up, and she caught the light in Lestrade's eyes.

'An accident?' she repeated.

He looked at her. She knew. 'No,' he said, 'not an accident.'

He watched her eyes widen. 'M'Travers was *murdered*?' she whispered.

Lestrade nodded. 'But that's not all of it, Fanny. Someone is trying to kill your father.'

Durham, Deceased

Lestrade had rarely seen so many women concentrated in one place at one time as were clustered, sorrowing, around the newly dug grave of the butler, M'Travers. The Widow M'Travers had become completely unhinged at her husband's untimely demise and became even more obsessed, viciously complying with the 'Kill That Fly' campaign then gripping the country. Even while the Reverend Penhaligon was helping M'Travers's passing with his handfuls of earth at the graveside, the butler's widow was seen flitting around the churchyard cheerfully committing insecticide.

'The ways of God are strange,' the vicar was heard to mutter, and Fanny Berkeley took command of the situation by removing the housekeeper's swat and leading her gently back to the house.

'Keep her away from the flypapers,' Lestrade had conjured Fanny before she left his side and busied himself attempting to fan his plaster lest it should melt in the June sunlight.

'. . . For man that is born of woman . . .,' he heard Penhaligon drone. How often had he heard those words? He tried to read the veiled faces opposite him. Nothing. Why would any of these country lasses want the chief constable dead? He motioned to Constable Stalker beside him, and at a few whispered words Tom Berkeley's driver wrote down in his ever-present notebook the names of the ladies ranged around the gaping hole in the churchyard. Even the elegant pannier dresses of the season could not disguise the fact that three of them at least were pregnant, and several of the children, forced into silence by the solemnity of the occasion, bore striking resemblance to the Late Departed.

When it was over and the burial party broke up to partake of the baked meats, Tom Berkeley wheeled Lestrade's chair below the spreading elms.

'I think it's time you two met,' he said. 'Reverend Penhaligon, Superintendent Lestrade.'

'Norman,' said the vicar, extending a limp ecclesiastical hand.

'Is it?' asked Lestrade, admiring the architecture behind the Man of God.

'Oh, no,' chuckled the vicar. '*That's* Perpendicular. *I'm* Norman.'

'Ha ha.' Lestrade tittered, slightly embarrassed at his misunderstanding. 'Sholto. Delighted to meet you.'

'And I you.' Penhaligon's other hand joined Lestrade's as though he was working the village pump. 'At last. I've heard so much about you. This is not the time to speak of it, of course.' He nodded towards the sextons hard at work with their spades. 'Be careful, Blake,' he called to one of them. 'But we have, I believe, a little matter of your forthcoming nuptials to discuss. When would you like the banns read?'

'Fanny and I have not discussed. . . .'

'Quite so, quite so,' Penhaligon intoned. 'Another time, of course.'

'Tonight, Norman,' Tom Berkeley cut in. 'Come to dinner tonight.'

'Oh, I couldn't impose, Tom. It's a bad time. Now you have no butler or housekeeper.'

'Ah, yes.' Berkeley glanced up the hill to the Georgian opulence of his house overlooking the lakes. 'I ought to let Mrs M'Travers go. But where would she end up?'

'Another night,' Penhaligon insisted.

'Very well. Er . . . next Thursday?' Berkeley suggested.

'Until then,' the vicar smiled. 'Abyssinia' – and he melted into the shadows to tend his flock.

*   *   *

Sergeant 'Buildings' Peabody stirred his tea with his pencil in the time-honoured tradition of the front-desk men at the Yard. He snapped to attention as Fanny Berkeley's arrival clattered the bell at his elbow.

'Ah,' she said archly, 'a sleeping policeman.'

Peabody cleared his throat. 'Can I help you, miss?'

'I am Fanny Berkeley.'

'Oh, yes?' The sergeant was inscrutable.

'My father is chief constable of Surrey.'

'Go on.' Peabody was as unimpressed as the granite of the tenements from whence came his sobriquet.

Fanny fumed inwardly at the arrogance of the Yard.

'I will soon be Mrs Lestrade.' It was her last barb, and it had found a home.

''Strewth!' Peabody spluttered into his mug. 'Of course, mum. Forgive me. I didn't recognise you for a moment there. Wexford!' he roared at a passing policeman.

'Sarge?' The confused constable whirled around.

'Take this lady up to Chief Inspector Dew's office at once. Savvy? Er ... it was the chief inspector you wished to see, mum?'

'It was' – Fanny giggled inwardly at this newfound power – 'and I am nobody's mum, Sergeant.'

'Quite so, Miss Berkeley.' Peabody looked suitably chastened. Er ... may I ask, how *is* the super?'

'Wonderful, Sergeant, thank you' – and she flounced in silk and taffeta to the lift.

Walter Dew, chief inspector of Scotland Yard, had gone snowy white with the strain of following other people's conversations. His moustache remained dark, however, lovingly pruned by Mrs Dew, and his eye and hand remained as firm as ever. For the past two years he had been working on his account of the Crippen case, in which both those parts of his anatomy, among others, had played leading roles. On the morning when Fanny Berkeley came to see him, he was still at the Remington, putting the final touches to chapter 1. He ordered tea for his guest in the time-honoured tradition of Lestrade, but no one quaked or moved with more than the usual speed.

'I'm afraid we have no sugar, Miss Berkeley,' Dew apologised, 'but certain constables who shall remain nameless – Dew' – he flashed out a lethal glance – 'neglected to do the shopping this morning.'

'Sorry, Dad,' a boyish whine rang through the frosted glass.

To Miss Berkeley's enquiring glance, the chief inspector nodded glumly. 'I'm afraid so, Miss Berkeley,' he said. 'Percival, my eldest. Apple of his mother's eye, of course.'

'And his father's, too, I've no doubt,' Fanny smiled.

Dew blushed a little.

'Dickens! Jones!' he bellowed. 'Get in here.'

The sergeants obliged.

'How is the guv'nor, Miss Berkeley?' they chorused.

'Not so laid up as to be unable to get round here on the double in the event of his hearing anything untoward about his sergeants,' snapped Dew, vaguely aware of having achieved a syntactical miracle.

'He is well, Sergeants, thank you,' smiled Fanny and, winking at them, 'He sends his love.'

She handed Dew a note in Lestrade's handwriting. He read it silently, trying not to move his lips. Then he scowled at Dickens and Jones. 'Miss Berkeley needs our help, gentlemen.' He paced the room with the air of a field marshal planning operations. 'A man is dead,' he said, in what he hoped was pure Lestrade. 'These' – he whipped upright the typed sheet of paper which had accompanied the superintendent's letter – 'are various ladies known to the deceased. Knowing that your one claim to police procedure and familiarity therewith is your phenon – phemon – amazing ability to regur – returg – throw up facts of mind-boggling detail, cast your peepers over this lot. Start with M'Travers – the deceased.'

Dickens and Jones looked at each other.

'Doesn't do anything for me,' said Jones. 'Does it do anything for you, Charlie?'

'Not a thing, John.'

'Any of these women, then?' Dew was irritated. 'Begging your pardon, ma'am – ladies.'

'There's an Arthur Adcock, a journalist here in London . . .,' Dickens ventured.

Fanny shook her head.

'I had a teacher called Adcock. He was a funny little t-tutor,' Jones offered.

Fanny shook her head again.

'Heycock?' Dew urged them on.

'Yes, Chief Inspector?' Jones turned to him.

Dew looked exasperated. 'The Miss Heycock of the superintendent's list.'

It was the sergeants' turn to shake their heads.

'Thomas, then?' Dew chanced.

'Well' – Dickens stroked his chin – 'one of the twelve Apostles, of course. . . .'

'An Aramaic word meaning "twin" . . .,' Jones joined him.

'Could be Thomas the Rhymer . . .,' Dickens ventured.

Dew slapped the sheet of paper down on his desk. 'This is hopeless,' he sighed. 'I'm sorry, Miss Berkeley. All I can do is run these names through the shoe-boxes and see if any of them matches, but frankly it's a long shot. I could always send Sergeant Blevvins down to make a few subtle enquiries. . . .' He noticed Fanny's face. 'No, I didn't think so. Constable Dew' – the lad promptly appeared – 'give Miss Berkeley the superintendent's mail and be quick about it.'

She thanked them with a smile and left.

There was one letter that caught Lestrade's eye, but Fanny bathed it gently and after a while he was able to read on. Amid a host of requests for Lestrade to speak at the next annual general meeting of the Haberdashers' and Milliners' Guild and several advertisements for cholera belts should the superintendent be venturing into the tropics, there was a single sheet of quarto, neatly folded and bearing the usual watermarks, which carried a single line in beautiful copperplate. It said: 'Four for the Gospel-Makers.' He checked the address: 'Lestrade, the Yard.' And the postmark: Lambeth.

'Sholto.' Fanny's voice brought him back to the moment. 'I'm sorry, my darling' – she kissed his head – 'you're obviously busy' – and she made to go.

'Fanny,' he said, getting the Bath chair into action, 'take a look at this.'

She transferred her hand quickly from the cloisonné vase she was gripping, just in case, and read the line. 'What does it mean?' she asked.

'I hoped you'd tell me,' he said. 'It was posted to me on May the eighth – that's nearly two months ago.'

'You were still at St Bledsoe's.'

He shuddered at the very name. 'What do you make of it?'

'The Gospel-Makers,' she murmured. 'Matthew, Mark, Luke and John. How odd. Is it important?'

Lestrade shrugged, and sideswiped the goldfish-bowl with his elbow. 'Some crank, I expect. We get them at the Yard from time to time.'

'Norman would know,' Fanny said.

'Norman?'

'The vicar,' she reminded him. 'He's coming to dinner tonight. He's bound to know about the Gospel-Makers.'

'All right, I'll ask him.'

The Reverend Penhaligon appeared as mystified by the missive as were Fanny and Lestrade. But the evening was convivial enough, and Fanny was the toast of the hour with her culinary arts, now that Mrs M'Travers was out of commission. The widow had spent most of the day in the kitchen preparing vast quantities of chalk and olive oil to cope with the gnat bites which were the inevitable result of her murderous attacks on the insect life of the garden.

'Fanny' – Penhaligon reached over and patted her hand – 'your tendrons is magnificent.'

Lestrade felt less than comfortable at that. After all, *he* was perhaps in a better position to judge that, and Penhaligon *was* a man of the cloth. They sat in Tom Berkeley's study, sipping his port and – all but Fanny – smoking his cigars.

'I was reminded of old Claverhouse the other day.' Penhaligon blew smoke-rings to the ceiling.

'Bonny Dundee, you mean?' Fanny had always enjoyed Scottish history.

'Bless you, no,' the vicar smiled. 'George Claverhouse, the Bishop of Durham. Of course, I'm going back a few years. You might remember the case, Sholto, for case it was, I'm afraid.'

'Claverhouse?' Lestrade's brow knotted with the effort. 'Good Lord – oh, sorry, Norman – yes, I do. Now, that *is* a long time ago.'

Penhaligon took up the tale. Lestrade listened, nodding at the memory of it, and through the swirl of the smoke and the fumes of the port his mind floated back through the years. . . .

'Constable Lestrade!' a voice barked in the gloom.

'Sir!' The young man snapped to attention. He was aware of a dark figure behind the green lamp.

'Do you know what time it is?'

The constable fumbled for his half-hunter. 'It's. . . .'

'It's six-thirty, laddie. A *real* policeman has a feel for the time, be it night or day. That's why they wrote a song about it. Which is . . .?'

'Er, "If you want to know the time, ask a policeman," sir.'

'Sing it.' The figure prowled behind the lamp.

Lestrade looked at the silhouette for confirmation, cleared his throat and broke into a noise reminiscent of a cat run over by a Bath chair.

'Thank you,' snapped the voice. 'Not a natural for the Cannon Row Glee Club, then.'

'No, sir,' Lestrade was forced to agree.

'I am Inspector William Palmer. Does that name mean anything to you?'

Lestrade looked blank. It was the start of a long career.

'My namesake was the Rugeley poisoner, hanged outside Stafford gaol on the fourteenth of June 1856.'

'I was three, sir,' Lestrade explained by way of expiation.

'I wasn't much older myself, son.' Palmer emerged from the shadows. He was in his late thirties, Lestrade guessed, with immaculately macassared hair, centre-parted, and a magnificent set of Piccadilly weepers. 'But I know my criminal history. Do you hope to be a detective one day?'

'I hadn't really thought about it, sir.'

'Well, I have, Constable, and I am about to be one.'

He whirled in front of a mirror. 'Quite elegant, this patrol jacket, but I shan't be sorry to get my best bib and tucker on. That's a nice watch.' He had spun to face Lestrade again. 'Fell off a passing cart, did it?'

'It was my father's, sir.'

'Dead?'

Lestrade nodded.

'What are your antecedents, Lestrade?'

The constable ran mentally through the possibilities. The inspector was obviously testing him. 'Would that be another name for testicles, sir?'

Palmer looked at him. 'No, Constable, it would not. I mean, what did your father do?'

'He was a policeman, sir, like me.'

Palmer's face fell. 'Not quite like you, Constable, I do hope.'

'No, sir.' Lestrade was suitably chastened.

'Right, then. As I was saying, I expect the letter from Scotland Yard any day now. Until then, it is my sorry duty to show you the ropes, as Mr Calcraft would say.'

'Mr Calcraft, sir?'

'The hangman, Constable. Can you write?'

'Yes, sir.'

'Good. Bring your notebook – and your bull's-eye. It's deuced dark in Whitechapel these winter mornings.'

The policemen walked through the crisp darkness that

preceded the December dawn, Palmer in his forage cap and patrol jacket, tapping the railings with his swagger cane, Lestrade in his blue cape and helmet, peering through the gloom by the aid of the lantern. The dark festering tenements watched their every move, and drunken shadows slid from alleyway to court at the sound of the measured tread of City boots. Carters and their horses clattered past them, too. They were all the people of the Abyss.

'Where are we?' Palmer asked him.

Lestrade looked around him. 'Flower and Dean Street, sir.'

'Good man.' Palmer was impressed for the first time. 'This is it.' He sprang up a flight of stone steps to a dark door.

'Bark your knuckles on that, Lestrade. That's what they're for.'

The constable complied, but no sooner had skin collided with wood than the door was wrenched back and an enormous rough smelling like a Thames lighter jerked him inside and the door was slammed in Palmer's face. Lestrade felt a sickening slap around the head that sent his helmet spinning down a passage.

'Waddya want 'ere, Peeler?' the rough asked him, in between lifting the constable bodily with repeated punches to his stomach.

'I'm not quite sure,' Lestrade gasped, desperately trying to hold on to his bull's-eye, knowing how expensive they were.

'Florrie!' the rough called up the stairs. 'There's a Peeler here. 'E's not sure what 'e wants.'

'Well,' a woman's voice whined from the end of the passage, 'we'll soon find out, won't we?'

Lestrade looked up through the slowly twirling view that the knock on the head had given him. A filthy blowzy woman with unkempt hair and a loose shift emerged in the rays of the lantern. 'Ooh, 'e's only a young 'un, Bert. Poor bleeder's pourin' with blood. Waddya done to 'im?' She knelt beside the recumbent rookie and began to mop his forehead.

'I only 'it 'im a little bit,' Bert explained, ''E 'ad 'is dad wiv 'im, outside.'

'Well, Jennie can 'ave 'is dad. I'm not up to old lechers this time o' morning.'

Lestrade's bull's-eye was now shining up the chemise of the lady in question, who had joined Florrie on the floor.

'Ooh, 'e's a one,' Jennie giggled, patting it aside.

'All the same, these bloody coppers,' Bert growled. 'Well, come on, where d'you want 'im?'

Lestrade was picked up bodily and dangled his way down the passage, his head crunching on the walls and door-frames until he felt himself flung on to an unmade bed, the sheets below him crawling with company.

'Oh, bloody 'ell.' Florrie dropped her chemise and began, stark naked, to empty the constable's pockets. 'Get 'im out, Bert. 'E's only paid fourpence and 'e's been 'ere all night.' She clearly wasn't talking about Lestrade.

'You're too good-hearted, you are, Florrie,' said Bert, and Lestrade was dimly aware of a second form on the bed beside him being lifted up by the obliging heavy.

'Now, then, dearie.' Florrie counted Lestrade's small change by candlelight. 'Oh dear, you won't get much for twopence halfpenny, ducks. Still. . . .' She fumbled with the constable's buttons. 'Oh, you 'aven't got much to start with, 'ave you?' She slapped his face gently. ''Ere, are you sure you're up to this, in a manner of speakin'?'

Lestrade groaned as his head swirled anew.

'Oh, well, 'e's got a nice watch, anyway.' Florrie held it up to the chink of light that showed dawn through the window. It was followed by a shattering and splintering of glass and wood.

'That's his dad's.' Inspector Palmer had just popped in.

Florrie screamed and fell against the wall.

'You are interfering with a police officer in the pursuance of his duty,' he said, brushing the dust and debris from his jacket. He took in the sordid room, the verminous bed and the bedraggled slut attempting to hide her embarrassment. 'Very nice, dear, but unfortunately I've left my wallet at home. Put this on.' He threw a curtain at her. 'Where is the man who was here?'

Bert, obliging as ever, put his head round the door and saw the inspector. But he wasn't fast enough, and Palmer's body hurtled against the frame, pinning Bert's head with a sickening crunch. The rough crumpled with a well-known Whitechapel expletive and lay groaning on the floor.

'Who else is in the house?' Palmer asked Florrie.

'Only me and two other girls – Jennie and Kate.'

'Where?'

Florrie pointed upstairs. Palmer looked around, found a jug and poured its contents over the groggy constable. Only afterwards did he smell the jug to reassure himself of its contents and vaguely wished he hadn't. Lestrade sat up, bewildered.

'Right, Constable. Now, let's stop playing silly buggers, shall we, and get on with this?'

Lestrade sheepishly fastened his flies and collected his watch and money from the equally sheepish Florrie. He followed Palmer up the stairs, finding his helmet and bull's-eye as he went. Palmer approached the first door. 'Lestrade,' he hissed, 'stealth would seem a little pointless now, what with the window and all. By the way, I'm sorry I was late on that entrance. I had to chance my manhood on the railings below.'

'What are we looking for, sir?' Lestrade's brain was as sharp again as it was ever likely to be.

'A body,' said Palmer. 'Probably a dead one. You take that door, I'll take this one. And, Lestrade. . . .'

'Sir?'

'You've got a tipstaff, Constable. Use it.'

Lestrade hooked out the truncheon from his belt.

'On the count of three,' Palmer whispered, bracing himself against the far wall. 'One . . . two . . . three!' – and he hurled himself forward disappearing into the blackness.

Lestrade was slower, largely because his left shoulder buckled on contact with the door and the thing wouldn't budge. He ended up kicking in the panels to shrieks of alarm from inside.

'Police!' shouted Lestrade, standing at last in the room. He took in the girl sitting on the chair. He took in the man lying on the bed.

'Who are you?' Lestrade asked.

'My name's Kate,' she muttered.

Lestrade lifted her up. 'How old are you?'

'Fifteen, sir . . . I think.'

'Who's this?' Lestrade pointed to the bed.

'A gentleman, sir,' said Kate.

Lestrade poked the gentleman with his truncheon. He didn't move. The constable lifted an eyelid. The pupils were dilated, the sight gone. He pressed an ear to the chest. No hint of breath.

'This man's . . .,' he began, standing.

'As deceased as a doornail.' Palmer had joined them.

Kate began to cry quietly. Palmer had the other girl, Jennie, dangling from his arm.

'Where are his clothes?' Palmer asked them.

Kate fetched the black breeches, stock and topper.

'And the coat?' Palmer asked. 'Ah, yes, I thought your fancy man was well dressed. Lestrade, get that later. Where's his money?'

Kate fumbled in a drawer behind her, still sobbing quietly, and gave the notes to Palmer.

''E died natural.' Florrie had arrived on the landing. 'Must have been 'is 'eart. Old man like that, 'e 'ad no business bein' 'ere.'

'Who was with him at the time?' Palmer asked.

Kate sobbed that she was.

''E liked 'em young,' Florrie explained.

'A regular, was he?' Palmer asked.

'I don' think he was a soldier.' Florrie looked confused.

'Neither do I,' said Palmer. 'Constable, this is . . . was . . . Mr George Claverhouse, the late Bishop of Durham.'

'Blimey,' Lestrade and the girls chorused.

'Get some men and a stretcher. There's not much point in him staying here.'

Lestrade hurried into the chill morning air to do as he was told. When he got back, paper and pencil ready for the depositions, it was in time to see Inspector Palmer buttoning up his flies as he left Kate's presence.

'Keep your notes brief,' Palmer said. 'Open-and-shut case, this.' He led Lestrade by the arm. 'We've got to stray into alien territory, Constable. The sunlit uplands of the West End.'

'But isn't that . . .?'

'The Metropolitan District? Yes, it is, lad. But don't let's be a snob about this. I told you, I'm destined for the Yard any day now. It's as well to know your new colleagues. Any questions?'

'Yes, sir. How did you know about the bishop?'

'I got a tip-off, Constable. Oh, not the usual source at all. I've got narks all over the City, but this one was from a gentleman; by his letter-writing, a secretarial gentleman. He told me His Grace was in the habit of frequenting a house of ill repute in Flower and Dean Street. He had seen him go in on Thursday afternoon, and no one had seen him since. So Flower and Dean Street it was – the place to start my inquiry. I must admit, I'd hoped for a bit more. Still, there it is. Enough to shock a good many people at their breakfasts tomorrow, I'll wager. My brother will be appalled.'

'Your brother, sir?'

'Yes,' Palmer chuckled. 'He's off to the University shortly. Going in for the cloth, of all things. That was to be my calling, too, only I was a little deaf, you see.'

'I see, sir,' smiled Lestrade.

'What?'

They hailed a cab in the Minories. Lestrade was paying.

'You are the Bishop of Durham's private secretary?' Palmer came to the point.

'I am, sir.' The lugubrious gentleman was dark-haired with the eyes of a hawk and the beak of a dodo.

'I am Inspector Palmer. This is Constable Lestrade, of the City of London police. I understand you wrote to me.'

'I . . . er. . . .' The private secretary mopped his brow.

'Come, sir.' Palmer threw the crumpled notepaper on the desk. 'Is that or is that not your hand?'

'It is,' the secretary confessed, covering his mouth as though he were about to vomit.

'Were you in the habit of following the bishop on his nocturnal ramblings?'

'What?'

Lestrade came to the man's rescue. 'Did you walk behind the bishop at night, sir?'

The inspector and the secretary withered the constable at a glance. 'I confess . . . ,' said the secretary.

Ah ha, thought Lestrade. There was more to this than met the eye.

'I confess I had taken to doing so. His Grace had become . . . odd. His manner furtive. Even in the most impenetrable of fogs, he would venture into the night, hail a cab and disappear.'

'In the direction of Whitechapel?'

'Quite so. Sir, I trust that His Grace will not be told that I. . . .'

'I doubt whether His Grace would listen to anything much at the moment,' said Palmer. He looked at Lestrade and, in so doing, his eye fell on the row of ecclesiastical hats on the pegs in the hall.

'His Grace has guests?' he asked the secretary.

'Why, yes. The Apostle Club meet regularly on the third Friday of every month.'

'The Apostle Club?' Palmer asked.

'A group of bishops. . . .'

'I think you'll find that's a bestiality of bishops,' Palmer corrected him.

'Er. . . . Quite so,' the secretary reflected. 'They meet in the town house of one of their number and discuss theological matters. They often have a guest speaker, as this afternoon. Only, His Grace has not yet returned home. They may well have begun without him. Is there any news, Inspector?'

Palmer smiled. 'How are your claws, Lestrade?'

'Sir?' The constable checked his fingernails.

'There is a flock of pigeons beyond that door, Constable. You and I are going to be cats' – and he prowled forward.

'Gentlemen, you cannot. . . .' Lestrade batted the private secretary aside and was at Palmer's elbow as the double doors crashed back.

'Constable,' said Palmer, 'the hat.'

Lestrade produced from below the cape a silk netted topper, of the type worn by bishops. On the nod from Palmer, he threw it into the centre of the gleaming mahogany table. Suddenly there were fourteen men on their feet in the room, eleven of them shouting incoherently and demanding to know what was the meaning of this. Only Palmer and Lestrade remained silent. And the guest speaker, who had been on his feet when the policemen entered.

'My lords,' Palmer yelled above the hubbub, 'and Mr Disraeli.'

'A player among gentlemen yet again,' the old Jew muttered, and bowed to the policemen.

'My name is Palmer, inspector of Her Majesty's City Police. Constable Lestrade and I are here, sadly, on official business. I would deem it an honour if you all sat down.'

One by one, led by Disraeli, they did so, with the creaking of episcopal knees. There was an empty chair. Palmer pointed to it. 'Would I be correct in assuming that that is the place reserved for the late George Claverhouse, the Lord Bishop of Durham?'

'Late?' Voices rose in astonishment.

'Only by an hour,' the private secretary piped from behind them. Lestrade didn't need the nod this time. With a deft kick of his right heel, he sent one door crashing back into the secretary's nose. The other closed of its own volition.

'Constable.' Palmer leaned against the door and waited while Lestrade placed his helmet on the table and produced his notebook.

He read: 'At approximately ten to seven this morning, Friday the thirteenth of December, I accompanied Inspector Palmer of Leman Street police station to a house of ill repute at number eight Flower and Dean Street—'

'Ill repute?' A bishop stood up.

'Yes, Your Grace,' Palmer replied on Lestrade's behalf. 'Proceed, Constable.'

'—where, after an altercation with a gentleman of the gutter—'

'Beautiful phrase, Constable,' Disraeli beamed. The novelist lurked in him yet.

'– we discovered the body of a gentleman in bed. On searching his clothes, it was discovered that he was the late Bishop of Durham.'

There was silence in the room. Beyond the doors, a dull thud as the private secretary floated gracefully to the floor.

'I don't believe it!' Another bishop was the first to find his voice. 'Constable, there must be some mistake.'

'Oh, there's no mistake, Your Grace,' Palmer assured him.

The bishops faced each other across the glittering table. One of them, as though reading the minds of the others, stood up and said: 'Mr Disraeli, Constable, I wonder if you would mind waiting in the lobby for a moment? Inspector, a word in your ear. . . .'

Lestrade checked his guv'nor. Palmer nodded, and the constable followed the leader of Her Majesty's Opposition into the hall, where the latter stepped gracefully over the recumbent secretary and Lestrade tripped headlong, to land in an undignified heap at Disraeli's feet.

'Let me help you, Constable.' The politician's breath was enough to poison a weaker man.

'Thank you, sir.' Lestrade dragged the secretary upright and propped him in the armchair in the corner.

'So here we are,' Disraeli said, 'relegated.'

'I'm Church of England myself, sir,' Lestrade felt it best to correct him.

'How old are you, Constable?' Disraeli looked at him oddly.

'Twenty, sir. Fast approaching twenty-one.'

'Ah.' Disraeli lowered himself with difficulty on to a sofa. 'When I was twenty, I had such ambition . . . such ambition. There was a greasy pole in front of me. . . .'

'Yes, sir,' Lestrade nodded grimly, 'there are lots of those in Whitechapel.'

'Talking of Whitechapel, is it all true? About Claverhouse I mean.'

'Yes, sir,' Lestrade assured him.

'Sit down, Constable.' Disraeli patted the sofa. Lestrade was loath to be on the same level as this man, but he had to admit that his dazzling rings, sparkling eyes and rouge did have a fascination for him. 'Your inspector in there. Is he straight?'

'Sir?'

'Is he honest, man?'

'As an arrow, sir.'

Disraeli smirked, smitten by a sudden thought. 'You didn't see the Prime Minister on your travels?' he asked.

'No, sir.' Lestrade was a little shocked. To find a bishop in such surroundings was one thing, but a Liberal!

'Oi vay,' muttered Disraeli, pressing his gardenia to his lips. 'You should grow a moustache, Constable.'

'Sir?'

'To make you look older. How long have you been on the beat?'

Lestrade checked his half-hunter. 'Nearly eight hours now, sir.'

'No, I mean, how long have you been a policeman?'

'This is my second day, sir.'

'Is it now? Well, you take my advice, young man. You grow a moustache. And when I'm Prime Minister come and see me. I'll make you Home Secretary one day.'

Lestrade looked at him. 'Are you pulling my leg, sir?' he asked.

Disraeli chuckled. 'Constable, I wouldn't dare.'

The door clicked open to reveal a beaming bestiality of bishops and a pleased Palmer.

'Mr Disraeli' – one of the bishops led the politician into the drawing room – 'I believe you were saying, "Where is your Christianity if you deny my Judaism?"'

Disraeli smiled at Palmer and Lestrade, shrugged and lifted his palms and allowed the bishops to shepherd him inside. On his way, he paused by the marble pillar. 'Do you see an angel there, Your Grace?' – and the door closed behind him.

'What now, sir?' Lestrade tucked his helmet under his arm.

'Let me see your notebook, Constable.' Palmer held out his

hand. He took it, perused the notes, then tore them out and threw them in the fire.

'Sir?' Lestrade rushed to grab them, but the flames had consumed them, snarling back at him. He looked uncomprehendingly at Palmer. 'What about the body?'

'What body would that be?' Palmer adjusted something large and pound-note-shaped in his patrols pocket.

'The one in Flower and Dean Street,' Lestrade persisted. Palmer put on his forage cap and made for the outer door. 'The Bishop of Durham,' Lestrade shouted.

Palmer turned to him calmly. 'His Grace the Bishop of Durham died peacefully in his sleep,' he said. 'In his bed, upstairs here, in Portland Place. And that's exactly where he will be by nightfall.'

'But the bishops . . .?'

'Do not wish a scandal, Constable.'

'Mr Disraeli . . .?'

'Old Clo'? There are more skeletons in his cupboard than you've had hot dinners.'

'Me?' shouted Lestrade.

'You?' Palmer laughed. 'A rookie copper, second day out. You're still wet behind the ears, lad. Who's going to listen to you?'

Palmer sensed the fall of Lestrade's crest. 'Look, Lestrade. You keep your nose clean and your mouth shut. Here' – he stuffed a five-pound note into the constable's helmet-strap – 'buy yourself a false moustache until you grow one of your own. . . .'

'Sholto! Sholto!' Fanny's voice swam through the balmy night air. He woke up with a start, jarring his leg as he did so.

'Fanny,' he said, 'I must have dozed off. Where's the vicar?'

'Norman left nearly an hour ago. He didn't want to wake you. Pa's gone to bed.'

'He must think me very rude, dropping off like that.'

'Pa knows you of old, Sholto. He's used to it.'

He threw *The Times* at her. 'I don't mean that old reprobate, as you very well know.'

She giggled. 'Norman didn't mind, either. It must be exhausting for you carrying that thing around.'

Lestrade blushed. 'Oh, we chaps get used to it,' he said.

For a moment she toyed with emptying the brandy over his head, but her father would never have forgiven her.

'I *meant* the plaster,' she scolded him gently. 'And what were you frowning at?'

'When?' he asked.

'While you were asleep. I was watching you. You were frowning.' She sat beside him, plumping his pillows on the chair.

He laughed. 'I was remembering the Claverhouse case – the one Norman mentioned. What did he say about it by the way? I'm afraid I didn't hear much.'

'He didn't say a lot. When he was a young man he met George Claverhouse. Apparently, there were a lot of rumours. There was some scandal surrounding the bishop's death. Something, he said, to do with a house of ill repute. Don't tell me *that* was why you were frowning!'

'No,' he said, 'I was just remembering how utterly green I was.'

'Not caused by my tendrons, I hope,' she smiled.

He kissed her hand. 'How do you like my false moustache?' he said.

Bridge Too Far

That day in August, Lestrade was alone in the house. At least, he was as alone as a man can be in the home of a chief constable with pretensions. Tom Berkeley had advertised for a butler, but no one wanted to assume the position. It had no class. No tone. And so the superintendent wheeled himself around the terrace and drank in the heavy August afternoon. There was no sound but the droning of bees and the distant clanking of the steam thresher, crawling like a black beetle over the golden arc of the hill. He watched through the haze of his last cigar, the sunlight playing on the waters of the lake and the solitary fisherman dozing in his boat.

'I let myself in, sir,' Lestrade heard a voice and cried out, upsetting the lemonade the maid Chrissie had made for him. 'Sorry, sir, didn't mean to startle you.'

'Startle me, Dew?' Lestrade roared, clamping the soggy cigar between his teeth. 'What on earth makes you think I've been startled?' He spun his chair round to face his visitor.

'There *was* a woman at the door,' said the chief inspector, 'but she asked me if I'd brought the fly-whisk. Seemed a little preoccupied.'

'Mrs M'Travers,' nodded Lestrade. 'She'll have to go. I would offer you some lemonade. . . .' Lestrade indicated the shattered jug. He rang a handbell on the table. 'Have a seat, Walter, but mind the—'

Dew shot upright with the air of a man with a problem.

'– broken glass,' Lestrade finished.

'We've had no luck, sir.' Dew gingerly removed the pieces from his serge and began staunching the blood. 'All those names Miss Berkeley gave us. Nothing.'

'Well, I didn't hope for much,' Lestrade said. 'Ah, Chrissie.' The maid bobbed to the policeman. 'Tea, Walter?'

'Very acceptable, sir.'

Chrissie bobbed and scuttled away.

'Mr Berkeley's got himself a nice little number here, hasn't he?'

'Don't give me that, Walter Dew. This is the country. If you're away from the pavements for more than an hour or two, your feet start to itch just like mine. Do you know, I've sneezed forty-three times today?'

'I'd have thought you'd have been too busy to count, sir,' Dew smirked. 'What with Miss Berkeley and all. . . .'

'Don't smirk, Walter; it doesn't suit you.'

'Blevvins has a theory about the late M'Travers, Guv'nor,' Dew said. 'Would you like to hear it?'

'No,' said Lestrade, 'but I suppose you're going to tell me anyway.'

'He said he knew one thing for sure.' Dew was concentrating hard on the verbatim report. 'The butler didn't do it.'

'That's what I like about Blevvins,' said Lestrade after a pause, 'his originality.'

Chrissie brought the tea, and Dew was mother. The Yard men were about to put lip to porcelain when a throat cleared behind them.

'Yes, Constable?' Lestrade squinted against the sun to make out the shambling form of Stalker.

'The afternoon post, sir.'

Lestrade took the letter and opened it. It contained a single line: 'Three, three, the Rivals.'

'Another one,' he murmured.

'Sir?' Dew looked up.

'Oh, it's nothing,' said Lestrade. 'Some crank playing games, that's all. Only. . . . Anyway, Walter, I appreciate your coming all the way out here. How are things at the shop?'

'Oh, all the lads send their love, sir. Hope to see you hopping round again soon.'

'Cases?'

'Well, some of them are, sir. You know. Oh, I see what you mean. . . . Well, there is *one* I wouldn't mind a little advice on, now you come to mention it.'

Lestrade smiled. He and Walter Dew went back a long way, since one was inspector and one was constable at the time of the Ripper case – and that *was* a long way. He knew there was something bothering that tiny befuddled brain.

'Let's have it,' said Lestrade.

'I've got a dead doctor on my hands – one Edmund Lucas, MD. Late, if you'll pardon the expression, of St Bartholomew's Hospital.'

'I've heard that name.' Lestrade rattled his cup for Dew to be mother for the second time.

'Yes, it's in Smithfield, sir. . . . Oh, I see. Doctor Lucas was Physician-in-Ordinary to Prince Arthur of Connaught, but when the field marshal went to Canada Lucas stayed here. Apparently, he didn't care for the climate.'

'Isn't Connaught grand master of the Masons?' Lestrade asked.

'I don't know, sir. Why do you ask?'

'Oh, protocol.' Lestrade waved it aside. 'How did your doctor die?'

'Well, that's the funny thing. Everybody assumed it was Russian roulette. Didn't you read about it in the papers, sir?'

'I've made it a rule not to open a paper, Walter. It's too depressing these days.'

'Well, there was the usual fuss about it. Couldn't move for news-hounds.'

'Where did he live?'

'He had a very nice little number in Harley Street.'

'Married?'

'No. A single man. Kept very much to himself. Stinking rich, of course.'

'Of course.' Lestrade tilted the panama over his eyes. 'But no knighthood?'

'Sir?'

'That's right. Most physicians of the royal family have a handle. Why didn't he? What do we know about him?'

'Er ... I wish I'd brought Jones or Dickens along now, sir,' Dew mumbled, 'but I'll do my best. He was educated at Uppingham and then, as I said, St Bartholomew's.'

'Go on.'

'He got his degree in – let's see – 1880, I believe it was, and continued to practise in the hospital for about ten years. He then became Professor of Anatomy—'

'Morbid?' Lestrade interrupted.

'Not unduly, sir. I suppose he had his moods like all of us.'

Lestrade let it pass.

'... Professor of Anatomy at Guy's. I suppose that's when he put in for the Prince Arthur job. He got that in 1901.'

'And when did he take up residence in Harley Street?'

'Ah, that would have been shortly afterwards – say, 1903.'

'1903,' pondered Lestrade.

'Oh, you didn't actually have to say it, sir,' Dew chortled.

Lestrade ignored him. 'Cause of death a bullet, then?' he asked.

Dew nodded. 'Point-blank range. Very messy.' He reached for his tea, but thought better of it.

'So what's your problem?' Lestrade asked. 'And why the Yard's interest?'

'Eminent man, sir.' Walter Dew was first and foremost a snob. 'We couldn't leave this to ... anybody else, sir, could we?'

Lestrade smiled and nodded. 'Doesn't it smell right, Walter?' he asked.

'No, sir.' Dew was emphatic. 'It most certainly does not.'

'Why?'

'Well, sir, just take an apothecarel case. Suppose you wanted to blow out your brains.' He threw a spoon down on the table. 'There it is, a Webley Mark Four. How would you do it?'

Lestrade picked up the spoon, checked that it was loaded, cocked it and placed it against his temple.

'Exactly,' said Dew triumphantly. 'Let me stop you there' – and he took the spoon away in case of accidents. 'The pistol was pointing at your head, am I right?'

'It's where some people say I keep my brains, Walter.'

'Exactly. Then, why, why, if you please, was there a wound in the clavicord as well?'

'Where?' Lestrade assumed the dead doctor had been musical.

'Here.' Dew pointed to his shoulder.

'The dead doctor wasn't much of a shot?' Lestrade ventured.

Dew tutted and shook his head as though dealing with a half-witted criminal. He had had years of experience.

'So what do you conclude, Chief Inspector?' Lestrade asked him.

'Murder, sir. By person or persons unknown.'

Lestrade looked at him. 'All right. You've got your weapon. Prints?'

'Clean as a constable's whistle,' said Dew. 'I gave it to Inspector Collins, and he did his usual black magic. Nothing.'

'Motive?' tried Lestrade.

Dew shook his head.

'Opportunity?'

The same again.

'Was there an exit wound in the neck?' Lestrade asked.

'Yes, sir, big as the palm of your hand.'

'Did you find the bullet?'

Dew looked blank.

'Oh, Walter.' Lestrade rang for Chrissie again. 'I'll leave a note for Fanny and Tom. It's time I got back in the saddle. Have you got transport?'

'A trap and constable,' Dew said.

'Good. Get me to Harley Street before dinner-time or the meal's on you.'

Lestrade was better on crutches than anybody thought he would be. Even so, it took the help of Dew and his constable to lift the superintendent up the steps into the consulting rooms of Edmund Lucas, MD.

'The doctor can't see anyone today,' the starch-fronted nurse on the front desk told them.

'Nor any other day.' Lestrade wobbled until the crutches took his weight.

'I really don't know what you mean. Good morning' – and she resumed her work in the ledger.

'She's good, Walter,' smiled Lestrade. 'Remind me to get her to give Peabody a few tips.'

'Nurse' – Dew took off his bowler – 'don't you remember me? I am Chief Inspector Dew of Scotland Yard. We spoke only the other day.'

The nurse grudgingly acknowledged the snowy hair and the kindly eyes and she sniffed.

'This is Superintendent Lestrade.'

She looked appalled at the spectacle of the senior man – the shirt-sleeves, the slouched panama. And surely that wasn't an unfastened collar-stud flashing before her?

'May we see the doctor's rooms?' Lestrade asked.

She snapped shut the ledger, making all three policemen jump. With a curt tug at her châtelaine, she led the way along the passage and unlocked a mahogany door. Then she proceeded to stand, like a rock.

'Yes?' Lestrade craned his neck to fix her with a stare. She sniffed again and left them to it.

'Where was the body found?' Lestrade hobbled to the settee and slumped sideways.

'Here, sir, at the desk.'

'Sit there, Constable,' Lestrade ordered.

'Go on, Per – Constable, do as the superintendent says.'

'Yes, sir.'

'Now, then, Walter. You've seen the body. I haven't. Angle of the wound?'

'Ah. . . .' Dew had been caught out.

'Well, didn't you stick your pen in it, man?'

The constable visibly paled.

'All right. Let's assume the shot came from in front. How tall was the deceased?'

'A bit shorter than young Per – policemen like this one,' Dew answered.

Lestrade aimed with his crutch. 'Right,' he said, lining up the shot. 'Constable, stay where you are. Chief Inspector, have a look under that fringed thing – no, to the left. Right a bit, right a bit, down a bit. There!'

'Good God.' Dew produced a smashed lead plug from the wall below the fringed thing. 'Well, I never. . . .'

'I fear you're right, Walter,' sighed Lestrade. 'What does this prove, Constable?'

The pale policeman opened his mouth. 'I don't know, sir.'

'Chip off the old block, eh, Walter?' Lestrade observed.

Dew blustered. 'How did you know?'

'Oh, it's the little things that gave it away. Like the constable calling you "Dad". I didn't get where I am today by missing the little things. What it proves, young Dew, is that, assuming the bullet-hole goes in at right angles – and the coroner's report should tell us that – then whoever murdered Dr Lucas was sitting here at the time. You've checked the room for prints, Walter?'

'Clean, sir.'

'Well, then. . . .'

'To the Yard, Guv'nor?' Dew asked.

'Ah, no, Walter. . . . Miss Berkeley would break my other leg if I so much as set foot beneath its portals. Who have you seen?'

'Well, the deceased was a keen bridge-player, sir. Apart from his three friends, as I said, he was something of a solitary type.'

'All right, Walter. Find out where and when the next game

takes place. I've an urge to play a rubber or two myself. Now, get me back to Virginia Water and keep me informed. I'm relying on you.'

'"Three, three, the Rivals,"' repeated Fanny. 'How odd. Another number letter.'

'Another?' Lestrade was poring over Tom's *Book of Gentlemen's Amusements for Winter Evenings*, though the season was against him.

'Why, yes. Didn't you have one recently for the Gospel-Makers?'

'Mm?' Lestrade was elsewhere. 'Yes, dear.'

She looked at him. 'I went to the moon today, Sholto.'

'Oh, yes,' he said, without taking his eyes off the book. 'See anyone you know?'

'Oh, the usual. Lots and lots of green cheese.'

'Well, there you are,' said Lestrade.

'Do you know your trousers are undone?' she tried again.

'All right, thank you,' he murmured.

Exasperated, she splashed him with water from the goldfish-bowl. 'It's raining, Sholto,' she shouted.

He shrieked in response. 'Good God, woman! Whatever is the matter with you?'

'With me, Sholto?' she smiled demurely. 'Nothing at all.'

There was no doubt that Harry Bandicoot had his uses. Not only, as policeman and private citizen, had he saved the life of Sholto Lestrade on at least two occasions; he had also brought up the superintendent's daughter and had now got him into the Portland Club, one of the most exclusive in London. Lestrade used the name of Latymer. His usual alias of Lister might raise too many awkward questions should the bridge-playing confederates of the late Dr Lucas prove also to be medical men. Harry went to dine while Lestrade hobbled into the games room, balancing manfully on a single stick.

'I believe you are short of a player, gentlemen,' he said to the three men under the fringed chandelier.

'As it happens we are, Mr . . .?' one of them said.

'Latymer,' replied Lestrade. 'Shame to waste the evening.'

'Indeed,' said another. 'Allow me' – and he helped Lestrade to a chair. 'I am Patrick Matthews.'

'Your servant.' Lestrade bowed a little and rested his stick against the table.

'May I introduce Abelard Johns?'

'Charmed,' Lestrade nodded.

'And William Marks.'

'Sir.'

Matthews produced an unbroken pack of cards and called for brandy. When it was poured, he held his glass aloft and announced in a powerful voice: 'Lord Brougham.'

'Lord Brougham,' the others chorused, and quaffed their glasses. The steward refilled them, and play commenced.

'Cigar, Mr Latymer?' Marks offered.

Lestrade accepted and began to take stock of the players. His partner was Matthews, tall, elegant, less hair than he would probably have liked, about forty years old. At Lestrade's left elbow sat the more ponderous form of Abelard Johns, glittering with rings and chains, not unlike those of the late Mr Disraeli whom Lestrade had met all those years ago. And at his right hand sat the cadaverous William Marks, whose huge cranium was crowned by a shock of silver hair and whose eyes shone in the myriad sparks radiating from the chandelier.

'I give you John Doe, gentlemen,' said Matthews.

'John Doe,' they repeated.

'My deal, I think,' said Marks, and proceeded to slide the glossy vellum through his fingers. At that moment Lestrade would have given his right leg for the photographic memory of Sergeants Dickens or Jones. He began to doubt himself.

'How did you know we were missing a fourth, Mr Latymer?' Matthews asked.

'The death of poor old Lucas,' Lestrade announced, sensing a way in.

Marks stopped dealing. Johns paused in mid-gulp of his brandy.

'Did you know Edmund Lucas?' Matthews asked.

'In a way,' Lestrade hedged. 'We dined together from time to time. And, of course, played.'

'Played what?'

'Bridge,' Lestrade replied.

'I thought Edmund only ever played bridge here,' said Johns, puffing on his cheroot. 'I've never seen you at the Portland, have I?'

'We played in his rooms,' said Lestrade. 'Just the two of us, you know.'

Johns opened his mouth to say something, but Matthews was quicker. 'Where did you meet Edmund, Mr Latymer?'

'At Guy's Hospital.' Lestrade remained calm. He had expected questions of this sort.

'Are you a medical man?' Marks asked, finishing his deal.

'No, no,' Lestrade chuckled, but offered nothing more.

'Strange Edmund never mentioned you,' murmured Matthews.

'The manner of his death was even stranger,' said Lestrade blandly, but his eyes flashed round them all.

'Tragic,' said Johns. 'Tragic.'

'Spades,' said Marks. 'Your bid, Mr Latymer.'

It would be, cursed Lestrade to himself. 'Er . . . Little Slam.' He watched their faces. Nothing seemed amiss.

Johns placed his card on the table. Matthews placed his. Marks's turn again.

'All right, partner?' Matthews smiled at him.

'Er. . . . No bid,' said Lestrade. 'I didn't even know Edmund had a gun.'

'Odd your not knowing that,' said Matthews. 'You being such a close friend as to play in his rooms.'

'Yes,' said Johns, downing his third or fourth brandy. 'An old colleague gave it to him. A Dr Watson.'

Lestrade looked up. 'Late of Baker Street?'

Matthews interrupted sternly. 'Your bid, Abelard.'

The heavy man shook a little and threw down the card.

Incomprehensibly, the others threw in their hands and Marks chuckled.

'Your dummy, Mr Latymer,' said Matthews.

Lestrade was about to protest that he was not, when Matthews announced the demise of the brandy-bottle and rose in search of the steward. Lestrade heard the click of a key behind him and sensed that all was not well. He half-expected an assault from behind, and his right hand gripped the brass knuckles that nestled in his pocket. It didn't come. Instead, Matthews spun the chair round so that he straddled it, blowing smoke into Lestrade's face.

'Now, then,' he said. 'Suppose you tell us who you really are.'

'I beg your pardon.' Lestrade decided to bluff it out.

'We knew Edmund Lucas for some time,' said Matthews. 'He never mentioned a friend called Latymer.'

'And bridge, Mr Latymer' – Marks edged his chair nearer – 'is never played by two persons, only by four.'

'And a Little Slam is the winning of twelve tricks,' said Johns, easing his girth towards Lestrade. 'It is not a bid.'

'Your game was that of an orang-utan, Mr Latymer.' Matthews leaned over the table. 'Once more, before I have you thrown into the street, who are you?'

Lestrade leaned back and lit another cigar. The heat from the chandelier began to singe Matthews's head, and he sat down.

'Very well, gentlemen. I am Superintendent Lestrade of Scotland Yard.'

The bridge-players moved back visibly, as though he were a contagious disease. Matthews was the first to find his tongue. 'Then, why the subterfuge? Why "Latymer"?'

'Your former partner-in-cards is dead, Mr Matthews. My job is to find out why.'

'Simple,' said Marks, gathering in the pack. 'Edmund shot himself.'

'While the balance of his mind was disturbed?' asked Lestrade.

'Presumably,' Matthews answered. 'Does anyone in his right mind put a bullet through his brain?'

Lestrade went for the weakest of them first. 'Mr Johns,' he began, 'may I ask how you came to know Dr Lucas?'

'Via the Club.' Johns downed another large brandy. 'I suppose I've known the man for about five years. We played most Thursday evenings. And occasional Tuesdays.'

'Do you find it warm in here, sir?' Lestrade began to rattle his man.

'A little.' Johns tugged at his wing collar. 'For the time of year.'

'May I ask your line of work?' Lestrade continued.

'Me? Insurance,' said Johns and, detecting a snigger from the others, sat up to his full height and underlined the fact. 'And my father before me.'

'Ah,' Lestrade smiled, 'the men from the Pru. Have you any idea, Mr Johns, why Dr Lucas should want to take his own life?'

Johns flashed a glance to his comrades-in-cards. 'None,' he said, a shade too quickly for Lestrade's liking.

'Look, Superintendent,' Matthews galloped to his rescue, 'we merely met Edmund Lucas to play bridge. We didn't know the innermost recesses of the man's mind – or his soul.'

Lestrade's eyes engaged the younger man's, but he continued to address Johns. 'How did you know that Dr Lucas's gun came from Dr Watson?'

'I . . . er. . . .' Johns was dabbing with his silk handkerchief at his forehead, running now with fear.

'When men play bridge, Mr Lestrade,' Matthews intervened again, 'they discuss many things. Oh, trivial, superficial. But the topics, like the cards, turn at random. I remember one evening we were discussing guns.'

'That's right,' said Marks. 'It was the day poor Dr Watson was found dead. The papers were full of it.'

'Come to think of it, Superintendent, weren't *you* on that case?' Matthews had turned the tables as deftly as he turned his cards.

'I was,' Lestrade answered.

'Well, that was it,' Marks went on. 'Edmund was saying that he was at medical school with Watson and the two of them had continued to meet on and off – you know, medical dinners and so forth. I understand that Watson's service revolver was the very one that he carried in all those marvellous cases with the late Sherlock Holmes.'

'Who?' asked Johns.

Ah, thought Lestrade. This may be a man with something to hide, but at least he has taste.

'And why do you suppose Dr Watson should give his favourite pistol to Dr Lucas?' he asked Marks.

'I really don't know, Superintendent – and it's a little too late to ask him, isn't it?'

'I suppose you only met Dr Lucas to make up a foursome?' Lestrade ignored the chuckle that rippled through the three of them.

'Well,' said Marks, 'Mr Matthews and I are solicitors, Superintendent. You've doubtless heard of Fortinbras, Fortinbras and Minney?'

'No,' said Lestrade.

Marks bridled. 'Oh, come now, Superintendent. A principal firm like ours respected the length and breadth of the country. . . .'

'Now, don't be a snob, William,' smiled Matthews. 'You must remember that Mr Lestrade is a policeman.'

'How long had you known the deceased?' Lestrade stayed with Marks.

'A trifle under two years,' said Marks. 'I am a relatively new member of this club. Incidentally, how did you get in?'

'Through the door,' replied Lestrade, whose opinion of lawyers, like most of his kind, was confined to a few carefully selected Anglo-Saxon phrases. 'Were you – that is, Messrs Fortinbras, Fortinbras and Minney – Dr Lucas's solicitors?'

'Now, Superintendent,' Marks leered, 'you know I cannot possibly divulge—'

'It's late, gentlemen,' Lestrade cut in. 'I don't think the Fortinbrases, not to mention the Minneys, would like being knocked up by my constables in the early hours with search warrants to go through their files.'

'We know the law, Lestrade,' Marks snapped. 'You can't do that. The confidentiality that exists between a client and his lawyer is—'

'William!' Matthews hissed.

Lestrade smiled. 'Thank you, Mr Marks. I don't suppose you'd also care to tell me whether your late client had any financial worries?'

Marks glared at Lestrade.

'No, I thought not. And so, Mr Matthews, we come to you. Would you say that Dr Lucas was a worried man?'

'Worried?'

'Yes. Did he appear nervous, preoccupied, particularly on the days leading to his death?'

'I suppose the last time I saw him – we all saw him – was on the day before he died. He seemed in perfectly good spirits.'

'The day *before* he died. That would be on the Friday?'

Matthews smiled. 'I wonder which of us has seen more cross-examinations, Superintendent? But, really, you'll have to do better than that. We both know that Edmund died on Friday. I said the day *before* he died. We played here at the club.'

Lestrade slid his chair back from the table. He toyed with rising, but wasn't sure enough of his balance. 'I have a chief inspector who works under me,' he told them. 'Oh, he's no genius. I doubt whether he has the agility of mind to cope with the rigours of Little versus Hampton – or even the hazards of double indemnity – but he *is* thorough. He knows his job. And when he smells something odd he digs, digs deep.'

'A sure way of catching typhus,' observed Marks coldly.

'Or a murderer or three,' Lestrade countered.

They looked at him.

'One example of my chief inspector's thoroughness,' Lestrade went on. 'He found an eyewitness.'

'To Lucas's death?' Johns gripped the rim of the table with white knuckles.

'No,' said Lestrade. 'To three gentlemen, impeccably dressed, who visited Dr Lucas in his rooms in Harley Street at approximately eight-thirty on the evening of Friday the sixteenth – the evening of the doctor's demise.'

They sat unmoving.

'One of them' – he leaned as though to examine Matthews more closely – 'was a man of about forty years, quite handsome in a bad light, with a receding hairline. The second' – he turned to Marks – 'taller, thinner, with a shock of white wavy hair, prematurely so, for he was no more than forty-five. The third' – he angled himself to face Johns – 'an older man, large and heavy. He seemed agitated, worried.'

'Who is this witness?' Matthews demanded.

'Abelard Johns,' Lestrade ignored him, 'I am arresting you for the murder of Dr Edmund Lucas on the night of Friday the sixteenth last. You are not obliged to say anything—'

Johns screeched and leaped from his chair. Marks stood up, shouting: 'Lestrade, this is monstrous. . . .'

'No, Mr Marks.' Lestrade's stick spun through the air to jab into his waistband.

'And that is assault!' Marks screamed.

'In fact it's a crutch.' Lestrade twisted the end in the man's shirtfront. 'And it's inches from yours. Shall we sit down?' The superintendent forced the solicitor back into his chair.

'Damn you, Matthews,' Johns was shouting from the darkened corner of the room. 'Where's the key? You've locked the bloody door!'

'Calm yourself, Mr Johns,' said Lestrade. 'That was designed, I suspect, not to keep you in, but to keep out any assistance I might need. Isn't that so, Mr Matthews?'

'You were operating under an alias, Lestrade. It was perfectly obvious something was amiss. I was taking no chances.'

'Any more than Mr Johns did when he shot Dr Lucas.' Lestrade glanced at him.

'No!' Johns bellowed. 'No, it wasn't like that. . . .'

'Shut up, Abelard, you idiot,' snapped Marks. 'Can't you see the man's bluffing?'

'I'm not a bridge-player, Mr Marks,' Lestrade answered. 'I never bluff.'

'Tell him!' shrieked Johns. 'William, Patrick, for God's sake. They'll hang me.' He slumped into a chair, sobbing dementedly.

Matthews was on his feet now and he patted the fat man's shoulder. 'William,' he said quietly, 'pour Abelard another drink, will you? I think he could do with one.'

Marks did so and passed it to the broken man.

'Very well, Lestrade.' Matthews sat down and leaned back in his chair. 'By fair means or foul you appear to have arrived at something. Oh, not the truth. Not by a long way. But to save us all any further embarrassment – not to mention whatever rubber-truncheon methods you Yard fellows may devise for us – let me tell you something about the good doctor Edmund Lucas. . . .'

All eyes were on him, even Johns's through the blur of brandy and tears.

'He was a cheat, Superintendent. He was also a liar, a braggart and a womaniser; but, then, he was a Harley Street physician. One could forgive certain peccadilloes, but not dishonesty. Marks and I were at Winchester, Lestrade. Even Johns went to – where was it, Abelard?'

'Manchester Grammar School,' sniffed the insurance salesman.

'Yes, well, there you are. But at Winchester, at any rate, we didn't put up with that sort of thing.' He leaned forward. 'We still don't. I think all of us had known for some time what Lucas was up to. We played all sorts of card games and he managed to win at virtually all of them. Money changed hands ... a considerable sum. . . . On that last night we caught him – or at least William did. "Dead to rights," I believe, is the phrase. He was arrogant about it, accused all of us in turn. It was pitiful.'

'So?' said Lestrade.

'So we went – in a body – to his rooms. We had it out with him, told him he knew what he must do. He didn't.'

'So I took the revolver from the wall,' said Marks. 'The one he'd been given by Dr Watson. He kept it loaded, he said, in case of miscreants. Apparently he'd once been visited by a Mormon. . . .'

Lestrade clicked his tongue and shook his head.

'We left the revolver on his desk in front of him,' Matthews went on. 'We made it clear he would be blackballed from the Club and indeed from any other. We took our leave.'

'What time was that?'

'About nine,' said Matthews.

'I heard the hall clock strike,' said Marks.

'So, you see,' said Matthews, 'as far as that goes, we are all guilty. But I doubt you'll get far in court, Lestrade.'

'So he finished his cigar and shot himself?' the superintendent said.

'His cigar?' said Matthews. 'Lord, no, not Edmund Lucas. Couldn't abide the things. Hated smoke of any kind. Always complained about the fumes here in the Club.'

'Then, who . . .?' Lestrade began almost to himself. 'One of you left a cigar behind – in his rooms?'

'No,' they asserted, remembering.

'We were anxious to make a point,' said Matthews. 'We were virtually asking a man to lay down his life for his friends. You don't do that with a cigar in your mouth.'

'Are . . . you taking me in, Superintendent?' Johns whispered.

'Mr Matthews, the door if you please.'

Matthews produced the key while Lestrade hobbled to the corner. He turned back, steadying himself on the frame. 'No, Mr Johns, I'm not taking you in. You see, Mr Matthews is right. I wouldn't get far in court. Conspiracy to murder may be a crime, but *suggestion* of murder? I'd be laughed all the way to the Temple. Besides, Dr Lucas did not go along with your suggestion, gentlemen.'

'What?' they chorused.

'You'll probably read it in the *Lancet* shortly. The dailies obviously missed it. Lucas was hit by two bullets. The one that killed him was in his brain, but another – an earlier one by seconds or minutes – passed through his neck. Not even a non-smoking suicide misses as wildly as that.'

The relief in the room was tangible.

'And the cigar . . .?' asked Matthews.

'I had assumed until tonight that it merely belonged to Dr Lucas,' said Lestrade. 'Now it's my guess that the doctor was not alone when you arrived. Presumably, he made no comment.'

'No,' said Marks, 'but we'd have noticed a cigar burning there. Or even the smell of smoke. It was unthinkable in those rooms.'

'Then, someone either appeared later or was already there in an antechamber when you arrived; shot the doctor, merely wounding him the first time, with his own gun, lit a cigar and left.'

'Why leave evidence like that?' Matthews asked.

'Perhaps he didn't know it was evidence. Perhaps he assumed, as I did until tonight, that the police would think it was Lucas's cigar.'

'So who is your someone?' Matthews asked him.

'Well, gentlemen' – Lestrade turned in the doorway in search of Harry Bandicoot – 'I've eliminated three from my enquiries. That only leaves thirty million to go.'

'Well, of course, I told him, but he doesn't listen.'

'Tut. Tut.'

'It's his age, you see, Vicar. And of course his pig-headedness.'

'Would you like me to talk to him, Mrs Runcie?'

'Oh, that would be a comfort, Mr Penhaligon; it really would. We . . . we were so happy once' – and the lady began sobbing into her handkerchief with a force that threatened to topple the castle walls. The Reverend Penhaligon patted her ecclesiastically and led her towards the station.

'Norman.' He looked up in relief to see the bright smiling eyes of Fanny Berkeley.

'Good morning, Fanny. Do you know Mrs Runcie of our parish?'

Mrs Runcie sobbed a greeting and sprayed tears liberally over Fanny's blouse.

'Hurry now,' said Penhaligon, 'or you'll miss your train. I shall call to see you and your good husband tomorrow. And don't worry; He moves in mysterious ways.'

'That's just it,' moaned Mrs Runcie, the wound gaping anew. 'But they can't touch him for it' – and she disappeared into the smoke and steam.

'Abyssinia,' Penhaligon called after her. 'My child' – the vicar linked arms with the chief constable's daughter – 'you have saved me from a fate worse than death. What brings you to Windsor?'

'Just a little shopping, Norman. And you?'

'Ah, I've been browsing in the bookshops. Did you know George III used to do the same? I've always found that odd. Imagine the King of England creeping out of the castle, no doubt past the dozing sentry, and rummaging among the volumes in MacConichie's.'

'Wasn't he mad?' Fanny asked.

'MacConichie? I've always found him reasonable.'

She tapped him with her fan. 'Norman, now that I've found you, would it be *too* terrible to lean on you as poor Mrs Runcie did? I hate to impose. . . .'

'Nonsense.' He patted her hand. 'Nothing is too much trouble for the daughter of an old friend. Lean away.'

'How long have you been at Virginia Water now?'

'Ooh, let me see; it must be nearly six months.'

'An *old* friend?'

Penhaligon laughed. 'Well, all is relative. Come on, I feel a strong desire for a Chelsea bun. One of my little weaknesses, I'm afraid.'

'Does your wife approve?'

'Jane?' He looked rather distant. 'Of most things, my dear, of most things' – and they entered the Tea Rooms.

'How's Sholto these days? I haven't seen him in weeks. The leg?'

'Let's just say I've got my hatpin back!' she giggled.

'Ah, the plaster is off. That's very good.'

'I'm afraid my intended is not the steadiest of men. I'm wondering what he's going to break next.'

'He was having a determined go at the organ in church a few Sundays ago.'

'Yes, I'm sorry about that. His stick got caught in the pedals.'

'The story of his life, I understand.' Penhaligon poured the tea.

'He's working on a case again,' she said, wielding the tongs with expert fingers.

'Ah, yes. What is it?'

She looked at him quizzically.

'Oh, forgive me, Fanny. Intellectual curiosity. I have to admit I am an avid fan of Father Brown.'

'Isn't that a little Denominational, Norman?' Fanny raised an eyebrow.

'Ah,' smiled the vicar. 'Know thine enemy. No, my dear, Father Brown isn't an *actual* cleric. He is a creation of Mr Chesterton, the novelist. A divine detective, you might say. A papist policeman. A theological thieftaker. . . .'

'I see,' Fanny interrupted, anxious to spare the vicar any further alliterative contortions. 'Sholto doesn't talk about his work. Policemen never do. And that's the problem.'

'With Sholto?'

'No, with Pa. He's still worrying. I don't seem to be able to shake him out of it. He won't confide in me, in Sholto. What can it be?'

'Well, you must remember poor M'Travers, Fanny. Most local ladies do.'

'I know, Norman.' Fanny was serious. 'But it goes deeper

than that. He's afraid. Sholto thinks. . . .'

'What does Sholto think?' He held both her hands across the Irish lawn.

'Sholto thinks someone is trying to kill him.'

As Superintendent Lestrade had feared, the cigar butt which had been found in the late Dr Lucas's consulting rooms, and which he now knew had not been smoked by the late Dr Lucas, had vanished without trace. Rumour had it that Dew Minor, the newest recruit at the Yard, had smoked it to calm his nerves when in the presence of a corpse. Not for the first or the last time at the Yard, vital evidence had been lost.

But all this was eclipsed by the news that loomed out of the banner headlines early in September: 'Brutal Slaying of Senior Policeman.' It jarred all the constabularies in the country into action. It forced the Yard to slide its current cases to one side. It gave Sergeant Blevvins a chance to use his muscles on a whole variety of subjects. And it galvanised Superintendent Lestrade into leaping, mercifully on his good leg, on to a northbound train.

The village of Burton Coggles lay in the flat broad expanses of the Lincolnshire Wold. Those walking encyclopaedias, Sergeants Dickens and Jones, had been of no help at all, especially over the telephone, since Lestrade was judged not yet fit enough for active service at the Yard. Dickens seemed to think that the village had once been the headquarters of Hereward the Wake. Jones was of the opinion that it was one of the few parts of the country where cress-growing still thrived. Neither piece of staggering trivia was of any relevance to the case.

The Case lay in his coffin in the library cum music-room by the time Lestrade arrived. The blinds were drawn, the shutters closed. The room swam and bobbed in the light of a cluster of candles, and an aged phonograph scratched out repetitively 'Safe in the Arms of Jesus', to be revitalised whenever the machinery wound down by a solemn youth who appeared to be the village idiot. Lestrade was shown by a local inspector into this shrine and he placed his panama on the piano. He looked at the deceased, cleaned and waxy in the silk-lined mahogany. The scent of death was heavy in the air, mingling with the flowers. There were wreaths from every constabulary in the country.

'Well, it's happened.' A voice behind him made Lestrade turn.

'Tom!' The superintendent was surprised to find the chief constable there. 'At the risk of asking the obvious, what are you doing here?'

'I've come to pay my respects, Sholto.' Even in the candlelight, Tom Berkeley looked as pale as the corpse.

Lestrade tapped him with the head of his stick. 'Yes, so have I. Only, I didn't know him. And my interests are purely professional.'

'I didn't know the Yard had been called in.'

'This morning apparently. It's John Kane's case.'

'Good man?'

'One of the best.'

Berkeley circled the coffin a few times. Then he clicked his fingers and sent the phonograph attendant scurrying through the door. 'Sholto,' he said, 'can you take the case?'

Lestrade lowered himself into a library chair and shook his head sadly, lifting the book that lay before him on the rest. 'I see the Late Departed had no taste whatever' – and he tossed the Conan Doyle into the wastebasket. 'Why me, Tom?'

'As a favour to me?'

Lestrade looked up at him, silhouetted as he was by the aurora of the candles. 'What did you mean when you said "It's happened"?'

Berkeley sat down heavily, burying his head briefly in his hands. 'All right,' he said. 'I think I owe you this after the past few weeks. I know I've been difficult to live with. Will you take the case?'

'I think I can get around John Kane. Tell me about it.'

Berkeley turned to the coffin. 'Gordon Ushant,' he said.

'Bless you,' observed Lestrade.

Berkeley continued undeterred, used as he was to the man's little foibles. 'Formerly chief constable of the county of Rutland. A good man. Honest. Efficient. Liked. You saw the men in the grounds? There are more coppers to the square inch here than the Bank of England's got. That's not just the measure of the rank. It's the measure of the man.'

'And you know something they don't.' Lestrade knew the signs.

'I'm surprised Edward Henry isn't here,' Berkeley nodded.

'The assistant commissioner? Why?'

'What I've always loved about you, Sholto, is that you're the least political policeman I've ever met. If His Majesty offered you the Crown tomorrow you'd probably fall over it.'

'Meaning?'

'Who died in June?'

'Er . . . the Pope?' Lestrade couldn't remember.

'John Gabriel, the commissioner of the Metropolitan Police.'

'Good Lord, yes. I'd almost forgotten "Angel." Funny how some men don't exactly stick in the mind, isn't it?'

'Which means a vacancy.' Berkeley was being his most patient.

'Yes.' Lestrade was with him so far.

'Well, practically every copper in the country, except you, put in for the job.'

'Yes.' Lestrade clung doggedly to the labyrinthine twists of the conversation.

'Three were shortlisted. Gordon Ushant, Edward Henry and myself.'

'I see.'

'Henry, as the local boy, so to speak, was in with the main chance, I thought. I don't know how to rate my own chances. Ushant looked strong.'

'What are you saying, Tom? That you or Edward Henry killed him?'

Berkeley paced the room. 'It looks that way, Sholto. We both had the motive. I dare say both of us had the opportunity.'

' "Three, three, the Rivals," ' said Lestrade.

'What?' Berkeley was elsewhere.

'You said there were three of you on the shortlist. And I received a note which said "Three, three, the Rivals". Who else knew about the job?'

'As I said, everybody. Or so I thought.'

'It hadn't come my way, Tom. Not even Fanny mentioned it.'

'You don't shit on your own doorstep, I was always told.'

Lestrade had been told not to shit on *anybody's* doorstep, but perhaps the times were changing.

'I try not to take my work or my worries home.'

'Well, at least you're in the clear, Tom,' Lestrade said.

'That's good of you, Sholto, but you can't let friendship cloud your judgement.'

'Friendship has nothing to do with it,' said Lestrade. 'We both know that M'Travers died by accident when the real target was you.'

Berkeley stared at him.

'You're not devious enough to have arranged that as a cloak to cover the murder of Chief Constable Ushant. I know you too well. Besides, there's something else. . . .'

'What's that?'

'I don't know whether it's my leg or this infernal heat, or what, but I'm slipping.'

'Well, use your stick a bit more.'

Lestrade circled the coffin, too. 'No, no, I mean the letter I received – "Three, three, the Rivals" – it's one of a series.'

'I don't follow.'

'Take four men,' said Lestrade. 'Matthews, Marks, Lucas and Johns.'

'What about them?'

'Do the names sound familiar?'

Berkeley pondered it. 'No,' was his conclusion.

'Change them a little. Matthew, Mark, Luke and John.'

'Ah.' Realisation dawned. 'The four Apostles.'

'Or the Gospel-Makers,' said Lestrade. 'And that's another note I received.'

'What does it mean?' Berkeley asked.

'I don't know – yet. But it goes back, Tom. A long, long way. Before this job of yours. Before Gordon Ushant. I'll take the case. And let's hope my memory hasn't gilded too many lilies.'

Black Caps, Black Ladies

All right, John, what have you got?' Lestrade rocked himself under the late chief constable's apple-trees, the shade dappling his features, roasted a darker parchment by his weeks in the sun.

'About twenty years to go to catch up with you, Guv'nor,' Inspector Kane sighed, turning his notebook first this way, then that.

Lestrade laughed, causing the patrolling policeman on the veranda to look up in distaste. 'And keep the noise down, Inspector. Chief Constable Ushant was well thought of in these parts. Let's not have any of your smart-alec Lunnon callousness here. Go on.'

Kane sat open-mouthed.

'Oh, all right, then, since you've asked so nicely,' sighed Lestrade and popped a cigar into his facial cavity, throwing a second to the inspector. 'Got a match?'

Kane fumbled for his lucifers and lit for them both.

'Cause of death?' Lestrade prompted him.

'Throat cut, from right to left. Windpipe severed. Various muscles lacerated. Neat job.'

'Meaning?' Lestrade blew rings to the boughs above.

'A powerful arm, certainly. Professional?'

'A paid killer, you mean?'

'It had crossed my mind, sir.'

'Why? This is sleepy Rutland, Inspector. The most excitement this place has seen in the last twenty years is the late King in search of female quarry, thundering out of Belvoir Castle of an evening.'

'You didn't know about the commissioner's job, then, sir?'
Kane was fishing.

'Ah, now you're getting warmer, John. Let's have it, then.'

'The fact that Mr Ushant was tipped to be the next
commissioner, standing in the way of two near-rivals.'

'And they were?'

Kane hesitated. He knew that one was Lestrade's immediate
superior. He knew the other was his oldest friend.

'Let me help you with the pronunciation, Inspector.' Lestrade
placed his tongue in his cheek, its most usual position. 'Edward
Henry and Thomas Berkeley.'

Kane nodded.

'So you think one of those did it?'

'Or paid someone to, sir.'

'Why use a woman?'

Kane flopped back in the rattan chair and tore up his notes
while Lestrade chuckled to himself. 'Don't let it get to you,
John,' he said. 'I'm not twenty years ahead of you, only a few
hours.' He leaned forward, checking the undergrowth for signs
of company. Only a white peacock tilted its head to catch the
conversation. 'And those few hours produced results. Time of
death?'

'No coroner's report yet, sir.'

'No one's gone to the moon yet, either, Inspector, but I know
it's not made of green cheese. No coroner's report is a positive
advantage. You've seen the corpse.'

'Well . . . er . . . judging by the state of the deceased. . . .'

'Yes, yes?'

'Thirty-six hours ago.'

'Nearer thirty-eight, but you're getting better. So death
occurred . . .?'

'Some time around dawn on Tuesday.'

'Right. Who was in the house?'

Kane was beginning to regret his hasty action with his notes.
'Apart from the deceased, a butler, six maids of various
descriptions, a cook and one house-guest.'

'Ah, yes, the house-guest. What did you make of Mr Casement?'

'Interesting chap. Irish, of course, but none the worse for that. A diplomat on leave from Brazil.'

'Isn't that where the guano comes from?'

'No, that's Chile. You're thinking of nuts.'

'Ah. Why is Casement here?'

'He's a . . . was . . . a friend of Ushant's.'

'What else about him?'

'A light sleeper. Given to turns in the grounds at unorthodox hours.'

'And on the night in question?'

'Claims he saw a figure crossing the orchard.' Kane found his bearings. 'Over there, I think.'

'What time was this?'

'Four-thirty or so. It was getting light.'

'And how good a view did he get?'

'Hopeless. "Human" was as far as he'd go.'

Lestrade puffed again at the cheroot. 'Let me draw your attention to the curious incident of the peacock in the night-time.'

Kane blinked. 'The peacock did nothing in the night-time,' he bluffed.

'The late Sherlock Holmes would have found that in itself a curious incident.' Lestrade smiled. 'Before your time, John.'

'I've heard of the great man, of course. Doesn't Sir Arthur Conan Doyle chronicle him still?'

'After a fashion, yes.'

'About the peacock. . . .'

'Ah, yes. They make the most marvellous watchdogs, John. Every bit as alert, twice as loud in their alarms and don't cost anything like a mastiff to keep.'

'I see.'

'Do you?'

Kane was one of the brightest of the Yard's jewels. 'So the peacock raised no alarm because it knew the intruder?'

'Or was it fast asleep or stone deaf? I always found Holmes's logic a little faulty. Let's gamble on the first supposition, shall we?'

'That the peacock knew the killer?' Kane caught a flash in Lestrade's eye. 'You know something else, sir.' He leaned back and waited.

'The woman in black,' Lestrade said softly.

Kane didn't move.

'How many people have you interviewed?'

'The cook, four of the maids and Roger Casement. Do you think he's all he seems, by the way?'

'Casement? Straight as a die. For all I know, John, he could be a German spy, but at the moment he's a witness and not a very helpful one at that. Come with me.'

The Yard men, one still limping, both swatting the heavy flies of summer, sauntered off in search of a solution. 'You didn't get to the butler, then?' Lestrade asked.

Kane tilted back his boater. 'He didn't do it, did he?'

'We've been through all that, John. How is Sergeant Blevvins by the way?'

'Homicidal,' Kane assured him. 'Same as ever.'

Lestrade nodded. 'Useful man, the butler. Soul of discretion, of course. Loyal to a fault. . . .'

'But?' Kane sniffed something in the wind. He wiped the peacock droppings from his shoe.

'But he disapproved of his master's little peccadillo.'

'I hadn't heard that about Ushant.' Kane frowned. 'Seemed a well set up chap to me.'

'He had a lady-friend,' Lestrade confided, as though writing to 'Madge' of *Truth*.

'Ah, you bachelors.' Kane tapped the superintendent with his boater and, realising the over-familiarity of the gesture, promptly stepped into the lily-pond to show his contrition.

'No, this way, John,' said Lestrade and vanished into a thicket.

'Sir? Superintendent?' Inspector Kane whirled this way and

that, vainly searching for his guv'nor. He also took the
opportunity to roll up his trouser-leg to wring out some of the
water.

Lestrade poked his head out of a hedge of privet. 'There's no
time for a lodge meeting now, John. We've work to do' – and he
dragged the damp confused inspector into a maze.

'It's a maze,' he said.

Lestrade applauded. 'The centre's over there. On sunny
evenings, the lady in black would meet Ushant there. She would
arrive, probably by the side-gate, which Ushant ordered to be
kept unlocked, would make her way through the gap you've
just negotiated. . . . You have negotiated it, John?'

The inspector spat out the leaves to put the superintendent's
mind at rest.

'The butler – Yeats – would leave sherry and almond trifles on
a tray for them. All the servants had orders to stay out of the
maze between the hours of seven and midnight. Then Ushant
and his lady made their way indoors. Follow me.'

Kane did so.

'We are walking, John, in the footsteps of a murderer.' He
swung one leg; Kane swung his other.

'Bandy, was she?'

Lestrade ignored it.

'Good God!' Kane stood stock-still. Before him, virtually
invisible in the boughs of an old gnarled tree, lay a small studded
door.

'It gets better,' said Lestrade. 'Watch yourself here. Some of
the—'

'Damnation!' Kane roared.

'– steps are a little uneven. There are fourteen of them—Oh,
Christ! Fifteen.' The policemen tapped, fumbled and cursed in
the darkness.

'And here' – Lestrade delivered a solid blow to the blackness
in front of him – 'is a brick wall. But here!' The stick made a
different sound as a panel slid back and the gloom of Ushant's
library came into view.

'Incredible!' said Kane, allowing the chinks of daylight to break again on his eyes.

'Not really,' said Lestrade, running his fingers over Ushant's brass fittings. 'It's a priest-hole. You know, the sort of hide-away escape-passage Catholics used to get away from Puritans. Or was it the other way round? Dickens or Jones would know.'

'How did you find it?'

Lestrade smiled. 'I'd like to claim it was a sixth sense,' he said. 'Actually Yeats showed it to me.'

'So this woman. . . .' Kane was intrigued. 'Shouldn't be hard to find a Negress in Rutland, eh?'

'What?' Lestrade was lost.

'The black lady.'

'I said she *wore* black, John; I didn't say she *was*. Do pay attention!'

'Sorry, sir. Description?'

'About as helpful as Casement's. At least Yeats could testify to her sex, which is an improvement on our dog-watching diplomat. Ushant began to bring her to the house – to this room and presumably upstairs.'

'Upstairs?'

'Yes, John, it's where they keep the beds.'

'Ah, I see. A liaison!'

'Brilliant! He began bringing her here nearly four months ago. He gave Yeats careful instructions that she was not to be addressed and on no account were they to be disturbed when she was . . . visiting.'

'So' – Kane's mind was racing ahead – 'Ushant, the peerless policeman, finds a floosy. They quarrel. She kills him.' He scowled. Even he saw the flaws in that.

'He wouldn't be the first great man destined for high office to be brought down by a woman.'

'No, I don't think they quarrelled. Look at this room, John. Nothing out of place. Nothing disturbed. That was how it was when Yeats found him. You found the bloodstain?'

'On the mat? Yes.'

'Right. Sit over it – in the position you assume Ushant was adopting.'

Kane took a chair, wedging himself next to the coffin. Lestrade stood in front of him. 'Right. We'll assume the coffin wasn't here that evening. I don't think our murderess would tip her hand by bringing one along, do you? Might put Ushant on his guard.'

'Go on.'

'Look at the desk.'

Kane took in the glittering mahogany, the brass clutter. Then he turned from the coffin to the desk.

'What's missing?' Lestrade asked.

'Er . . . a photograph of the lover? The black lady?'

Lestrade tutted and shook his head. 'Ushant did all his own paperwork,' he said, as a clue.

'No pens!' Kane was triumphant, until his eyes fell on them, neatly tied beside the inkstand. 'No blotting paper?' His enthusiasm was waning.

'No letter-opener, man,' Lestrade broke in. 'Remember Ushant's throat. The cut.'

'Jagged,' Kane threw back.

'As though made by a blunted knife or—'

'—a letter-opener,' they chorused.

'But she'd be covered in blood,' said Kane.

'She may have been,' said Lestrade. 'Who saw her go? Casement of the consulate, half-asleep in a deceptive light? She could have been twelve feet tall and bright green, and he wouldn't have noticed.'

'But Ushant was a big man. And a copper. He'd have seen it coming.'

'Not if,' said Lestrade, and he swept behind the inspector, bringing his stick up horizontally under his throat, 'she attacked like this' – and he drew the wood gently across Kane's larynx.

'So that's it,' the inspector said smugly.

'Perhaps.' Lestrade sauntered to the window. 'Or perhaps the peacock did it.'

'Sir?'

'There's something else, John. Come into the garden again. I've got a little story I want to tell you. It's a few years old, I'm afraid, but I don't think you'll have heard it. . . .'

Constable Lestrade had been on mounted duty that day in 1874. He had grown the moustache that Mr Disraeli had suggested, but the new-found swagger in his stride had been easily upset by his mount. Burned into the animal's bay flank were the initials and numbers of the City force – CL 81 – but the beast was affectionately known as the Destroyer. From the very day Lestrade had clapped eyes on it gently chewing its handler's tunic-sleeve in its stall, it had been hatred on a mutual basis. After three days, the insides of the constable's knees were raw with mounting and dismounting, his undress uniform trousers in tatters. And the Destroyer had taken against a pair of dray-horses in Leadenhall Street and had hurtled after them, leaving the constable to bounce around like a sack of potatoes, much to the delight of the watching crowd. Worse had followed the next day when the Destroyer had taken a fancy to a pretty dapple grey ridden by a lady along the river at low tide. In vain did Lestrade haul at the snaffle, insisting he thought the animal 'had been done.' Nature nearly took its course until Lestrade hauled the erotic equine sideways so that both landed with a splash in the slime. Try as he might to make the embarrassing beast drink the fatal water, the Destroyer merely rolled upright, his ardour temporarily cooled, and Lestrade, black as a Nigger minstrel, had no option but to roll upright with him.

So here he was, on that April day, lining the route taken by the Prime Minister on what was to be his last triumphal visit to the City. It was to be less than a triumph. Mr Gladstone had managed to outrage nearly everyone in a whirlwind reforming spree of six years. Above all, they screamed vengeance to a man, because he had closed their pubs on Sundays. Only a little knot of gaudily clad ladies, whose virtue seemed to Lestrade not very difficult, waved and cheered. The-Not-Yet-Grand-Old-Man smiled and waved back. He seemed to know them.

Lestrade sat in his place on Ludgate Hill above the stinking sewer of the Fleet. Behind him the imposing granite of St Paul's; below him the rattling, whistling track that ran into Blackfriars Station. The Prime Minister's cavalcade approached him, the People's William leaning out and nodding his balding grey head to the less than faithful. As the open landau reached him, Lestrade saw a figure jump forward against the barricade of blue-caped constables. In an instant he saw the pistol raised and, tugging hard on the rein, attempted to wheel the Destroyer into action. The dumb beast, clearly of Tory tendencies, stood rooted to the spot. Lestrade did the only thing left open to him; he leaped, whirling his long truncheon, into the milling mass of the crowd. The Destroyer succeeded in blocking the way of Gladstone's horses, and screaming and panic filled the air. Lestrade struggled upright and found himself locked in an iron grip with a lady of the Temperance persuasion who fetched him a smart one across the temples with her Rechabite banner. Lestrade was not at all sure that was in order, independent or not. By the time his vision had cleared, he could only fling himself at the gent who was preparing to make a hasty exit, and together they rolled on the cobbles below Christopher Wren's steps. The crowd cleared for them as Lestrade battled with the would-be assassin, tugging him first this way, then that. At last he sat on the assailant's head, pinning him to the stonework.

'Feed the birds, guv'nor,' the old bird woman croaked next to him. 'Tuppence a bag.'

'Not just now.' Lestrade's mind was elsewhere, and his grip was around the other man's throat.

'Unhand me, poltroon!' the gent was hissing, but Lestrade sat resolutely until help arrived in the form of two other constables and a sergeant.

'Bloody coppers!' snarled the crowd.

'Police brutality, that's what it is!' the cry was taken up.

'Don't worry.' A sergeant handed Lestrade his helmet. 'They're just miffed 'cos the bloke missed old Gladeye, that's all.'

Lestrade whistled for the Destroyer, and three dogs came bounding over to him.

'Next time I'll let him fire,' he murmured, wiping the potato peelings from his tunic.

'Constable!' A Lowland Scots accent with a trace of genteel Liverpudlian rent the air.

'Yes, sir.' The nearest twenty coppers clicked to attention.

'No, you,' called the voice from the carriage, 'with the battered helmet and recalcitrant horse.'

Gradually the crowd parted to leave Lestrade alone with his Prime Minister. The People's William thrust out an Undenominational hand. 'My thanks to you, Officer,' said Gladstone. 'It's good to know our lives are safe in your hands. Catherine' – he nudged his poker-faced wife – 'give this man a shilling. He's earned it.'

'No, thank you, sir.' Lestrade saluted. 'We of the City force do not take money, sir.'

'The City force? My dear chap,' Gladstone apologised, 'I thought you were with the Metropolitans. Drive on, Morley. I hope one day', bellowed Gladstone as the landau picked up speed, 'you will come within the pale of the Constitution.'

'What did he mean?' A constable handed Lestrade the Destroyer's reins, the last thing on earth he wanted, but at least he was grateful for the fact that there was no horse at the end of them. The beast had bolted.

'Perhaps he thought I didn't look well,' said Lestrade.

'You want *me* to interr – inter – ask him a few questions, sir?' Lestrade was nonplussed.

Inspector Palmer lolled back in his chair, counting the wad of pound notes in his hand. 'Why not, laddie? He was your collar, wasn't he? How long have you been with us now?'

'Just over a year, sir.'

'Well, then. Hop to it. You've watched me do it often enough. It's time you won your spurs. Anyway, come the end of the week' – Palmer carefully lit his cigar with a note and chuckled at the incredulity on the constable's face – 'I'll be out of this bloody patrol jacket and residing at Great Scotland Yard. Who'll hold your hand then?'

Lestrade saluted and clattered down the winding stairs to the cells.

'How are your plates, Bert?' he hailed the constable at the bottom.

'Somethink chronic, Sholto. How are yours?'

'Horse patrol, Bert.' Lestrade hung his helmet on the hook. 'It's not my plates I'm bothered about.'

The cell was lit by a solitary oil-lamp. There were no windows, and the whole thing reeked of ammonia and tobacco.

'Mr Hesketh?' Lestrade grated back a chair and sat down.

The prisoner, slumped in his shirt-sleeves, looked up at the constable's entrance. 'Who the devil are you?' he snarled.

'Constable Lestrade, sir,' he said. 'I was the one who apprehended you.'

'Why has my bail been denied?' The prisoner began to pace the room like a caged cat, the flickering lamp throwing lurid shadows as he moved.

'I don't know, sir. You are entitled to a lawyer.'

Hesketh stopped pacing and looked levelly at Lestrade. 'Poltroon,' he growled, 'I *am* a lawyer.'

'Oh.' Lestrade had not done his homework.

'Has my wife been to see me?' Hesketh was softer.

'Not that I am aware, sir. Tell me' – he tried to recollect Palmer's tone in these situations – 'why did you try to kill Mr Gladstone?'

Hesketh turned away. 'Constable, I've answered that question a couple of dozen times in the past few days.'

'I have not been privy to any of that, sir. Would you mind answering it again?'

'All right,' Hesketh rounded on him angrily. Lestrade stayed calm, seated, although the pain was intense. 'All right' – the lawyer was calmer now – 'I will answer it once more. And once I have I reserve my right under the law to remain silent. Understand?'

Lestrade nodded.

'I had to see a new client in the City on Wednesday last, and as I walked up Ludgate Hill I became enmeshed in the crowds watching the Prime Minister's entourage.'

'Did you know that Mr Gladstone would take that route, sir?' Lestrade was trying his best.

'I didn't know he was taking any route, man. I told you, I just happened upon it.'

'And then?'

'I thought I'd wait until the carriage passed. It was impossible to get through the throng of people. As the landau came nearer I felt someone push me from behind and found myself in front of the police cordon. A man behind me was pointing a gun at Gladstone. There was confusion. It all happened so quickly. . . .'

Lestrade had heard that one before.

'Then an idiot constable of the City Police leaped off his horse and succeeded in jumping on everybody but the right man. While you were floundering at my feet, I found a hand in my pocket. I thought it was being picked.'

'And was it?'

'No. The man with the gun had put his weapon into my pocket. I had been put in the frame, so to speak.'

'And then?'

'And then you and I had our little contretemps, Constable. As I was turning to stop the real assailant, you stopped me.'

Lestrade produced the pistol from his tunic. It was a crude wooden carving, painted metallic blue.

'And that's the biggest piece of nonsense in the whole affair.' Hesketh threw himself down on the chair. 'Why me? And why a harmless wooden toy?'

'What did you do with the real gun, Mr Hesketh?' Lestrade leaned forward as he had seen Palmer do on several occasions to worry and fluster his man.

Hesketh merely returned the posture, so that their noses virtually touched. 'In the struggle,' he said. 'Surely you noticed me secrete it deftly up my posterior?'

Lestrade's mouth hung slack. For a moment he toyed with calling a doctor, then reason got the better of him. He stood up. 'Is that your final word on the matter?' he asked.

Hesketh nodded.

'Then, God have mercy on your soul' – and he turned to go.

'Very dramatic, Constable, but really it has no significance. No one is going to hang me for waving a bit of wood at Mr Gladstone. Disraeli does that all the time. Not,' he hastened to add, 'that I did any such thing.'

The constable reached the door.

'Lestrade, you've seen the roster by now. Who's on?'

'Which beak?'

'Yes' – Hesketh was appalled by the lack of reverence – 'which chief justice?'

'I am afraid I am not at liberty to—'

'Lestrade!' Hesketh broke forward. 'Lestrade, I am not a well man. Tussling with you on the steps of St Paul's; my heart. . . .'

Lestrade was unimpressed.

'Please,' the lawyer wheedled.

'Firkett,' said Lestrade.

Hesketh staggered back.

'No, sir, I am not being disrespectful. Chief Justice Firkett.'

'Oh, yes.' Hesketh's voice was scarcely audible. 'I know what you mean.'

Lestrade could not sleep. Since he had talked to Hesketh in his cell, something niggled. An indefinable sense of unease; an itch he couldn't scratch. And when he heard that Hesketh had refused to eat, refused even to see the wife he had asked for, he was convinced that something was very wrong. Accordingly, on his rest day, he found his way to the chambers of Mr Herbert Uriah Hesketh in a particularly unimposing corner of the Temple, where Father Thames regularly threw up his litter of deceased dogs, cadaverous cats and endemic effluent. His tread up the spiral staircase and along the gloomy passage had by chance been noiseless, and when he reached the door he found it slightly ajar and had no need of Hesketh's key, which he had appropriated – and signed for – the previous day. He had hoped that something in the lawyer's papers would provide a clue to his behaviour, an explanation of why the cocksure counsel should now become the silent recluse. He found more than he bargained for. As the door swung open, he heard muffled sounds from the inner office. This was Saturday. It was unlikely anyone would be working, and of an afternoon especially. He realised the sounds were rhythmic, grunting, male and female, and getting louder. With all the majesty of his profession he put his shoulder to the second door and nearly fell over a couple writhing on Hesketh's desk. They sprang apart immediately, he stuffing shirt-tails and all sorts of things back into his trousers, she desperately smoothing down the layers of petticoat and bombazine and attempting to cover her pert breasts.

'Who the devil are you?' the gent roared, crimson with exertion and embarrassment.

'I might well ask the same of you, sir.' Lestrade felt he held the whip hand, so to speak.

'I shall call the police!' shouted the gent.

'And I shall come running,' Lestrade answered him.

'What?' Outrage began to subside.

'I am Constable Lestrade of the City Police. Who are you?'

The gent snatched the girl's hand and dragged her past Lestrade out of the room. 'Someone who knows that he is not obliged to answer any question put by a constable who is out of uniform, has no means of identification and is signally out of his jurisdiction. Good day!' – and he slammed the door behind them.

Lestrade's interest lay inside. He rummaged through the solicitor's briefs, but all he came up with of interest were the lady's drawers. He never knew when such things might come in handy, so he stuffed them into his pocket and was on his way.

'Constable Lestrade!' the name boomed and rang down the corridors, reverberating by octaves as it turned corners and climbed stairs. The officer of that name slicked down his moustache for the umpteenth time that morning and, cradling his helmet with his white gloves, entered number 2 chamber of the Central Criminal Court.

He took the oath as he had often before, although this was his first appearance in such august surroundings.

'You are Constable Lestrade of B Division, City of London Police?' Counsel for the prosecution gripped his robe-lapels in time-honoured fashion.

Lestrade appeared not to notice, but stood staring open-mouthed at the judge.

'Are you Constable Lestrade of B Division?' Counsel for the prosecution, never a patient man, assumed the witness was deaf.

'Er . . . yes, sir. I am,' Lestrade responded at last.

'Did you apprehend the prisoner at the bar on Wednesday the eighteenth ult. while in pursuance of your duty?'

'Er . . . I . . . er. . . . Could you repeat the question, please?'

'Oh, really, m'lud,' counsel bellowed to the bench, 'is it possible to have an ear-trumpet brought into court for the purposes of cross-examination? *I* am having difficulty. I fear it will be beyond my learned friend. . . .'

Counsel's learned friend flashed him a withering glance.

Chief Justice Firkett leaned forward till his wig dragged over his gavel. 'Do you have a hearing deficiency?' he bellowed at Lestrade.

'No, sir,' the constable answered.

'Then, pray, answer counsel's questions in a manner. . . .' And the judge's voice trailed off, too.

Counsel looked at each other. For a long moment, Lestrade and Firkett looked at each other across a crowded courtroom. One recognised the other. In Hesketh's office. On Hesketh's desk. In his wig, vertical, the judge looked different. But they all looked the same lying down. Firkett looked away, to the gallery above. Lestrade followed his gaze. Their eyes fell on a dark-haired beauty sitting demurely in the front row. She, too, had looked different lying down, but Lestrade still had her fol-de-rols at the station.

He gave his evidence. He coped with counsel. He watched Hesketh, pale, unresponsive, weak. He watched the Chief Justice Firkett. He watched the dark beauty in the gallery. He listened while the Prime Minister's evidence was read out. Hesketh had intended to defend himself, but at the last moment he had hired a colleague. As prisoner at the bar he was allowed no word in his own defence. Neither did he attempt any. On the fifth day, defence counsel, ashen-faced and tight-lipped, announced a change of plea. Guilty as charged. Chief Justice Firkett directed the jury accordingly, and those twelve just men declined to leave the box. They delivered their obvious verdict where they stood.

Herbert Uriah Hesketh asked to see Sholto Lestrade when it was all over. The former lawyer sat in his cell slumped over the table.

'You wanted to see me?' Lestrade's voice brought him for a while out of himself.

'This is my wife.' Hesketh handed Lestrade a crumpled photograph.

'My God!' The constable stared blankly at it.

'Yes, you've probably seen her before. She was in court of course. Nominally to give me her support. The girl I love sat up in the gallery.'

'Mr Hesketh, I. . . .'

'No, Lestrade, please.' The lawyer held up his hand. 'I asked to see you. And I'm grateful to you for coming. I know the law, Lestrade. Firkett gave me the hardest sentence he could. The toy *could* have been a gun. The gun *could* have been loaded. Six people swore they saw me waving it about. That adds up to circumstantial evidence, Lestrade, and if I'd not changed my plea—'

'Why did you?'

'Why?' Hesketh looked old and tired. 'Look at my wife,

Lestrade. She's a lovely woman, isn't she?'

The constable nodded.

'Everybody thinks so, naturally. Chief Justice Firkett thinks so, too. Oh, it wasn't obvious at first. He's old enough to be her father, and she pretended she wasn't flattered by it. High Court judge and all. There's talk of the attorney-generalship. Well, she became less and less . . . happy. With me, I mean. One day, I found them together. . . .'

So did I, thought Lestrade to himself.

'I forgave her. There were tears, vows. We even went away together for a while, and for a time I thought her infatuation was over. Then this business. As soon as I knew it was Firkett on the bench, I realised. . . .'

'What do you mean?'

'Don't you see, Lestrade? He fixed it. Perhaps they both did. Firkett paid some thug to cause that scene on Ludgate Hill. It must have been meticulously planned. The whole reason for my being there – to meet a new client – was almost certainly spurious. Firkett's man waved the gun, thrust it into my pocket. And you did the rest.'

Lestrade looked suitably chastened. 'I didn't know,' he said.

Hesketh patted his shoulder. 'Of course not. How could you? I didn't know myself. He – or perhaps it was her – forged the letter they found in my office.'

'Letter?' Lestrade had been back on horse patrol, wrestling with the Destroyer, in the closing days of the trial.

'A letter which I was supposed to have written to some Fenian, expressing my profound hatred of Gladstone. If it weren't so appalling, it would be laughable.'

'We've got to get this sorted.' Lestrade reached for his helmet.

'Oh?' Hesketh looked at him. 'I've had my moment in court, Lestrade. I pleaded guilty, remember? I'm on my way to Dartmoor now and they'll throw away the key. I'm not coming back, you see. I don't want to.'

'But Firkett? Your wife?'

'They're guilty, Lestrade. She of breaking the sixth

Commandment, he probably of breaking many more. But I know the law, Lestrade. And I know Firkett. He'd stop you as he'd squash a fly. I only called you here because . . . because I think you're an honest man, and that's a rare thing nowadays.' He looked up at the constable, and held out his hand. 'Goodbye. . . .'

John Kane puffed his smoke-rings to the evening sky. Bobbies' bull's-eyes darted like fireflies in the shrubbery near the house.

'Well . . . Firkett,' he mused.

'Of course,' said Lestrade. 'All that was a long time ago.'

'The black lady!' Kane dropped his cigar. 'That's why you reminisced. Our murderess is Hesketh's wife!'

'No, no, John.' Lestrade stubbed out his smoke. 'That's not why I told you the story. I went to Palmer straight from Hesketh's cell. I told him what I've told you.'

'And?'

'And, as Hesketh would probably have guessed, he laughed. Said that morally, of course, I was right. But legally. . . . And that was the end of it. Except. . . .'

'Except?'

'Except that Herbert Hesketh hanged himself in his cell at Dartmoor a few months later. Nobody was surprised. When decency permitted, Mrs Hesketh married Chief Justice Firkett. I hope they were happy together. Between them, they'd succeeded in killing a man. But the thing was. . . .'

'H'm?'

'A few days after the trial was over, I got a letter at the station. Addressed to me, personally.'

'Who was it from?'

'That's just it – I don't know. All it said was "Ten for the Ten Commandments". The Commandments that Firkett had broken.'

'How odd. Mrs Hesketh, do you think? Remorseful?'

'From what I saw of her, which was quite a bit, she didn't have a remorseful bone in her body.'

'Firkett, then?'

'I doubt it.'

'Then, who?'

'The same person, John, who is behind the murders of M'Travers, Lucas and Ushant. The butler, the doctor, the policeman. Like a game of Happy Families. And you know the card who comes out on top, don't you, John? The Undertaker. Every time.'

The Baker's Dozen

In deference to the late chief constable of Rutland, the commissioner's post was allowed to remain vacant throughout the autumn. The Home Secretary put pressure on Sir Edward Henry, and the little nutbrown man put pressure on Superintendent Frank Froest of the Serious Crimes Squad. Apart from putting considerable pressure on his braces, Froest leaned heavily on Inspector John Kane, who instinctively and at his own request looked for guidance and inspiration to Lestrade. Such was the chain of command, and not for the first time the buck stopped there.

'It's Mr Lestrade, isn't it?' The superintendent turned to the low woods behind him.

'Who's that?' Lestrade had been miles away, ruminating over the depositions Kane had given him.

'We haven't met,' the voice went on. 'I am Jane Penhaligon.' She seemed to float over the russet leaves on the hill, leading a pony by the bridle.

'Ah, Norman's wife.' Lestrade tipped his bowler.

She took his outstretched hand. 'Yes, yes, I can see it.'

For a moment, Lestrade wondered whether his Donegal had flapped open and all was not well beneath it, but Mrs Penhaligon spared him any further embarrassment. 'I can see why Fanny has chosen you. Clear eyes. Firm jaw. That hint of loneliness. Your face says it all, Mr Lestrade.'

He was unused to such directness in women, and wives of vicars in particular were a breed unknown to him. 'Were you riding, Mrs Penhaligon?' was all he could think to say.

'Schooling the grey,' she explained. 'How is your leg?'

'Better every day, thank you.'

'Good. Fanny says you are working on – what is your phrase? – a case, although not yet free to return to work. Admirable dedication, Mr Lestrade.'

He found himself staring for longer than he had intended into her deep dark eyes. A man, he knew, could lose himself in there.

'Take my arm, Mr Lestrade' - and they walked by the river. Thunder rumbled in the distance, and the pony jerked its head. Lestrade reached back to catch the bridle, stroking its neck.

'Thank you,' she said. 'You have a way with horses.'

Lestrade laughed. 'That's kind of you,' he said, 'but if you knew me better....'

'I should like that.' She held his hand. 'I should like that very much.'

He felt something inside leap at that, then he remembered. He was a superintendent of Scotland Yard, nearly sixty years of age, and there was Fanny.

'It looks like rain,' he said. 'Perhaps you'd better get home.'

Her dark eyes flashed reproachfully. 'Tut, tut. Are you trying to get rid of me, Mr Lestrade?'

He smiled. 'No, of course not.'

'Tomorrow, then.' She drew the reins over her pony's neck, and he helped her into the saddle. She bent towards him, and the warm scent of her hair tumbled over him in waves. 'Will you be here?'

He nodded. She smiled and lashed her pony across the hill.

'Well, Sholto, so you've met Jane?' Fanny looked up from her sewing.

He looked up from his book. 'Yes,' he said. 'How did you know?'

Fanny chuckled. 'I met her later in the village. What do you make of her?'

'Not a lot,' Lestrade lied.

'You must admit she's very attractive.'

'Oh, I wouldn't say so.' He was at least consistent.

'Sholto Lestrade, you liar.' She threw a cushion at him.

'Billiards, Sholto?' Tom Berkeley stood in the doorway. Lestrade was grateful for the escape.

'Can you stand another tear in the baize?'

'Can you stand to lose another quid?'

'How much is it now?'

'Three thousand and twenty-four pounds,' Fanny told him.

'Ah, well,' laughed Lestrade, 'in for a penny. . . .' And he took up his cue in the billiards room. Stalker poured the brandies and left quietly. Lestrade rolled up his shirt-sleeves and lit a cigar.

'I hear you met Jane Penhaligon today,' Tom said, and Lestrade's cue clacked uselessly on the cue-ball.

'Is that the Berkeley family's sole topic of conversation?' he asked.

'Rather a stunner, isn't she? I hadn't met her myself until recently. For a while everybody thought Norman was a bachelor. Married to his work and all that.'

'Ah, who isn't?' Lestrade watched Berkeley sink his first ball.

'That's an odd remark for an engaged man,' the chief constable commented.

'You know what I mean, Tom. But I thought vicars' wives were an integral part of the community. You know, cucumber sandwiches, garden fêtes, that sort of thing.'

'This one isn't. Fanny says she's hardly known in the village. And she's not often in church, either. Apparently, there's a sick relative. Your shot.'

Lestrade assumed the position.

'Both feet on the floor.' Berkeley tapped Lestrade sharply with the business end of the cue.

'Who's been talking?' Lestrade complied.

'Ah, if I were a younger man. . . .'

'And if she wasn't the vicar's wife,' Lestrade reminded him.

'Oh, quite, quite.' Berkeley crouched for his shot. Lestrade sipped his brandy. It was good to see Tom in humour again. He had accepted the situation now. That someone had a grudge against him, that it went with the job. Lestrade had discreetly increased the group of men around the chief constable. Stalker never left his side during the day, and Lestrade himself was in the room next to his at night. For safety's sake, Lestrade had also asked Frank Froest to put a close watch on Edward Henry.

'That grey horse reminded me of something, though.'

'Oh?' Berkeley was clearing the table with his usual skill. 'What's that?'

'Do you remember Valentine Baker?'

'Baker? Baker? Wasn't he that explorer chappie?'

'His brother. My first arrest in the Metropolitan Police.'

'What's he got to do with Jane Penhaligon's horse?'

'Nothing, directly. It just reminded me. And, while I've got nothing else to do, I thought I might tell you about it.'

Tom Berkeley yawned. 'Go on, then, Sholto. But don't stand in my light, there's a good chap.'

The helmet plate was different, and the beat. But the rest was the same. The pay, the aching feet, the abuse. People asked him why he'd changed. Why he'd gone over to the other side. He didn't really know. Except that his dad had been with the Metropolitans. In a way, it was like coming home. 'You'll be sorry,' they'd told him. 'You won't get anywhere.'

He thought he detected a disapproving growl from the iron griffins that flanked Fleet Street and guarded the arches of Temple Bar as he passed them, but it was probably only a cab-horse breaking wind. He put on his new boots and began to wander the wilderness of Seven Dials. At least his transfer, written out in triplicate, long hand, copperplate, had got him off the horse patrol. And he still had all his fingers.

It was a fierce month, that June of 1875. Constable 312 Lestrade of H Division, Metropolitan Police, tucked himself behind the angle of the building and pulled off first his helmet, then his boots. He toyed for a moment with dabbling his toes in the horse-trough, but it was rather unseemly and people might talk. As it was, he was getting ready for a doze when shouts roused him.

'Help! Police! Police! There's never one around when you want one!'

Lestrade tugged his boots on and, grabbing his helmet, emerged before the grimy façade of Victoria Station.

'What seems to be the trouble?' he asked the agitated-looking guard twirling this way and that by the entrance.

'Ah, at last. Come on. There's been a 'orrible crime' – and he leaped back into the smoke and steam. People scattered as the two men dashed through them. A burly man grabbed the guard. 'I've got him, Constable!' he shouted.

Lestrade unhooked them both. 'I'm *with* him, not *after* him,' he explained, 'but I appreciate the thought, sir. Perhaps next time, Mr . . .?'

'Crigh,' shouted the man. 'Hugh N. Crigh.' But Lestrade had gone.

The guard dashed past the ten o'clock from Liphook, snorting and hissing in the morning sun that flooded the station. The engine made funny noises, too.

'There it is,' the guard pointed, hanging back in terror.

A tall mustachioed gentleman stood in frock-coat and topper beside a first-class carriage. Some yards from him, a young lady was sobbing violently, being consoled by a dowager and her companion. Quite a crowd had gathered at a safe distance from them, and were hurling abuse at the gentleman.

'Now, then.' Lestrade pushed his way through. 'What's all this?'

'Rape,' jabbered the guard who was cringing at Lestrade's elbow. A powerful blow from the dowager's parasol dented the man's hat and beneath it, conceivably, his head.

'You needn't exacerbate the appalling problem by using foul language, my man,' she pointed out.

'Excuse me, madam, who are you?' Lestrade asked.

'My name is irrelevant, Constable.'

Lestrade reached for his notebook. 'Could you spell that, madam?'

'Davinia,' the companion attracted the dowager's attention, 'do we really want any truck with a man whose boots are on the wrong feet?'

Lestrade followed their gaze. This was almost as bad as being caught with his trousers down.

'Are you really a policeman?' the dowager asked.

Lestrade staightened. 'Will you give me your name, madam?' he repeated.

'Oh, very well. I am Davinia Cruise. *Lady* Davinia Cruise. This is my companion, Miss Ethel Hinch.'

'Doubtless you've heard of the Hertfordshire Hinches,' the companion gushed.

'No, madam. Who is this young lady?'

'This' – Lady Davinia clutched the sobbing girl to her daunting bosom – 'this poor creature is Miss Hannah Dickinson.' She broke away to take Lestrade by the arm and whispered in his ear with that special venom only the gentry can muster, 'That despicable beast over there tried to force his attentions on Miss Dickinson. Do you have a truncheon?'

'Yes, ma'am,' Lestrade assured her.

'Then, I trust you will be bending it over the swine's head on your way to the police station.'

'Er . . . we shall see, madam.'

'Tut!' Lady Davinia broke away, creaking in her whalebone armour. 'Papa was right. Blue Devils indeed! Weak namby-pambies, that's what! And as for you,' she rounded on the railway guard, 'I shall see to it personally that you never work again as long as you live. Whatever was Lord Beaconsfield about, giving creatures like you the vote? I shall be suing, of course!' she shouted to the train. 'When I've finished the Southern Railway Company will have ceased to exist.'

'You must sell your shares first, dear,' warned Miss Hinch.

'Shut up, Ethel,' Davinia retorted. 'I'm in full flight.'

'Sir.' Lestrade thought it best to leave the ladies alone for a moment, especially in view of Lady Davinia's prowess with a parasol. The tall mustachioed gentleman looked from under his topper at the young constable.

'Well?' he said.

Lestrade looked at the bristling walrus whiskers, the piercing dark eyes. 'Your name, sir, if you please?'

'Valentine Baker.' He flashed a vicious glance at the dowager. 'Colonel Valentine Baker, late Tenth Hussars. Currently Assistant Quartermaster-General at Aldershot.'

'Hmmph,' snorted Lady Davinia. 'Assistant!' – and she swirled away to apply more smelling salts to the trembling Miss Dickinson.

Lestrade observed the crowd at his back and was glad to see a couple of coppers coming at the run to break it up.

'All right, Sholto?' one of them called.

'Hold the train, Ben. It doesn't go anywhere until I've got this one sorted. Would you mind getting into this carriage, sir?' Lestrade held open the door. It was the first time in his life he had sat inside a first-class compartment. The padded seats unnerved him.

'Will this take long, Officer?' Baker asked. 'I have a pressing engagement.'

'Not long, sir. Could you give me your address, please?'

The colonel did so.

'Now, sir,' said Lestrade, 'what happened here?'

'This really is tedious, Constable,' Baker sighed. 'I caught the train at Southampton and was alone in the carriage until Bishop's Waltham when the lady you see sobbing over there got in.'

'You were alone in the carriage?'

'Yes. I was reading my manuscript.'

'Manuscript, sir?'

Baker produced a leather travelling case. 'I am writing a book on my travels in the East, Constable.'

'Please go on.'

'I barely noticed the girl, save to tip my hat, when suddenly she stood up, tore open her bodice and began screaming.'

'"... began screaming,"' Lestrade wrote it down with his stubby pencil. 'And what did you do, sir?'

'I stood up as well. Thought the woman was having some sort of fit. Seen it in Ceylon of course.'

'Seen what, sir?' Lestrade asked. This smacked of a confession.

'People having fits, Constable. Do pay attention. It's the heat, you see. Damned hot today, what?'

'What did the lady do then?'

'The damnedest thing. Started trying to get out.'

'Out?' said Lestrade. 'Of a moving train?'

'Quite. In a trice, she was out of the door, hanging on like grim death. I was reaching out trying to get her back in. At any moment she might have plunged to her doom.'

'But you' – a parasol-point skewered the colonel in the shoulder as Lady Davinia lunged at him through the open window – 'represented the Fate Worse Than Death, didn't you, you monster? I shudder to think what might have befallen poor Miss Dickinson had she succumbed to your offer of so-called help.'

'Thank you, madam.' Lestrade closed the window to save the colonel further injury. Lady Davinia wrenched open the door.

'My man' – she prodded Lestrade above the bull's-eye – 'it will not, clearly, have occurred to you, but I have a fainting young lady out here who has been subjected to the most revolting assault upon her person. I am taking her to my hotel.'

'With respect, madam' – Lestrade removed the parasol-point from his tunic – 'that will not do. You may take Miss Dickinson into the next carriage, and I shall be there to ask her a few questions.'

'You impudent puppy.' She snatched his paper and pencil and ostentatiously made a note of the metal numbers on his collar. 'I shall be reporting you to your superiors' – but she and Miss Hinch helped the victim into the next carriage even so.

'Do I have your word, sir, that this *is* your address?'

'It is my London address, yes. If I am not there, I shall be in the camp at Aldershot.'

'Then, I need not detain you, sir, but we will need to talk again.'

Baker tipped his hat and walked away.

Lestrade straightened his uniform, removed his helmet and braved the lionesses' den behind him. Amid the whistles and snorts of the platform he tapped on the carriage door.

'I would like to talk to Miss Dickinson alone,' he said.

The dowager levelled her parasol. 'Never,' all three of them chorused. Lestrade knew when he was beaten. 'Very well, then' – and he sat beside Miss Hinch, who quickly crossed the narrow carriage to sit on the other side of Miss Dickinson from Lady Davinia. Lestrade was left like a pariah on the other seat.

'Why are there no ladies on the force?' Miss Hinch asked him.

'How grotesque, Ethel!' Lady Davinia remonstrated with her. 'Ladies could not possibly do so bestial a job.'

'Indeed not, madam,' Lestrade was the first to agree. He looked at Miss Dickinson. She was about his own age, he guessed, very attractive under the tears and the red nose, and her bodice and blouse were torn. There was something about the way her calves showed above her high-laced boots that did not sit easy with him. Perhaps it was the boots that Colonel Baker had seen. Perhaps it had stirred something in his blood.

'Can you tell me what happened, Miss Dickinson?' Lestrade sat poised, pencil and notebook in hand.

The lady was calmer now, as poised as the constable, and she took up the tale.

'I caught the train at Bishop's Waltham,' she said, 'to visit my aged grandmother in Kensington' – and she crumpled on to Miss Hinch's shoulder.

'Imagine,' said Lady Davinia soberly. 'That poor woman. How will her heart take the strain?'

'Do you know this lady's grandmother, madam?' Lestrade was nearing the terminus of his tether.

'That is irrelevant,' the dowager said.

So they *were* related, Lestrade mused.

'Womankind must suffer. But not, *not*,' her voice mounted with the fury of a hell-fire preacher, 'in silence.'

'You caught the train at Bishop's Waltham,' Lestrade reminded Miss Dickinson. 'Why did you take a carriage with a single gentleman in it?'

'Miss Dickinson is young and naïve,' Lady Davinia answered. 'She clearly mistook him for a human being.'

'Answer the question, please, miss,' Lestrade ignored her.

'By the time I realised I *was* alone,' she said, 'the train had started.'

'What happened next?'

Miss Dickinson hung her head. Miss Hinch clasped the girl to her. 'There, there, child,' she soothed her.

'I have to know, Miss Dickinson,' Lestrade persisted. 'You want this beast behind bars, don't you?'

'Ah,' Lady Davinia crowed, 'your first sensible statement, Officer. This is more like it.'

'We had been travelling for a while when the . . . gentleman—'

Lady Davinia and Miss Hinch snorted in unison.

'— the gentleman put his hand on . . . my knee.'

There was an audible silence in the carriage.

'Under or over your skirt?' Lestrade asked.

'Revolting!' hissed the dowager.

'Disgusting!' recoiled the companion.

'Under,' affirmed Miss Dickinson. 'Then he . . . tried to kiss me.'

'My child!' Lady Davinia held out her arms.

'No' – Miss Dickinson stood up – 'I must go through with this,' she said, staring tearfully and with resolution at the sign which proclaimed to the world the wonders of Margate. 'You have been so kind to me, but this officer has a duty to perform. When I tried to pull away,' she continued, 'he tore my blouse and bodice. He was . . . undoing the buttons on his trousers.'

Miss Hinch fainted in a corner. Everyone ignored her. Lady

Davinia was on the edge of her seat.

'What then?' she blurted out.

Miss Dickinson and Constable Lestrade looked at her, and she had the grace to wither a little.

'Then I climbed out of the door and clung there for dear life until the train stopped at Liphook.'

'Did Colonel Baker say anything to you?' Lestrade asked.

'He kept trying to make me get back in.'

'We can well imagine what for, my dear,' Lady Davinia commented sagely, and she fixed Lestrade with a stare. 'What beasts men are!'

'And at Liphook?' Lestrade went on with his questioning.

'A clergyman who had seen me clinging on for dear life took me into his compartment.'

'You weren't afraid?' Lestrade challenged her.

'He was a Man of the Cloth,' Lady Davinia explained. 'Besides, vicars aren't men in the accepted sense of the term.'

'Where is he now?' Lestrade asked.

'He went in search of a policeman,' the dowager explained. 'Unfortunately, so did that disgusting little railway chappie. And *he* found *you*.'

'Do you wish to press charges, Miss Dickinson?' Lestrade asked.

'Of course she does!' Lady Davinia snapped.

'I fear I must,' Miss Dickinson answered him. 'For the sake of decent women everywhere.'

Lestrade took down the lady's particulars, careful to do so while Lady Davinia's back was turned as she did the decent thing and roused her companion.

The constable was shown into the riding school at the Duke of York's barracks a little before midday. The smell of manure and pipe smoke was horribly redolent of the horse patrol, and he almost recoiled. The room was vast, whitewashed walls slashed with shafts of sunlight streaming in through the high windows. The orderly who had escorted him thus far ran the length of the sanded floor to the two horsemen exercising at the far end. One

Lestrade recognised as Colonel Valentine Baker, AQMG, wearing the dark blue and gold-laced stable-jacket of the Tenth Hussars and sitting a magnificent grey charger, arching its neck and carrying its tail high. The other, in civilian dress, on a chestnut, he did not know, but behind the full beard the Baker features were evident. Both men looked up as the orderly saluted and pointed at the policeman.

Colonel Baker turned his grey to the far corner, reached down a lance from the rack and rammed home his spurs. Lestrade stood stock-still in the centre as man and horse whistled past him, the lance slicing into the earth inches from his feet. Baker whirled the animal back and reined in at Lestrade's back while the other horseman caracoled across to his front.

'Constable,' Baker said, 'I could have killed you then.'

Lestrade turned coolly to look at the cavalry lance nodding in agreement with Baker as it yawed backwards and forwards.

'I don't doubt it, sir,' he said, hoping his voice did not betray the fact that his heart was in his mouth. 'Why didn't you?'

'The same reason' – Baker hooked his leg over the pommel of his saddle and dismounted – 'I didn't get off the train at Liphook. The same reason I waited until you arrived at Victoria. The same reason I gave you my correct address and left instructions with my valet to tell you I was here.' He waved to the room. 'When I need to, the garrison kindly give me permission to use their school.'

'Constable,' the bearded man barked behind him.

'My brother Samuel,' the colonel introduced him. 'Baker Pasha.'

'Bless you,' offered the constable.

'My brother' – Samuel Baker dismounted, too – 'has fought in the Kaffir and Crimean Wars, witnessed the Austro-Prussian and Franco-Prussian Wars, has travelled extensively in the Far and Near East, and is the country's leading authority on cavalry tactics. . . .'

'Now, Sam, you're boasting again. You know I've never been to the Far East.'

'The point I am making, Constable, is that a man of Colonel

Baker's enormous reputation does not molest ladies in railway carriages.'

'With respect, sir, I only have his word for that. The lady in question is adamant that he did.'

The Bakers loomed over him. 'You've got nerve, Constable,' Samuel said, 'or do you have a platoon of men outside?'

'I came alone, sir,' Lestrade answered.

'More questions, I suppose?' Valentine grunted, digging out the lance and throwing it to the orderly.

'In due course, sir. But now I am afraid it is my duty to place you under arrest.'

'What?' fumed Samuel.

'You are not obliged to say anything, but anything you do say will be taken down and may be used in evidence.'

Valentine stood to his full height. 'What is the charge?'

'Attempted violation,' said Lestrade.

The brothers looked at each other. Samuel reached into his pocket. Lestrade steadied his truncheon, ready to parry an attack, but found himself facing the deadliest weapon of all – a wallet.

'Constable, I . . .,' Samuel began.

Colonel Baker gripped his arm. 'Put it away, Sam. We'd never live with ourselves. Besides, I don't think the constable's the type. Mr . . . er . . .?'

'Lestrade, sir.'

'Mr Lestrade, my wife and daughters are due to meet me here in a few moments, as well as Samuel's wife and his children. I wonder if. . . .'

'I shall walk on the other side of the road, sir,' Lestrade said. 'Can you meet me at Bow Street within the hour?'

'You're taking a chance, Lestrade,' the colonel said.

'All life's a chance, sir.'

The colonel shook his hand, and he and Samuel left their horses with the orderly and walked away.

'Colonel Baker,' Lestrade stopped them. 'Talking of life, sir. What does life mean to you?'

'They wouldn't give him life, Constable?' Samuel was horrified. 'He didn't do anything, man.'

'I've been in prison before, Sam,' confessed the colonel.

'Oh?' For a moment Lestrade's suspicions were aroused.

'In France five years ago,' Baker explained. 'I was accused of being a German spy. Iron bars don't frighten me, Constable. Why do you ask about life? It certainly isn't a bowl of cherries, is it?'

'Oh, just something Miss Dickinson said, sir.'

'What was that?'

'She used the phrase, when she was hanging on outside the train, "clinging on for dear life".'

'So?' Samuel asked.

'So,' said Lestrade, 'she used the phrase twice, as though. . . .'

'As though what?' asked the colonel.

'As though she had been rehearsed,' he said.

The Bakers looked at him and then at each other. 'I shall never doubt the intelligence of the force again,' said Samuel, and the inference that he habitually did offended Lestrade more than somewhat.

'Rehearsed by whom?' Valentine asked.

'That, sir, I don't know but. . . .'

'Yes?'

Lestrade took off his helmet. 'Look, sir, I'm sticking my neck out here. I lost six weeks' rest days for not arresting you at the station. . . .'

Colonel Baker patted his shoulder appreciatively.

'. . .I've seen her since, I think.'

'Who?'

'Miss Dickinson.'

'Well, naturally,' frowned Valentine. 'In the course of your enquiries.'

'Not exactly, sir. Are you familiar with Duke Street?'

'Know it like the back of the Albert Nyanza,' Samuel said. 'Off Oxford Street, isn't it? Near Manchester Square.'

Lestrade nodded. 'Part of my beat, sir. A lady who looks

astonishingly like Miss Dickinson lives at number thirty-two.'

'I don't follow you, Constable,' the colonel confessed.

'Number thirty-two, like most houses in the road, is a house of ill repute, sir.'

Valentine's chin-strap pinged up under his nose.

'Do you mean that Miss Dickinson . . .?' Samuel was the first to find his voice.

Lestrade held up his hands. 'I don't know,' he said. 'I only saw her fleetingly. I could be mistaken.'

'That makes a difference, doesn't it?' Valentine's brain was whirling.

'I can make no promises, sir,' Lestrade said.

'But you will be investigating,' the colonel urged. 'If I am convicted, Lestrade, it will mean the end of everything.'

The air was suddenly filled with the squeals and chatter of children. The Baker offspring and the Baker wives came tripping over the sawdust towards the men. Valentine made embarrassed introductions.

'Constable Lestrade is here, dear, to—'

'To enquire whether your husband would give us his expert advice on our mounted division, ma'am,' Lestrade finished the sentence for him.

All the Bakers smiled. Valentine, his wife and two daughters, Samuel, his wife and their seven children tripped back the way they had come. When the Bakers' dozen had left, Samuel reappeared at the door.

'Lestrade,' he said. 'Thirty-two Duke Street. The house of ill repute. . . .'

'Yes, sir?'

'I've been in some bordellos in my time, from here to Khartoum. They're rough places.'

'Some of them, sir.' Lestrade spoke of his single experience, cudgelled into semi-consciousness in Whitechapel the morning he and Inspector Palmer had found the body of George Claverhouse.

'Here.' Baker produced something from his pocket. 'I bought

that in Cairo. A damned sight more useful than that tipstaff you
carry.'

Lestrade made as to protest, but Baker Pasha had gone in
search of his family. The constable looked down. In his palm lay
a set of brass knuckles with a catch at one end. Lestrade pressed
it and a murderous blade clicked out. He smiled to himself. An
equaliser at last. A companion of a mile.

In the year of the Great Public Health Act, Constable Lestrade
picked his way gingerly through the reeking flotsam the Thames
and the hot summer had contrived to throw up on the dark
dingy reaches of the Arches. No doubt the ghost of David
Garrick would have been at home there. He crossed from
Villiers Street into the sunlit court that fronted Charing Cross
Station, negotiating as one had to the myriad piles deposited by
the Strand's busy hansom service. The pigeons got him at least
twice before he crossed Trafalgar Square and he found his way
through the labyrinthine alleys to Oxford Street where the
better sort of person was beginning to be found in those days. It
being a Tuesday afternoon and admission to the Entomological
Society's museum being free, he was swept along by the tide for
a while and at no point did his feet touch the ground. It was
noticeable that no one hurried the other way to the Panopticon
of Science, since admission there cost a shilling.

It was the oldest science in the world that drew Lestrade to
ring the bell at number 32 Duke Street. He felt conspicuous in
his only suit, and the freshly starched collar rubbed his neck. A
lady's maid answered the door, as freshly starched as he was.

'Yes?'

'My card,' said Lestrade, heart pounding. The printing of the
thing had cost him nearly a week's wages. His inspector had
disapproved of the whole venture. If he must do it at all, he must
do it in his own time, and at his own expense. He must indeed
do it incognito, although Lestrade had told him several times it
was in Duke Street.

'Won't you come in?' the maid bobbed. He was ushered into a

plush room, glittering with glass and candelabra, festooned with velvet and flock. Twice he nearly bolted for the door. He was twenty-three years of age, unused to bordellos at any level, but this one smacked of opulence far above his bowler. He fingered the three pound notes in his pocket. How far would they get him? he wondered. Probably not much above somebody's ankle.

'Lieutenant Lister?' A warm voice made him turn. Miss Dickinson swept in in feathers and paint, her breasts jutting deliciously over her bodice.

'At your service.' Lestrade attempted to click his heels as he assumed cavalry officers did.

'Oh' – she tapped him with her fan – 'you wicked man. Leave the servicing to me. Now' – she lolled back on the vast pile of Turkish cushions – 'who recommended me?' she asked.

'A brother officer,' Lestrade hedged.

'In the Tenth?'

'Yes.'

She smiled and rang a tiny silver bell at her side.

'I believe in business before pleasure,' she said. 'What is your taste?'

Lestrade felt his colour rise. 'I ... er ... hoped to be surprised,' he said.

'Oh, I'm sure you will be.'

The door swung open and three large men stood there.

'Ah, Auguste,' she said, sweeping upright, 'Lieutenant Lister wishes to be surprised.'

'Lieutenant 'oo?' asked the largest man. He was immaculately dressed in the manner of the heavy swell, with loud check suit, monocle and huge Dundrearies.

'You know the officers of the Tenth Hussars, don't you?' she asked him. 'Baker's Light Bobs?'

'Intimately,' Auguste replied. 'Zere is no Lieutenant Lister among zem.'

'Oh, I've just been gazetted,' Lestrade bluffed.

'Zat is nussing to what will 'appen to you now.' The men

behind Auguste pushed forward.

'First, I should warn you, Miss Dickinson,' Lestrade said, 'that I did not come here alone.'

Miss Dickinson was visibly rocked. 'I think you have mistaken me for someone else.'

Lestrade began retreating slowly. There was not much room to manoeuvre. 'You have a very short memory, Miss Dickinson,' he said. 'Perhaps without my helmet and whistle I look different. I am Constable Lestrade of the Metropolitan Police.'

'Well, a Peeler!' growled one of the men. 'I shall enjoy this even more.'

'Wait.' Miss Dickinson took charge. 'What are you doing here?'

'Carrying out my duties,' he said, 'in the interests of justice.'

One of the men spat copiously.

'Not on ze carpet, Warwick! It is best Persian. Do you zink I am made of money?'

'There was something about your story,' Lestrade went on, hoping for inspiration, 'not to mention your boots.'

'My boots?' she repeated.

'Not the boots of an innocent young lady visiting her dear old granny, who had the misfortune to be ravished by a wolf in man's clothing. They are the boots of a professional, madam. A harlot.'

'Auguste,' Miss Dickinson turned to her protector, 'I don't think you need me for what follows' – and she swept from the room.

'Miss Dickinson sees only ze clients of which I approve,' smiled Auguste.

'You are a pimp, sir,' said Lestrade.

'Ah, no, zis is a phrase of ze gutter,' Auguste corrected him. 'I am 'er patron, as we 'ave it in Paris.'

Lestrade had no idea how they had it in Paris, and in desperation he jumped upwards to grab the chandelier, intending to lash out with his feet and bring two of his opponents down. As it was, he couldn't reach it and found himself being knocked backwards over the chaise-longue behind him. The two roughs hauled him upright and pinned him against the flock wallpaper while Auguste put on his gloves.

'Officers of ze British army cannot spoil zere 'ands,' he explained, and proceeded to aim a savage kick into Lestrade's vitals. The second time, the constable was ready and blocked Auguste's kick with one of his own. It was better-timed, and the Frenchman hobbled back, cursing. Lestrade wrenched his left arm free and hauled one rough across his front, slamming down his fist on the man's head for all he was worth. The second coiled an iron forearm across his throat until Lestrade's boot gouged a hole in his shin. He remembered the brass knuckles Samuel Baker had given him and drove them into the face of the first rough. The man spat teeth and blood in all directions, and Lestrade turned to face the Frenchman and the henchman. Auguste had a heavy-topped cane in his hand, and the other a knife. It was getting ugly, especially Warwick, and Lestrade decided it was time to call a halt to his enquiries. Behind him was a plate-glass window. In front of him were several weeks in hospital, at best. He had no real option and found himself rolling under the hoofs of rearing cab-horses, pieces of glass embedding themselves in his body as he threw himself this way and that. It was merely his bad luck that one of the the cabmen was not of the calibre to appear in the pages of *Mogg's*, and the hackney caught the constable a nice one which sent him sprawling into a doorway opposite.

When Lestrade awoke, it was to a warm wet sensation around his face and an indescribable stink. As his vision returned he realised that, apart from a swollen head and various lacerations to the body, he was being revived by a mangy alley dog, which had probably had nothing to chew on but Lestrade's collar for days. Perhaps it was from this experience that Lestrade's aversion to dogs stemmed. His money had gone, so had his return ticket by omnibus. All that remained, clutched maniacally in his fist, were the brass knuckles which had probably saved his life.

* * *

'So you got Baker off?' Tom Berkeley chalked his cue anew.

'For a senior policeman, you've got a damned short memory,' said Lestrade, lighting another cigar. 'I had no evidence, Tom, not a shred. My inspector had warned me not to go to Duke Street. I lost three days' pay owing to my injuries, and it took me four months to afford a new bowler.'

'What about Auguste? Who was he?'

'*Hart's Army List* helped me there. He was a captain, would you believe, in the Twelfth Lancers. Apparently he'd been a Chasseur d'Afrique in the Crimea. Much travelled. A member of the Army and Navy Club. Quite a Man About Town.'

'And a pimp,' Berkeley asserted.

'They were different days.' Lestrade blew smoke-rings to the ceiling. 'Many respectable gentlemen, otherwise pillars of society and sons of the Church, had secret rooms here and there.'

'So Auguste paid Miss Dickinson to implicate Valentine Baker?'

'So I thought,' Lestrade answered. 'Now I am not so sure.'

'What happened to Baker? Didn't he go to Egypt?'

Lestrade nodded, with a chuckle. 'Ended up as commander of gendarmerie.'

'Policemen?' Berkeley paused from his shot.

'Do they have policemen abroad?' Lestrade asked. 'I suppose they must. Better ask Walter Dew; he's our foreign correspondent. Baker stood trial in August of that year. I remember the court was bursting at the seams. And hot! You wouldn't believe it. There he was, like the villain in *Maria Marten*, twirling his waxed moustaches and flashing those fierce eyes. Hannah Dickinson was of course innocence itself. Weeping pitifully now and again, lifting her tear-stained face to the jury. She had the judge of course round her little finger – one of the favourite positions at Duke Street in the seventies, I understand.'

'Well, you'd know,' Berkeley chuckled. 'Couldn't you put forward any of that at the trial?'

'It wasn't a good time for the force. My inspector told me to drop it. Without evidence, he said, I'd be torn apart by counsel.'

'He was right. What happened?'

'Baker got twelve months and a fine. What was worse for him, of course, was that he was dismissed the service.'

'Cashiered?'

'Bless you. Apparently the Queen wrote to say she had no further use for his services.'

'Would it be disloyal, do you think,' asked Berkeley, 'after this passage of time, to make the observation that that woman was a cow?'

'Utterly fair, I'd say,' Lestrade answered him. 'I met Samuel Baker by chance when his brother had sailed for Egypt. He took with him nothing but his white horse.'

'Yes, well, you *can* take a white horse anywhere,' said Berkeley.

'He died of a heart-attack, so the papers said. When I joined the Yard I remember Inspector Palmer saying he deserved all he got.'

Berkeley nodded. 'It comes to us all. Tell me, Sholto, apart from whiling away the minutes while I have thrashed you yet again at billiards, what's the point of all this?'

'Yes,' sighed Lestrade. 'That's three thousand and thirty-four pounds I owe you now, isn't it? I got a letter, a few days after Baker's trial.'

'From whom?'

'That's just it. I don't know.'

Realisation dawned on Tom Berkeley. 'Another of those jingles? Like the others you received?'

Lestrade nodded.

'What did it say?'

'It said "Nine for the Nine Bright Shiners".'

'What did it mean?'

'For a long time I didn't know. Then I got it. What was the nickname of the Tenth Hussars, back in the seventies?'

'Er . . . Baker's Light Bobs you said, I think.'

'Or, alternatively, the *Shiny* Tenth.'

'Ah.' Berkeley had caught Lestrade's drift. 'And Valentine Baker was the brightest of the Shiny Tenth.'

'Exactly,' said Lestrade.

'So Miss Dickinson sent it?'

'Perhaps.'

'Or Auguste?'

'Perhaps him, too.'

'But this is ludicrous, Sholto. Why should some idiot send you snatches of rhyme over the past – what – forty years? And what's it got to do with me?'

Lestrade shrugged. 'I wish I knew, Tom. Somebody else paid Miss Dickinson to bring down Colonel Baker that summer. The same person who killed M'Travers and the others. The same person who sent me the notes for the twelve Apostles and the rest. But there's one curious thing.'

'What's that?'

'The pattern – and I wish to God I'd kept those notes now – is from twelve in descending order.'

'How far have you got?'

'Currently to three – you, Edward Henry and Gordon Ushant, the Rivals.'

'Two and One to go. Is that your curious thing?'

'No. My curious thing is that I can't remember receiving number Eleven.'

Berkeley shrugged. 'Lost in the post?' he ventured.

'Entirely possible,' said Lestrade, and he made for his bed.

Whenever he could, Sholto Lestrade liked to spend time with his daughter. They strolled together in St James's that day at the end of September. There was family news in plenty. Harry was Harry, gallant, reckless, yet a rock in the sea of change at Huish Episcopi, the Bandicoot manor for centuries. Letitia, his wife, who had insisted that Lestrade's daughter should be taken under her wing when the girl's mother died, was a little older, a little sadder. Since her own son Rupert had died, there was an emptiness in her life, but she tried not to let it show. Ivo, Rupert's twin, had gone up to Cambridge, to read Law, and had met a young poet there, who was writing a dissertation for a fellowship at King's College. Emma had met this young man and fallen a little in love with him.

Then she broke her news. 'Daddy. . . .'

He recognised the tone and sat down heavily on the nearest park bench. 'I am sitting comfortably,' he said. 'You may begin.'

'You won't be cross, will you?'

'Is it this poet chappie?' Lestrade felt his working-class morality rising. Poetry and Pimlico didn't mix.

'Paul Dacres?' she laughed, clouting him with her handbag. 'Oh, no, he's far too dilettante.'

'That's easy for you to say,' he commented, and she pushed him off the bench. He landed badly, and the old familiar feeling swept over him: the pain, the nausea, the tears filling his eyes.

'My God, Emma, I think I've broken my leg!'

She peered over the edge of the seat. 'My God, Daddy, so you have!' – and she flagged down passers-by, who lifted the superintendent bodily and carried him with much puffing and ado to the Greycoats Hospital nearby.

'Are you a Quaker?' they asked him.

'Not usually,' he said, 'though I have to admit to being a little shaky on my pins at the moment.'

They closed the door on the little huddle around Lestrade.

'Get him a cab, someone,' Emma insisted, and one of the party hailed a passing hansom.

'Disgusting,' growled the growler on his perch. 'To be in that state at this time of day. You should take more water with it' – and he cracked his whip and rattled away.

Eventually, by stages, and with many gasps and moans from Lestrade, they got him to St Mary's, Paddington, where one of them knew a doctor. He was bundled into a makeshift bed, strapped and weighted, and watched dusk fall over Praed Street, his daughter by his bedside.

'Oh, Daddy, I'm so sorry.' She took his hand in hers and wept quietly.

'It's nothing.' He stoked her hair. 'Just think, I was going back to the Yard next week. Now I've got a few more months' convalescence.'

She looked at him with tear-stained cheeks pale in the half-light. She knew the Yard was the man's life. Fanny Berkeley had not changed that. A few more months' convalescence was the last thing Lestrade wanted.

'What was your news?' he asked, trying to brighten the situation.

'News?'

'Yes. Before you pushed . . . I fell off that park bench, you had something to tell me.'

'Oh, yes.' She shuffled uncomfortably. 'There was something. It was about the Yard, actually. . . .'

Lestrade propped himself on both elbows. The nightshirt he had been given fitted him nowhere, but it cut in sharply as he moved and he plummeted back again on the pillows. 'What about the Yard?' he hissed as the pain swept over him.

'Well . . . you remember Miss McDougall?'

'No,' he answered.

'Yes, you do. Sir Edward Henry called her in to help with the questioning in . . . delicate cases. . . .'

'No, Emma!' Lestrade shouted. 'I absolutely forbid it! On no account are you to—'

'There, there.' She patted him gently. 'That's more or less what Sir Edward said you'd say.'

'You mean, you've been working with Lord Love Us?'

'No, of course not. I merely asked him if he thought it could be a good idea. I *am* Lestrade's daughter,' she reminded him. 'It's in the blood.'

'I knew a girl who wanted to be a policeman once,' he said. 'She killed to prove she was good enough' – and he shuddered at the memory of it. 'Once and for all, Emma, no.'

'Now, then, what's all this?' a voice rang from the far side of the screens. Was it a copper? The phrasing was right, but the tone too articulate. Sergeant Blevvins? Too human.

'What a noise.' A young man with a firm jaw and a white coat stuck his head round the canvas. 'You'll be waking the dead. Ah' – and he straightened his tie when he caught sight of Emma – 'is it Miss Lestrade?' he asked.

'It is.' She offered her hand, which he graciously kissed. 'And you are?'

'Enchanted,' the young man said. She smiled.

'My daughter wants to know your name.' Lestrade was fast losing his sense of humour.

'Oh, Fleming. Alexander Fleming,' he said. 'I'm the new house assistant here. Miss Lestrade, I'm afraid I must ask you to leave now. May I get you a cab?'

'Thank you, Dr Fleming, but I can manage. Daddy, I've sent a telegram to Fanny and Tom. They shouldn't be long.'

'There'll be no more visitors for your father tonight, miss,' he said. 'Excitement at his age. . . .' And he shook his head, frowning.

Lestrade considered aiming a pillow at him, but thought better of it. 'You whippersnapper,' he snarled. '*I'll* decide how much excitement I can stand.'

'Miss Lestrade,' Fleming ignored him, 'may I have a private word wi' ye?'

They stopped outside the screens.

'What is it, Doctor?' She looked at him earnestly. 'No complications, are there?'

'Och, no' – he took her hands in his – 'your da's as right as rain. A wee bit cross-grained, I fancy, but his leg'll be as good as new. I was merely wondering if . . . but I'm being forward. . . .'

'Go on, Doctor.' She arched an eyebrow. 'I'm all ears.'

'There's genetics for you,' he smiled, nodding beyond the screens. 'I would very much like to see you again, Miss Lestrade.'

She leaned tantalisingly towards him. 'You will, Dr Fleming,' she whispered. 'I shall be back in the morning' – and flicked his stethoscope so that the end pinged painfully across his nose. He emerged from behind the screen.

'Well?' Lestrade snapped.

Fleming ripped back the bedclothes and began heaving and hauling. Lestrade screamed and rolled.

'Isn't that comfortable?' Fleming asked in mock amazement.

Lestrade winced through clenched teeth. 'You're a Scot, aren't you?' he asked.

'I am,' the doctor replied. 'And you're a Peeler, aren't you?'

'Old-fashioned, but essentially correct.' Lestrade subsided in the bed. 'Have you got a minute?'

'Time and the medical profession wait for no man,' said Fleming. 'I'm young, Mr Lestrade. I've got places to go.'

'Ah.' The superintendent lolled back with as much decorum as the knots and splints would allow. 'An assignation.'

'No, merely another eight hours' duty before I can stagger off to my truckle bed. If you're lonely, I have a Bible some-where. . . .'

'I have something on my mind, Dr Fleming. I want to use you as a wall to bounce ideas off. It's important.'

Fleming checked his half-hunter. 'Ah well,' he sighed. 'A few minutes, maybe.' He sat down and produced a paper parcel from his pocket. 'Would you care for a sandwich, Mr Lestrade?' – and immediately withdrew them. 'Och, will you look at that?' His face twisted in disgust. 'Mouldy bread! I ask you, what is the use of that?' He threw it into the bed pan. 'Now,' he said, 'what was it you wanted to tell me?'

'You being a Scot reminded me,' Lestrade said and reached for a cigar until the wagging finger of the doctor stopped him.

'Not in the ward, Mr Lestrade,' he said. 'Do you chew?' – and produced a quid of tobacco.

Lestrade shook his head as the doctor munched.

'It all began with a Scot, Dolly Williamson.'

'Och ay?' mumbled Fleming. 'Who was she?'

'Not she – he,' Lestrade corrected him as the gas-lamps were lit in the ward around them. 'All rather a long time ago, I'm afraid. If you're chewing comfortably, then I'll begin.'

He crossed the slush that coated the cobbles and mounted the steps to the side-entrance. The wind whipped the cape around his head as he fumbled with the door and he staggered into the hall, unable to see where he was going or indeed where he had been.

''Ello, 'ello, 'ello.' The tone was familiar, but he couldn't, until he unwrapped the cape, gauge the direction.

'Constable Lestrade,' he mumbled. 'Reporting to see Superintendent Williamson.'

'I see,' said the voice. 'May I point out, Constable, that you are talking to the 'at-stand? I am over 'ere.'

Lestrade saluted.

''Elmet off, lad,' the desk-man said. 'I am Sergeant Dixon. This is my post. To get up there' – he pointed to the stone steps – 'you will 'ave to go through me. Sign 'ere. You can write?'

'I could a while ago, Sarge.' Lestrade's fingers would not obey him.

'What's your name again?' Dixon did the honours.

'Lestrade.'

He wrote it down in his best copperplate.

'You'll be at 'ome 'ere. Got a lot of furriners in the Detective Department.' He clicked his fingers at a passing constable. 'I thought you were in the dock, Green,' he said.

''Ave a 'eart, Sarge. That's tomorrow.'

'All right, lad. Just testin'. Take Lestrade 'ere up to the super's office. Double up.'

Lestrade caught his groin on the desk-corner as he turned, and jack-knifed in pain.

'Not you, lad.' Dixon leaned over to view the spectacle. The constables took to the stairs, one considerably more gingerly than the other, and they spiralled upwards until they reached the mahogany door. Green knocked and responded to the snarl from within.

'Constable Lestrade, sir.'

The man in the chair was a sandy-haired sour-faced individual; Lestrade guessed about fifty. He wore a loud suit and immense side-whiskers.

'Well, laddie.' His Scots accent was as broad as his facial hair. 'So you want to be a detective?'

'Yes, sir.' Lestrade's fingers burned fiercely as the fire in the room began to take its toll on his digits. He dripped melted snow over Williamson's carpet.

'Why?'

It was a fair question, but Lestrade had never thought of an answer to it.

'Er . . . because I want to catch criminals, sir.'

Williamson scowled at him, stood up, walked around him, lit his pipe and tapped the falling glass. After what seemed to Lestrade an eternity, he smiled at him and said: 'So you will.'

The superintendent sat back in his chair and allowed the tobacco to tumble from his pipe.

'Born in Pimlico.' He clenched again on the briar stem.

'Yes, sir.'

'Father on the Force, I understand.'

'Twenty-three years, sir. Man and boy.'

'I remember your daddy, laddie.' Williamson relit the pipe.

'With me at Bow Street when I arrested Constance Kent. Wonder what happened to her? School?'

'Er . . . Blackheath, sir. Mr Poulson's Academy.'

Williamson's face fell.

'It *was* the school Lord Beaconsfield attended, sir,' Lestrade reminded him. Nothing wrong with keeping in with the Prime Minister.

'We don't discuss that here, young man,' the superintendent reminded him. 'It's enough of a mess without religion and politics. You've done some pretty nifty work over the past three years.' He stood up again and placed his nose near Lestrade's ear. 'And quite a bit of it in your own time, I see.'

Lestrade shifted uncomfortably. 'I can explain Duke Street, sir.'

'No need, laddie. No need. I'm looking for new blood, Lestrade.' He slapped his shoulder and glanced around him. 'Fresh, uncontaminated blood. Right, Lestrade. You're hired. Your predecessors secured you a pay rise of four shillings per week. Buy yourself a decent suit. Hebbert's do a nice little number for one pound, three shillings and eightpence. And get a bowler if you haven't got one. You'll need a top-coat for inclement surveillance. By the time you're a sergeant, you'll be able te afford a Donegal. Report to Inspector Palmer – I believe you've worked with him before.'

'Yes, sir.' It was just like old times.

Williamson reached for his half-hunter and began to toast his backside over the fire. 'You'll find him at this time of day in the Clarence across the yard. And, Lestrade. . . .'

'Sir?'

'I want you to keep your eyes and ears open, d'ye ken ma drift?'

'Yes, sir,' lied Lestrade. It was an inauspicious start.

'By the wa',' Williamson stopped him. 'That moustache is real, isn't it?'

The Clarence was crowded with coppers that December morning. Lestrade had taken his savings, bought himself a grey

whistle and flute from Messrs Hebbert, Haberdashers and
Tailors to the Constabulary, and trudged through the snow to
the cheery fume-laden atmosphere of the saloon bar. He
searched the rows of bowler-hatted mustachioed faces for signs
of Palmer, and in so doing tripped headlong over the feet of a
lounging customer and rammed his head into the groin of
another.

Amid howls of laughter mixed with indignation, the head-
butted man hauled Lestrade upright. 'You stupid clumsy
Sassenach!' he hissed.

Another Scotsman, Lestrade realised. No wonder the place
was called Scotland Yard. 'I'm sorry,' he said, 'I tripped.'

'Yes,' said another with an unplaceable accent, 'over *my* feet,
you careless oaf.'

'I said I was sorry,' repeated Lestrade.

'Oh, well, that's all right, then,' said the Scotsman. 'Whad-
dyou think, Nat? The horse-trough?'

'Well, it'll help to break the ice,' he said.

Lestrade was manhandled though a side-door and out into a
yard still thick with untravelled snow. It was walled all the way
round, the Clarence in front of him and red bricks everywhere
else. In one high window to his left he caught sight of the sour
face of Superintendent Williamson glowering down at him.

The two men began walking slowly towards him, fanning out
as though to outflank him. They were putting on gloves in the
way Lestrade had seen Captain Auguste do. It did not bode well.

'I think I should tell you', he tried a desperate tack, 'that I am
Constable . . . Detective Constable Lestrade of Scotland Yard.'

The men laughed. 'Is that right?' asked the Scotsman. 'Well,
that's all right, then. We can keep this in the family. Y'see, I'm
Detective Inspector Meiklejohn and this is Chief Inspector
Druscovich, though he doesnae like ta brag about his senior
rank. Isn't that right, Nat?'

Druscovich nodded. 'It's rather appropriate that you're a new
boy,' he said. 'The lads would have given you your cold bath
sooner or later anyway.'

Lestrade caught sight of the horse-trough behind him as he

retreated. The top was white with powdered snow, lying on the thick slab of ice. He tried a second tack. 'I think I should also tell you that Superintendent Williamson is at the window. . . .' He pointed to it, but the Scotsman had vanished.

'Oh dear,' Meiklejohn chuckled. 'Has teacher gone away? Never mind.'

Lestrade's last gamble was to run the gauntlet between the two and make for the Clarence's doors. In this he was thwarted by those very doors opening and a crowd of coppers emerging, led by a sharp-suited man in a Donegal.

'Good morning, Inspector Palmer.' Lestrade saw a face he knew.

'Do you know this man, Bill?' Meiklejohn asked him.

Palmer shook his head. 'Never seen him before in my life, John,' he smiled. 'Have I, Lestrade?'

With that, the Scotsman and the Pole rushed at Lestrade, who was dragged backwards through the snow and dumped bodily into the ice of the trough. Whistles and shouts drowned his gurglings and splutterings, and Meiklejohn and Druscovich, tired of their sport, turned back to the Clarence.

Palmer sauntered over and extended a hand to lift Lestrade out. 'Come on, Constable, before you freeze to death.'

Lestrade grabbed hold and staggered out, slipping and sliding, but as he did so he called out, 'Inspector Meiklejohn,' and hurled a slab of ice. The inspector turned just in time to be hit full in the mouth, and he went for Lestrade, snarling and cursing.

Palmer stopped him. 'That's enough, John,' he said quietly, and Druscovich joined them to lead the bleeding Scotsman away.

'I'll have you, Lestrade,' Meiklejohn jabbered. 'You watch your back. One dark night in an alley somewhere. There'll be somebody behind you. It'll be me.'

And, still protesting, he was dragged from the scene by the others.

The detective in winter wrapped himself up in his muffler, kept his head down, buried as it was in paperwork, and tried, as

Adolphus Williamson had ordered he should, to keep eyes and ears open. It was a raw day in the February of the new year that Williamson sent for Detective Constable Lestrade again.

'Well, Lestrade? What news?' 'Dolly' came straight to the point.

'It looks like war between Russia and Turkey, sir,' was the best he could do at a moment's notice.

'Damn it, y'idiot. Not in the world; here at the Yard!'

Lestrade shifted his bowler from crook of left arm to right. 'Nothing untoward, sir.' He stared fully frontal.

Williamson slammed his fist down so that his quills jumped in all directions. 'Is that so, mister?' he snarled. He rang a bell, and a uniformed constable appeared. 'Send in Mr Abrahams,' he said. 'And then on no account are we to be disturbed.'

'Very good, sir' – and the constable left.

'Sit down, Lestrade. Oh, here.' Williamson fumbled in his pocket and produced a five-pound note.

'Sir?'

'Take it, man. It's your monthly cut. Here we are, February, and I haven't slipped it to you yet.'

'I've been paid, sir.' Lestrade was confused.

'By Meiklejohn?' Williamson was glowering more than usual.

'No, sir, by the Pay Office.'

'Well.' Williamson lightened his approach. 'A little extra never did anyone any harm.'

'No, thank you, sir.' Lestrade stayed polite.

'Wassa matter?' Williamson's Gaelic intruded when he was angry. 'Are you some sort of plaster saint, or something?'

Lestrade stood up. 'Sir, I don't understand this conversation. Neither do I understand why I have been sent for.'

Williamson looked relieved. 'All right, laddie. Sit you doon again. I chose right' – and he put the money back in his pocket.

There was a knock.

'Ah, Mr Abrahams.' A Jewish-looking gentleman entered, carrying a battered briefcase and squinting through thick pebble glasses. 'I'd like you to meet the Detective Department's newest recruit, Constable Lestrade.'

Lestrade saluted.

'No, we don't do that here, laddie,' Williamson sighed.

'Sorry, sir.'

'Is he . . . er . . .?' Abrahams began.

'Kosher?' Williamson finished the sentence for him. 'Oh, yes. He may not be able to stop saluting now he's out of uniform, but he's clean, I'll vouch for that.'

So would Lestrade. The cost of Pears soap these days. . . .

'Tell Lestrade what you have told me, Mr Abrahams.'

The three of them sat down.

'Are you familiar, Mr Lestrade, with a small-time crook called William Kurr?'

'No, sir,' said Lestrade.

'A rogue, sir,' said Abrahams. 'Kurr by name and cur by nature. What about Harry Benson?'

Blank again.

'Hugh Montgomery?' Abrahams had perseverance.

Nothing.

'What about', Williamson came to his rescue, 'the comte de Montagu?'

'Ah, yes.' Recognition was seeping into the frozen brain of Lestrade.

The others smiled. 'How do you know him?' Williamson asked.

'He is a regular at the Clarence, sir. A friend of Chief Inspector Druscovich.'

Williamson looked at Abrahams. 'Is that right, laddie?' he murmured. 'Tell me. When the comte and Druscovich are in their cups, what do they talk about?'

'I don't know, sir. They speak in French.'

Williamson slammed his fist again on the desk.

'But . . .,' Lestrade began.

'Yes?' the Scot and the Jew chorused.

'I have noticed a number of betting slips changing hands, sir. I expect the chief inspector likes a bit of a flutter.'

'Oh, I expect he does,' nodded Williamson gravely. 'The only problem is that most of the comte's betting establishments don't exist. And if Nathaniel Druscovich is one of the Fancy I'll eat ma hat. Mr Abrahams, will you explain to the constable?'

'Of course, Superintendent my dear.' Abrahams's ancestry showed occasionally. 'I am a solicitor acting on behalf of a client whose name need not concern us here. . . .'

'A French lady named de Goncourt,' Williamson broke in. 'I'm sorry, Mr Abrahams, but if we are to use Lestrade it is vital he knows the whole story. We may be asking him to place his life on the line.'

'Oi vay.' Mr Abrahams raised his hands in time-honoured tradition. 'The comtesse de Goncourt is the unwitting dupe of an unscrupulous rogue named Hugh Montgomery. . . .'

'Alias the comte de Montagu, alias Harry Benson. He's about as French as my horse, but he was brought up in Paris and speaks the language like a native.'

Lestrade had never heard a native speaking French, but he nodded sagely.

'Montgomery has persuaded the comtesse to part with thirty thousand pounds with a bookmaker whose credentials are "impeccable",' Abrahams went on.

'So?' asked Lestrade.

'So the bookmaker is either Benson or his partner-in-crime William Kurr,' said Williamson.

'Kurr by name and cur by nature,' Abrahams reminded him.

'I don't see how this involves me, sir,' said Lestrade.

Williamson leaned forward over the desk, whiskers bristling in the firelight. 'It involves you, Lestrade, because as of now you are the only man I can trust. At least the only man with anything resembling a brain. They're in it, Lestrade, up to their necks. Meiklejohn, Druscovich, God knows who else. I want you to find out who – and I want proof.'

Lestrade flopped back in his chair. 'You mean that senior officers at Scotland Yard are taking bribes? And you want me to rat on them? On my superiors? Men I hope one day to call friends?'

Williamson and Abrahams nodded.

'When do I start?' Lestrade asked.

It was a routine investigation. An inclement surveillance in the worst of the winter, watching the movements of Mr Larchlap, the fence. Lestrade put on his old suit and passed muster as a road-sweeper. Palmer, more capable with matches and tongs, sold chestnuts to blue-faced passers-by. The Strand had never looked so dreary as at that tail-end of winter. Pigeons dropped dead of cold in the gutter. Growlers had to be lifted down from their cabs. And in mid-sweep of some horse-droppings from the road Lestrade saw a face he knew – the comte de Montagu, with a prison record longer than the Yard's arm. And the comte seemed to have an extraordinary passion for hot chestnuts.

'There's something going on,' he heard Palmer mutter to the comte. 'Williamson's sniffing around.'

'Can he be reached?' The comte turned up his astrakhan collar.

Palmer shook his head. 'You'd better get out. Chestnuts, 'ot chestnuts. They're lovely, madam. Some as big as your 'ead. Where will you go?'

'Rotterdam.'

'Where?'

'Rotterdam,' repeated the comte, somewhat irked. 'It's in Holland.'

'Have you got the . . . er . . . ?'

The comte passed him a package and wandered off. At the next corner he threw the chestnuts into the gutter.

Lestrade swept nearer, and before Palmer could stop him he snatched the packet.

'Guv'nor?' He looked at Palmer.

'For God's sake, Lestrade,' the inspector hissed. 'What the devil's the matter with you? You'll rumble us.'

Lestrade ripped open the brown paper, and his jaw dropped at the bundle of notes therein. 'You're rumbled already, sir,' he said.

Palmer looked frantically from left to right. 'You,' he growled. 'You!'

'No, sir. You.'

'You're a copper's nark, Lestrade.'

'I'm just doing my duty, sir.'

Palmer jabbed his man in the chest with a livid finger. 'I'll tell you this, Constable; you'll never do any duty again. Not in this or any other city' – and he kicked over his chestnut-cart and vanished into the dusk.

The surveillance forgotten, the fence lost in favour of bigger game, Lestrade trudged through the gathering night towards the Yard. He was sprayed by passing gigs and curricles, jostled by the gay ladies who thronged the Haymarket, and as he entered the maze of alleyways that led to Whitehall Place he suddenly realised he was not alone. Night in the Metropolis. The sound of gaiety died away. His boots scraped and rattled on the glistening cobbles. A cat sprang from the shadows, screaming in disgust at the interruption as it foraged for food. Lestrade's heart descended from his mouth, and he rounded the corner where the light from the gas-lamp did not reach.

'Are you good-natured, dearie?' The familiar cry of London hit his ears.

'Go home to your mother,' Lestrade hissed at the girl. She flounced away. But he heard her ask her question again behind him, and a Scots voice barked: 'Not just now, lass. I'm after a bit of brown.'

A shadow loomed from the darkness ahead. Lestrade turned back and saw the bulk of Inspector Meiklejohn cross into the light, a lead-weighted cosh strapped to his wrist.

'I warned you, Lestrade,' he cooed, relishing what was to follow. 'I told you we'd meet one dark night. Well, this is it.'

Lestrade edged back into shadow. The other figure coming from the other direction he recognised as Palmer, still in his costermonger's outfit.

'Now, go easy, John,' he called to Meiklejohn.

'Easy?' the Scotsman snarled. 'This wee bastard has the

evidence in his pocket to put us twa away for a long time, Bill. I'm not accepting that as a condition of service.'

'That's it,' said Palmer, gripping the Scotsman's arm. 'He's got money in his pocket. Money from Harry Benson. That puts him in the same position we are.'

'Not quite,' said Lestrade. 'You see, I no longer have the money.'

'What?' growled Meiklejohn.

'I passed it to that doxy back there. I'll bet she's never earned so much money so fast in her life.'

'Get her, Bill. I've got a little score to settle with the good constable here' – and Meiklejohn slapped the cosh into the palm of his hand, beckoning to Lestrade. 'Come on, laddie. Get it while it's hot' – and as Palmer fled in search of the girl Meiklejohn lunged at Lestrade. The constable leaped aside, bringing his leg up into the pit of the Scotsman's stomach. Meiklejohn cursed in Gaelic and swung round to whirl his cosh with a sickening thud into Lestrade's ribs. The men sprang apart and faced each other across the court. Meiklejohn beckoned again, circling his man warily.

'I've got her!' Palmer returned with the struggling girl.

'Search her!' Meiklejohn hissed.

''Ere, I need payin' first!' she shrieked.

'I know what you need, hinnie, and when I've finished wi' this I'll give y'it.'

He lashed out with his boot, but Lestrade caught it and held him there. 'Palmer,' he shouted, 'don't just stand there. Get the bastard!'

Lestrade yanked Meiklejohn over and rolled sideways still holding the leg until a dull cracking sound followed by a long howling moan told the world that it was broken. Palmer straddled the rolling bodies, throwing the girl against the wall. He brought his fist down hard on Lestrade's head and his knee into his groin. The constable staggered back, but as Palmer closed in on him he brought his switchblade up under his chin.

'One move, Inspector,' he fought for breath, 'and I'll cut your nose off, so help me.'

Palmer stood back. He had no more stomach for the fight.

'Never believe a constable,' said Lestrade, hauling the girl upright. 'She never had the money.' He patted his inside pocket. 'It was here all the time. I'll leave you to clear up the mess here' – and he dragged the girl into the lights of Carlton Terrace. Sure they weren't followed, he stopped and held up her face to a gaslight. 'I'm sorry,' he said. 'You could have been hurt.'

'Wouldn't be the first time,' she answered.

He looked at her. A pretty girl beneath the paint.

'How old are you?' he asked.

'Sixteen come the summer. 'Ere, are you a Peeler, or wot?'

'Wot, I should think, after tonight' – and he winced as the chuckle caught him.

'You're 'urt,' she said, steadying him against the railings.

'Riff-raff!' a voice called from an overhead window. 'Get away from there!'

''Ere – you got somewhere to go?' she asked.

He smiled, feeling fainter by the second as the pain tore through his lungs. 'I thought I told you,' he said. 'I'm not good-natured.'

'No, but you've got money, aintcha?' She patted his package.

'It's not mine,' he breathed.

'Never mind, ducks. Come on. It's not a night to be out. And you need 'elp. Reckon that bastard's broke your ribs.'

'Wait.' He leaned on her. 'What's your name?'

'Gertie, sir,' she said. 'Gertie Clinker. Wot's yours?'

'Sholto Lestrade,' he told her.

'Right, Mr Lestrade. Let's get yer ter bed, eh?'

'So you were twenty-four before you lost your virginity, eh, Superintendent?' Fleming giggled.

'I thought you'd gone to sleep,' grunted Lestrade. 'And what I did with Gertie Clinker in the wee small hours thirty-three years ago is no concern of yours, Doctor.' He caught the twinkle in Fleming's eye. 'Let's just say she had the knack of making men out of constables.'

'What happened to the detectives? Meiklejohn and Palmer?' Fleming asked.

'They went down. Hard. Two years' hard, to be exact. Druscovich was sent by Williamson over to Rotterdam to get Benson. Benson and Kurr stood trial in April – fraud and forgery. They got twenty years between them.'

'Ah, and they blabbed at the trial. Put the finger on your Yard colleagues, eh?'

'It worries me when doctors of today are conversant with underworld slang, Mr Fleming, but in fact you're wrong. Nothing came out at the trial. But a month or so later Benson sang like a canary. With that evidence, and mine against Palmer and Meiklejohn, it was a foregone conclusion. But there was more to it.'

'Oh?'

'A few days after the trial of the detectives, I received a letter. It was unsigned, but it carried a single line: "Eight for the Eight Bold Rangers."'

'What was the significance of that? I don't follow.'

'Neither did I. Except that in those days policemen patrolling the parks were called Rangers sometimes. Endlessly moving on park women and vagabonds.'

'Who sent the letter?'

Lestrade threw up his hands. 'To this day, I don't know. When I walked from the courtroom a man came up to me and said: "Sergeant Lestrade, can I have a word with you?"'

'Who was that?'

'I didn't know. I told him it wasn't "sergeant", but "constable". Constable Lestrade. He shook his head and asked if I knew what the initials CID stood for. . . .'

'And did you?'

Lestrade chuckled. 'Not at the time. No one did. Except the man outside the court. His name was Howard Vincent, and he said he hadn't made a mistake about my rank. He was the new director of criminal investigations. He had a job for me. For many men like me.'

'You must have felt pleased with yourself,' smiled Fleming.

'Pleased?' Lestrade looked at him through withering eyes. 'No, Doctor, I felt sick. Sick and ashamed.'

'But Meiklejohn, Palmer and the others were guilty men, Lestrade. They deserved all they got.'

'Yes,' Lestrade remembered. 'That's what Palmer had said about Valentine Baker.'

'Who?'

'Nothing. Yes, I thought they were guilty then. Now, after all these years, I'm not so sure.'

'What happened to Palmer?'

'After his two years' hard? I don't know. Benson was released eventually. He stumbled from fraud to fraud, a marked man and never so successful again. He topped himself one day in prison by jumping off a roof.'

'Well, there we are,' mused Fleming.

Lestrade chuckled, remembering Abrahams's sentiments years earlier. 'Palmer by name and palmer by nature,' he said. His smile vanished. 'Then the murders started.'

'Murders?' Fleming's ears pricked up.

'Yes. What I haven't told you is that the letter, the one with the Eight Bold Rangers, was one of a number. Twelve, Ten, Nine, then Eight. . . .'

'No Eleven?'

'No Eleven,' nodded Lestrade. 'And after Eight, men began to die.'

'Mince,' Fleming suddenly said.

'What?'

'Mince. It's my turn to check the mince. Your evening meal tomorrow. We have the occasional outbreak of food poisoning here. Oh, nothing to worry about, but I must dash. It's been fun hearing your stories, Mr Lestrade. Now, you get a good night's sleep.'

No sooner had he gone than another head appeared round the curtain. It had a helmet on it.

'Superintendent Lestrade, sir.'

'Blevvins?' Lestrade narrowed his eyes to make out his sergeant in the gas-lamp's glimmer. 'What the devil are you doing here? And why are you in uniform?'

'Er . . . as to the last, sir. A little disciplinary matter involving a magistrate. Nothing major, sir. He'll be out in a few weeks.'

'Out? Out of where?' Lestrade gripped his blankets, afraid to hear the answer.

'Out of Charing Cross Hospital, sir. Though not of traction. Talking of traction. . . .'

'Blevvins!' Lestrade screamed. 'Touch those ropes and you're a dead man. Understand?'

'What is all this row?' A muscular little nurse arrived from behind the screen.

'Look, Miss-bloody-Nightingale,' Blevvins rounded on her, 'how would you like to spend the rest of the night with a bedpan up your—'

'Blevvins! That will do!' barked Lestrade. 'I'm sorry, Sister. This is urgent police business – and it *is* private.'

She glowered at the sergeant and spun on her heel.

'So why are you here?' Lestrade asked him.

'Ah, a bit more bad news, I'm afraid, sir. Miss Lestrade informed us that you would not be joining us on Monday. A great pity, if I may make so bold, sir—'

'Get to the point, Blevvins.' Lestrade was beginning to feel the effects of a very long day.

'Well, sir, while she was with us at the Yard, a telegram arrived for you. It was sent by a Constable Stalker, sir.'

Lestrade's heart skipped a beat. 'Well?'

'They weren't sure where to find you, sir, but there's been an accident. Chief Constable Berkeley is dead.'

Murder Made Easy

Fanny Berkeley stood by the little bridge that spanned the lake. The sunset was glorious behind her, and she stood immobile against it, like the statues in some stately home. The herons lapped their way to the trees across the dark waters, startled by the grating of the Silver Ghost on the gravel. Fanny did not look up at the house. Nor at the dark figures, one with a white leg thrust awkwardly out and swinging its way wildly between crutches, the other moving alongside in case he fell.

'Fanny.' She heard her name, then quieter as he reached her: 'Fanny.'

She turned as though from the dead and gazed into the steady burning eyes of Sholto Lestrade. She recognised beside him the smaller frame of Emma, acting as a third crutch for her father. The Lestrades stared back at her.

'Fanny. . . .' Lestrade balanced himself as best he could and reached out with one hand. She turned back to the water, ringed by the darkening trees.

'I know, Sholto,' she said, her voice hollow and empty, like the house behind her.

He looked at Emma, and she at him. He let the hand fall.

'There's nothing to say. Nothing to do,' Fanny went on. 'Not now. Not yet.'

As she passed him, she turned to him. By the light of the last rays of the sun he saw her face, pale and suddenly old. There was so much he wanted to say and, if it could not be said, he wanted to hold her to him and to feel her tears soak into the Donegal.

His tears would join them. He had loved Tom Berkeley, too. But she looked at him and through him. He knew why. He had been staring Death – sudden, violent Death – in the face for nearly forty years. He had seen what it did to people – to enemies, to friends, to lovers, to strangers. Even now she must find her own way, and the way twisted through the tangled woods of pain. It was not a road he could walk with her.

As she climbed the steps that led to the orchard, where M'Travers had died in the spring, he unhooked himself from Emma's velvet-wrapped shoulders. 'Go with her,' he said and, as if to remind her of something, let his hand linger on her pelisse.

'I know,' she smiled up at him. 'Close, but not too close. I'll send Harry to you.'

The giant Old Etonian passed both women on their various journeys and reached Lestrade utterly confused. Nothing amiss there, the superintendent realised. It was Harry's usual state.

'What happens now, Sholto?' Bandicoot asked.

'I need a hand, Harry,' he said.

'Or a leg?' the blond man quipped.

'I don't think we need the jokes, Harry.' Lestrade turned with the air of a man on his last legs.

'Sorry, Sholto.' Bandicoot was easily crushed. 'Bad form. I'm sorry. Will Fanny be all right?'

Lestrade gazed at the Georgian house that had been Tom and Fanny's home. 'I don't know,' he said. Then he slapped Bandicoot on the shoulder. 'Come on. We've got a murder on our hands, and two heads are better than one. Last one to the house is a superintendent' – and he began to jerk his body into action, driving the crutches into the ground like a man possessed. Faithful Harry stayed at his elbow, ready to catch the crippled copper should his supply of laudanum suddenly run out.

Lestrade had been winched together and his leg plastered as an emergency by Dr Fleming early that morning. Putting his faith in his God and in Sergeant Blevvins (never the act of a truly balanced man), Lestrade had somehow got across London and had reached Emma, then staying at the Moribunda, and told her the tragic news. She in turn had telephoned her guardian, Harry, who had paused only to throw his topper and smoking jacket into the Silver Ghost, had kissed his wife and had roared furiously at nearly thirty miles an hour to join his erstwhile guv'nor. Lestrade had given Harry scant details on the journey through Surrey. It wasn't wise to overburden the intellectual capacities of a man like Bandicoot. 'One man in a thousand,' said Solomon and Rudyard Kipling, 'stuck closer than a brother,' but Harry needed time to absorb facts, and something told Lestrade time was running out.

They sat at length in Berkeley's study, the oil-lamps burning into the night. Emma arrived briefly to say that Fanny was sleeping.

'Right, Harry.' Lestrade eased himself as best he could on the chaise-longue, gripping the cigar with his teeth whenever the pain swept over him. 'You were a copper once. Talk me through it.'

Bandicoot opened his waistcoat and loosened his tie. He was about to go fifteen rounds with Bob Fitzsimmons or he was about to think. 'Tom Berkeley died at approximately half-past three yesterday afternoon.'

'Where was he?'

'The town hall, Chertsey, guest of honour at the toy bazaar.'

'One of two guests of honour – the other was the Bishop of the Indian Ocean.'

'Odd, that,' Bandicoot observed. 'I thought they were all Hindus or Muslims.'

'This one's as white as your hat,' said Lestrade. 'Poses as a Christian.'

'Have you met him?'

'No. That treat's in store tomorrow.'

'You're going to *him*? Sholto, you're not well enough.'

'Tom Berkeley's dead, Harry. He and I go back a long way. I owe him this, whether I'm well or not.'

'But the Surrey police ...,' Bandicoot began, only to be stopped by Lestrade's look.

'All right, then, the Yard. Walter Dew. ...'

The same look silenced him altogether.

'No, Harry, this one's mine.' He clenched down on the cigar. 'You see, somehow the pattern has been broken. It's all gone wrong.'

'Pattern?' said Bandicoot, sensing the ground shifting under him.

'Never mind that now. The night is young. Which reminds me – you haven't eaten. Ring that bell, will you? I'll ask Mrs M'Travers to make us something.'

He did so. 'The housekeeper?' Bandicoot paused. 'I thought you said she'd become unhinged.'

'She has, but she can manage a ham sandwich. If she gives you Garibaldis, check the black bits very carefully. Cause of death?' He returned to Tom Berkeley.

'Yes, gentlemen?' The much sedated Mrs M'Travers had answered the call and stood like a ghost at the feast before them. But, then, the poor woman had lost her husband, her master and her mind in the space of six months.

'Ah, Mrs M'Travers. Could we have a pot of tea, please?'

'Better make that coffee, Sholto.' Bandicoot's etiquette was perfection to the last. No one in the better houses drank tea after four these days.

'As you wish,' said Lestrade. 'And ham sandwiches, Mrs M'Travers. Lots of them.'

'We only have cheese, sir.'

'So be it.' Lestrade waved her away. To be honest, the melancholy countenance irritated him.

'Shall I order the baked meats, sir?' She remained motionless.

'Baked meats?' Lestrade repeated.

'For the master's funeral, sir' – and she sobbed convulsively, reliving the horror of it all over again.

Harry rushed to her side. He had servants of his own. 'There, there, Mrs M'Travers. Don't take on so.' He patted her ample

arms and ferreted in his pocket for the monogrammed handkerchief. He held it to her nose. 'Big blow,' he beamed.

'Yes, sir, it has been, sir,' she wailed. 'Nice of you to be so
concerned.'

'Yes, well, these things are best if the heart is busy,' Bandicoot
observed. 'We'll have our cheese and coffee now, Mrs M'Travers, if you please.'

She curtsied and dragged herself from the room, brightening
her step a little as she used Bandicoot's handkerchief as a swat for
the flies she imagined to be buzzing around her head.

'I keep telling her they've gone to sleep for the winter,' sighed
Lestrade. 'In my more callous moments, I sometimes wish she'd
do the same. Cause of death?' The superintendent was a
tenacious man.

'Arrow,' said Bandicoot, still not believing it even though
he'd said it himself.

Lestrade shook his head, talking to himself. 'An arrow,' he
repeated. 'Extraordinary.' Then: 'What time is it?'

'Nearly eight.' Bandicoot checked his hunter.

'Right. Get me the Yard. See if Jones or Dickens is on duty. If
you want to know the time, ask a policeman.'

'No, Dickens,' Lestrade screamed over the jangle of static
wires when Harry had got through. 'Crossbow. Crossbow. C
for Charlie, R for Rat, O for Orange. . . .'

There was a series of squeaks and clicks.

'Orange. Orange,' Lestrade repeated. 'O for Oswald, R for
Ringworm, A for Aardvark— Oh, forget it!'

He was about to hang up when Constable Stalker entered the
study. He carried in his hand an arrow, nearly a foot long, heavy
and steel-tipped. Lestrade took it from him. 'Are you still there,
Dickens?'

Squeak.

'It's an arrow, nearly a foot long.'

Squeak again. Lestrade placed his hand over the receiver,
frowning at Harry. 'Dickens has gone mad. He just called me a

dolt. What? Look here, Dickens ...,' he bellowed into the instrument. 'What? A bolt? Oh, I see. Yes. Yes.' His face froze as Sergeant Dickens launched himself. 'Yes, yes. All right, thank you, Sergeant. Yes. Yes. Thank you. Thank you. Keep me posted' – and he replaced the receiver with gratitude.

'Well, Stalker.' The superintendent's eyes scorched the constable from head to foot. 'Where were you, man?'

'With him, sir.' Stalker's face was gaunter and paler than ever. He seemed to have aged ten years in a day. 'As near as I am to you.'

'Harry, take notes, will you? I would, only my leg ... you understand.'

Bandicoot smiled indulgently. Lestrade's temperature was soaring, his leg throbbed, his father-in-law-to-be was dead, his lady-love numb with grief. He could probably stand a little secretarial help about now. On the other hand, he might not be able to stand at all.

'What happened?' Lestrade asked.

'We were at Chertsey town hall, sir. An engagement the chief constable was looking forward to.'

'The toy exhibition?'

'Yes, sir. We got there shortly before eleven—'

'In the chief constable's landau?'

'No, sir. The Ford. The chief constable wanted to go on into Town.'

'Why?'

'To see you, sir, I understand. Of course, he didn't know about the leg.'

'At that point, neither did I. Tell me, Stalker, did the chief constable give a reason for wanting to see me? As far as he knew, I would have been home for the evening.'

'He said he had a clue, sir. To the death of M'Travers and the others.'

Lestrade raised himself up on one elbow from the chaise-longue.

'What clue, man?'

The constable shook his head. 'He didn't say, sir.'

Lestrade subsided again. 'Back to the toy fair,' he said.

'Excuse me, gentlemen,' Bandicoot butted in. 'Are there two tees in Chertsey?'

Even Stalker's look was withering.

'Just the essentials, Harry,' Lestrade sighed.

'There were the usual speeches. One made by' – Stalker resorted to the inevitable black notebook – 'the Bishop of the Indian Ocean.'

'What *was* he doing there?' Lestrade asked.

'Making a speech, sir,' was the best gloss Stalker could put on it.

'Then what?'

'The mayor declared the exhibition open. You've never seen so many jumping monkeys in your life.'

'You forget, Constable,' Lestrade reminded him, 'I'm from Scotland Yard. Go on.'

'I followed the chief constable as he met various people and inspected the toys. He seemed very taken with Stein and Bucher's Cat Simulator and the Maischin's Dirty Trick. Then he sort of . . . fell. Lurched forward on to a model of that tower they've got in Paris.'

'Eiffel,' Bandicoot as the Most Travelled Man Present helped him out.

'That's what I said, sir. He fell. Clutching his back, he was. I thought he'd tripped.'

'What did you do?' Lestrade asked.

'I got to him and realised he was bleeding badly.'

'A wound in the back?'

Stalker nodded. 'And that was in it.' He pointed to the bolt in Lestrade's hand.

'Did your man help with that?' Bandicoot asked.

'Dickens? After a fashion,' Lestrade told him. 'Not wishing you to turn white during the duration of the story, I'll prays – prais – cut it short for you. Dickens says the crossbow, or arbalest, was a weapon popular in western Europe in the Middle Ages. It is composed of a bow fixed crosswise upon a stock with a notch to which the cord is stretched and released by squeezing a trigger. It fired one of those things – a bolt.'

'So who had a quarrel with Tom Berkeley?' Bandicoot asked.

'When we find our crossbowman I'll let you know. You didn't see such a weapon, Stalker, among the toys, perhaps?'

'No, sir.'

'Harry. Give the constable your pencil and paper. Stalker, I want you to think hard and sketch your relative positions, yours and the chief constable's.'

Stalker took the pencil and did his best. Lestrade turned the paper round several times. 'So you were behind Berkeley?'

'Yes, sir, and to one side.'

'Luckily for you, or that thing would have been in *your* back. What was behind you?'

Stalker screwed up his face in an effort to remember. 'Er . . . a turquoise curtain, sir.'

'A bolt from the blue,' Bandicoot commented.

Lestrade nodded. 'And behind that?'

'A murderer,' said Bandicoot.

'What a copper you'd have made,' said Lestrade drily. 'Did you look, Constable?'

'Yes, sir. Nothing.'

'Where was the nearest door?'

'Er . . . to the left, across the hall. No one left that way.'

'Are you sure?'

'Yes, sir. I had it in view the whole time.'

'The *whole* time?' Lestrade checked.

'Well. . . .' Stalker realised the uncertainty of his position. 'No one left carrying a bow, sir, of any kind.'

'How did you know it was a crossbow, Sholto?' Bandicoot was intrigued.

'Blevvins told me the arrow was a short one. That gave it away. You see, I've tangled with the greenwood before. Nottingham. Ninety-seven, it was. Remind me to tell you some time about the Wild Goose Case. You couldn't move for longbows. Besides, a longbow is a big weapon to smuggle into a town hall full of people.'

'So is a crossbow, sir,' Stalker ventured.

'That it is, Constable.'

'What was in front of the curtain? Immediately in front of it.'

'Um . . . a table, set out with toys.'

'What toys, exactly?'

Stalker's brain failed him.

'All right, because I'm not mobile, I'll be Tom, lying here on the floor – that's the chaise-longue to you, Harry.' Lestrade wanted no misunderstandings.

'And to you, Sholto,' the big man quipped.

'Stalker, you stand where you were yesterday morning.'

The constable assumed the position.

'Right, Harry. Get over by the door. You're hiding behind the curtain. Stalker, I haven't seen poor Tom's body yet. Where precisely did the bolt strike?'

'A little left of the spine, sir, here.' Stalker fumbled behind him.

'Right. So, Harry, you're either crouching down or you're a dwarf. Which would you like?'

'I think I'll crouch,' Bandicoot beamed.

'Very wise,' said Lestrade and waited while he got into the mood. 'Release your shaft,' he ordered.

Bandicoot's arm came back abruptly, colliding as it did so with the passing posterior of Mrs M'Travers, in the act of depositing the cheese sandwiches. She bellowed, visibly moved, and hobbled into the darkness.

'I do believe you've goosed the cook,' said Lestrade. 'You've also proved something to me.'

'What's that?'

'It wasn't a crossbow. At least, not one carried by a man. Stalker, your sketch of this area behind the curtain, is it to scale?'

'Approximately, sir.'

'About the size of a urinal, then?'

'I don't follow,' said Bandicoot.

'When was the last time you knelt – and pulled back a bowstring – in a urinal, Harry?'

It wasn't a thought that had occurred to Bandicoot. His life had not been as lavatorial as Lestrade's.

'There simply would not have been room. Not if – as Stalker assures us – his measurements are correct. So, Stalker, once again, what was on the table in front of the curtain?'

Blank.

'Harry, pour me some brandy, will you? These sandwiches are inedible.'

'Meccano!' Stalker suddenly roared, causing Bandicoot to douse Lestrade's outstretched hand liberally with the amber nectar.

'You haven't improved, Harry. When I first knew you you poured boiling water over me. Only your tastes have got richer. Are you ill, Constable?' Lestrade sensed Stalker's agitation.

'I've just remembered, sir.' Stalker fluttered an eyebrow and flexed the muscles of his jaw. It was his way of registering euphoria. 'The toy in front of the curtain. It was called Meccano.'

Bandicoot exchanged glances with Lestrade.

'Never heard of it,' was their chorally expressed verdict.

'It was a series of metal strips with holes in it, screwed together.'

Bandicoot looked at Lestrade again.

'Harry,' said the superintendent, 'get me the Yard again.'

'Is Meccano important, sir?' Stalker asked; but, before Lestrade could answer, the door burst open to reveal a pair of parsons in capes and collars.

'Sholto, my dear chap, I had to come to see Fanny.'

'Norman.' Lestrade tried to rise, but the pain defeated him and he sank back on the chaise-longue.

'My dear boy, not a relapse, surely?'

'No,' grimaced Lestrade. 'The damn thing snapped again.'

'May I present' – Penhaligon swept his cape – 'His Grace the Bishop of the Indian Ocean? Superintendent Lestrade.'

'Not *the* Lestrade?' The Bishop's grip crushed the policeman's fingers, though there was scarcely an inch over five foot of him and he must have been threatening seventy.

'*The?*' Lestrade repeated.

'The famous foil to the Great Sherlock Holmes. I know young Norman here is an avid reader of this Chesterton fellow, but I cherish my Conan Doyle. It remains one of my great regrets not to have met the Great Man.'

'Forgive me, sir, I would dearly love to stroll down Fiction Lane with you, but we have matters more pressing. Pray be seated ... er ... I mean.... I don't believe you've met my old friend Harry Bandicoot?'

The three men shook hands. 'Your Watson, eh?' His Grace kept up the literary boredom, beaming at Lestrade.

'No, I'm Harry Bandicoot,' the Etonian repeated, sensing that years in the Cochin had obviously reduced the churchman's intellect. 'Your call, Sholto.'

Again the line crackled and jumped. 'Peabody? Is that you?'

Squawk.

'Get me Sergeant Dickens again .'

Squawk.

'Lestrade.'

Rattle. Squawk. Crack. Squawk.

'Dickens?'

Crackle.

'Oh, it's you, Jones. What do you know about Meccano?'

Squawk?

'Meccano. It's a toy – for kiddies. You know, like you and Dickens. M for Monkey, E for Elephant, C for Curate – oh, I'm sorry, gentlemen.' He remembered their Presence. 'Got that, Jones?'

Squawk. Rattle. Rattle. Bleep. Crack.

'Right. And don't be damned cheeky.' Lestrade was tired, and his leg and the long night were beginning to take their toll. 'Stalker. Get along to the chief constable's office. I want the address of a Mr Frank Hornby. And I want it by morning.'

'Who's he?' Bandicoot asked.

'He's an inventor, Harry. Architect, designer, physicist, businessman, call him what you will. I have reason to believe he can help us with our enquiries. Get along to the kitchen, will you, and see if Mrs M'Travers can manage any more ham sandwiches. You've no aversion to ham, your Grace?'

'I'm a bishop, not a rabbi, Superintendent.'

'And you're a detective-story reader,' Lestrade focused through his throbbing head and steamy eyes.

'Avid,' the bishop smiled.

'There isn't any ham,' Harry reminded Lestrade. Everyone ignored him.

'It's a hobby of ours,' Penhaligon chirped. 'But I did come to see poor Fanny, Sholto. I'll tell you what I can later.'

'Tell me what you can?' Lestrade repeated.

'Why, yes,' said Penhaligon, somewhat taken aback. 'I was there when poor Tom died, along with His Grace here.'

Lestrade's mouth fell open. It was a pose not unbecoming to him. 'I'm sorry,' he said. 'I hadn't realised. Er ... Fanny's sleeping, Norman. The shock of it all – you understand. My daughter, Emma, is keeping an eye on her.'

'Ah,' Penhaligon nodded sagely, 'marvellous comforters, the young. Wouldn't you agree, Arnold?'

'Indubitably, Norman.' His Grace lounged back in Tom's old chair, letting the firelight dazzle on his spectacles and gleam on the shiny expanse of his dome.

'Well, gentlemen. You were both there. You are both armchair detectives. Tom Berkeley was a friend of mine. Suppose you catch his murderer for me.'

Fanny tossed and turned in her sleep while Emma did her best to soothe her. In the end Harry called the doctor, and he administered a sedative. Best, he said, under the circumstances. She would sleep more soundly all night, and probably all the next day, too.

'Hello, Sholto.' The soft voice rose and fell, as though on a breeze. It couldn't be Fanny? No, the hair was too dark, the form too shaped. Sarah? No, Sarah was dead. Was it Emma? Too sensuous, too ripe. Not Constance Mauleverer, after all these years? Or the battling Emily Greenbush, still hot from her tilt with the windmills of mankind? The women who had filled Lestrade's life floated on a dream before him.

'Hello, Sholto,' the voice said again, and he focused. The fire was out in the big old-fashioned grate. The lamp still burned at his elbow, and someone, probably Harry, had thrown a travelling rug over him.

'Jane?' He peered into the vastness of Tom Berkeley's library.

'Jane,' she said and sat beside him, sweeping the long dark hair from her face.

'I'm sorry,' he chuckled, 'I was dreaming.'

'Were they happy dreams, Sholto Lestrade?' she asked.

He tensed, sending the old pain searing down his leg again. He moved as though to speak, and she put a finger to his lips. 'I know,' she said. 'You are a superintendent of Scotland Yard, about to be married, and I am the vicar's wife. The year is 1912 and we should not be alone together in the wee small hours.'

He chuckled again. 'Something like that,' he said. 'What time is it?'

'Nearly five,' she said. 'It will be light soon' – and she lit his cigar for him. 'All this is true,' she said, 'but you're alone and in pain and you need help.'

He puffed gratefully on the cheroot. She poured them both a large brandy.

'I've got Harry,' he said. 'And Stalker. My lads at the Yard.'

'And Fanny?' Jane Penhaligon's voice hardened. 'Where is Fanny, Sholto?'

'Upstairs,' he said. 'Asleep. The doctor thought it best to give her a draught.'

She bounced to the window, gazing out to where the first streaks of light were breaking to the east.

'Her father . . .,' Lestrade began.

'Yes, I know.' She turned to him, softer, wiser. 'Was he an old friend, your Tom Berkeley?'

Lestrade nodded.

'I'm sorry,' she said. 'You're tired, and I shouldn't have come.'

'No.' He caught her sleeve as she crossed by him. 'Don't go. Sit down.'

She did, leaning towards him. He looked up at the deep dark eyes, like the lakes beyond the orchard. The full lips parted into a smile.

'Why did you come?' he asked.

'You didn't turn up,' she said.

'What?'

'That day we walked in the woods. You promised to meet me the next day. You didn't. Why was that?' She lowered her face to his.

'Because I am me and you are you,' he said.

She shook her head slowly. 'That won't do at all,' she said softly, and their lips met in the dawn light.

'Jane,' he said, running his fingers along the line of her cheek. 'Jane.'

She held his hand fast, running her own fingers over the scarred haunted face, ruffling the tousled hair.

'Do you know what it's like to be married to a man of God?' she asked. 'A man as cold as the crypt of his church? He never touches me, Sholto. Never.'

'Jane . . .,' he said again.

She sat upright, took his hand and placed it on her breasts, heaving under the purple velvet. 'Is your leg very painful?' she asked.

'How do you mean?' he asked by way of feeble riposte.

'Does it hurt if I do this?' She folded forward again to lie beside him on the chaise-longue, kissing his cheeks, his hair, his lips. Her expert fingers unhooked the buttons above the plaster and gently squeezed what they found within. Lestrade gulped. His hands were busy with the bodice-hooks, and in the dim light the smooth roundness of her naked shoulders filled the room. The chemise fell away to reveal her pert breasts, with the dark nipples firm under his touch. She sighed and shuddered as he touched them.

'What of Norman?' he whispered.

'Who?' she asked and then stopped her kissing.

'What of Fanny?' he said more loudly.

'Sholto. Let's forget Norman. Let's forget Fanny. For one hour, in this silence, in this dark, let's just be ourselves' – and she lowered herself on to him.

'Come, come, Mr Lestrade. I am a very busy man, and I want you to know this is, to put it mildly, an imposition.' Frank Hornby stood in the drawing room before Lestrade's recumbent form. 'Good God, what a perfectly ghastly Bath chair. Mind if I have a look?'

'Feel free,' said Lestrade and instantly regretted it as the inventor's hand jabbed him in the vitals with all the precision of modern engineering. 'Well, perhaps not as free as all that.'

'Sorry.'

'You are the Mr Hornby who is the manager of the Meccano Company of Elmbank Road, Sefton Park, Liverpool?'

'The same.' The inventor buried his head in the wheels of Lestrade's machine. 'But you didn't ask me all this way to tinker with this, did you? Although, I must admit, it's an interesting little job. I'll get Hatton to oil it for you.'

'Who?'

'Hatton. My driver. He's outside.'

'Not now, Mr Hornby. I am more interested in your Meccano.'

'Are you?' Hornby produced a variety of tools from his coat pocket. 'Why?'

'Could you describe it to me?'

'Well, originally it was called Hornby's Improved Toy or Educational Device for Children and Young People. Mechanics Made Easy. I should have thought you were a bit old for all that. Brace yourself.'

Lestrade clutched the machine's arms convulsively as it tilted backwards. There was a metallic grinding sound, and Lestrade's body rang in time to the peal Hornby hammered out with the end of his pliers.

'Put an engine on that and it'll outrun a Silver Ghost. Is that yours on the drive, by the way?'

'No, it isn't. Mr Hornby, I am conducting a murder inquiry.'

'Murder?' Hornby stood up. 'Who's dead?'

'The chief constable of this county.'

'Good God. I must tell Hatton. He'll be delighted.'

'Delighted?' Lestrade felt his plaster crawling.

'Oh, it's nothing personal. Hatton's got a thing about people in authority. The Establishment. Between you and me, Mr Lestrade, I think he's a closet socialist.'

'A . . . *closet* Socialist?'

'Yes. I found a copy of the *Communist Manifesto* in the servants' privy once. I'll swear it was Hatton's.'

'To come to the point, Mr Hornby. . . .'

'I wish you would, Mr Lestrade. As I said, I'm a very busy man.'

'Can your mechanical contrivance kill a man?'

'Well, Hatton says the cost of it can. But, no, of course not.'

'What about a crossbow?'

'I didn't invent the crossbow. It's a bit before my time, if you know what I mean.'

'Come with me.' Lestrade released the brake, and the chair shot forward with a horsepower the Household Cavalry would have envied. The foot-rest destroyed Tom Berkeley's remaining jardinière.

'There,' beamed Hornby. 'That's better already, isn't it?'

Lestrade led the way, slicing and gouging the wallpaper as he went to the library where the assorted pile of Mr Hornby's invention lay in pieces on the desk. A crossbow bolt and string lay with it.

'I want to test your ingenuity further, Mr Hornby,' said

Lestrade. 'Build me a crossbow with that lot.'

Hornby circled the desk a few times, crouched, rotated, closed one eye, licked his finger and held it in the air.

'It's a challenge, all right,' he confessed. 'You see, there's not much call for crossbows alongside model railway lines. Give me ten minutes.'

Lestrade sat and watched in astonishment as the inventor whipped off his coat, stripped to his shirt-sleeves and proceeded to set to with spanners and screwdrivers on the desk. Lestrade found himself glancing at the grandmother in the corner. In just eight and three-quarter minutes, Hornby stood back and said: 'What do you want me to shoot at?'

On the desk stood a metal frame, riddled with holes, a series of bars, nuts and bolts, and the crossbow bolt jutting from the centre.

'That picture.' He pointed to a cow on the wall behind the door.

'I can't guarantee accuracy,' said Hornby and brought his hand down on a lever. As he did so the door opened and Mrs M'Travers entered, only to exit again with a scream as the deadly bolt thudded into the cow's posterior and the plaster-work and brick beyond.

'Bull's-eye!' said Hornby. 'Will that old lady be all right?'

'Oh, yes,' said Lestrade. 'I'll tell her it's a new flykiller. That'll please her.'

'Of course, with more time I could make it stronger,' said Hornby.

'I'm not sure that's necessary,' said Lestrade, watching the inventor turn purple as he dislodged the bolt from its target.

'Am I free to go now?' Hornby asked. 'I'm a busy man.'

'Thank you, Mr Hornby, you have been most obliging.'

'More brandy, Sholto?' Harry Bandicoot stood by the decanters.

'I can't stay here much longer, Harry.' Lestrade held out his glass.

'Why ever not?' Harry asked. 'Tom doesn't need the house any more. And you can't leave Fanny, not just now.' He sensed Lestrade's mood. 'How is she?'

'I'm worried about her,' Lestrade admitted. 'She just goes through the motions of living, Harry. You know, she hasn't spoken of Tom since the funeral.' He changed the subject, ruminating on the women he loved. 'Emma wants a job at the Yard, you know.'

'Yes, she told me. Do you approve?'

Lestrade raised his eyebrows over his glass. 'Do you?'

Bandicoot shrugged. 'I don't think her mother – sorry – I don't think Letitia does.'

'I don't think her mother would have, either,' said Lestrade. Suddenly, he changed tack again. 'Right, Harry. Who killed Tom Berkeley? Got the paperwork?'

'Right here, Sholto.'

'Start pinning them up.' Lestrade lolled back in the Bath chair, praying the motions of his body wouldn't ignite the engine Frank Hornby had fitted to it before he left. He had a constant sense of ill-ease about it. It was like sitting in a Lanchester in the living room. He watched as the pages appeared under the massive thumbs of Harry Bandicoot. '"Twelve for the Twelve Apostles,"' he read. 'Bishop George Claverhouse, found dead in an East End brothel, 1873. Natural causes. My first year with the City force. My first case. Next?'

Bandicoot obliged.

'"Ten for the Ten Commandments." Chief Justice Firkett presiding and meting out sentence without mercy. The victim was Robert Uriah Hesketh, solicitor. Committed suicide in his cell, 1874.'

'And this one?'

'"Nine for the Nine Bright Shiners." Assistant Quartermaster-General Valentine Baker. Tried, convicted and cashiered for an assault in a railway carriage, 1875. Died of a broken heart.'

'A broken heart, Sholto?' Bandicoot had once read a copy of

the *Lancet*. He knew the impossibility of such things. Or was his old guv'nor getting soft?

'A broken heart,' repeated Lestrade and waited for the next sheet. 'Ah,' he said, '"Eight for the Eight Bold Rangers." Messrs Druscovich, Meiklejohn and Palmer, senior officers of Scotland Yard, all dismissed for fraud and bribe-taking, 1877.'

'Is there a pattern in the dates?' Bandicoot asked.

'You tell me.' Lestrade rattled his fingers on the desk-top and blew smoke through his nose. He emptied his glass and held it out to Bandicoot. 'The late Dr Watson used to say that the late Sherlock Holmes would play his violin hour upon hour as he thought.'

'Cogitated.' Bandicoot, after all, had read every word to drip from the pens of Doctors Watson and Conan Doyle.

'Probably,' said Lestrade. 'But that would have been the least of his problems. Holmes fiddled. I drink.'

Bandicoot replaced the decanter-stopper and smiled engagingly.

Lestrade shrugged and put the empty glass down.

'Then the numbers jump to four,' Bandicoot said. '"Four for the Gospel-Makers."'

'No, they don't,' Lestrade corrected him. 'Seven, six and five are there all right. And, perhaps, among them we have our clue. Perhaps, among them we have our man.'

'Man? I thought you said Chief Constable Ushant died at the hand of a woman?'

Lestrade nodded. 'So I did,' he said. '"He" is a figure of speech, Harry. Don't let it confuse you.'

'But what do these numbers mean? Twelve, and so on. And why no number eleven?'

Lestrade sighed, shaking his head. 'Damned if I know,' he said. 'There were twelve members of the Apostle Club to which George Claverhouse belonged. After that, they don't fit. The trouble is, Harry, I'm guessing. I'm supposing. I could be hopelessly off the track.'

'What about the missing numbers, then?' Harry sat down.

'It's late.' Lestrade checked the grandmother. 'Do you realise, Harry, it's Christmas in a day or two? Go home to your family.'

'I will when you've told me about number seven, Sholto.'

'Number seven? God, how the years roll by. Ah well, here goes. . . .'

The dead man lay propped against the angle of the stage, his head fallen on his chest, his arms brushing the ground. An ugly knife protruded from his glittering waistcoat, the silver threads darkened with his blood. The doctor had cleared a space, and the auditorium was empty now except for himself. He half-turned to the click of steel-shod heels on the boards above.

'Who are you?' the arrival asked.

'Dr John Watson, medical practitioner. And you?'

'Sergeant Lestrade, Criminal Investigation Department, Scotland Yard.'

'Indeed? One of Mr Vincent's boys, eh?' Watson wiped his hand before extending it to grip Lestrade's.

'Who called you?' Lestrade sprang down from the footlights, impaling himself briefly on a violin bow in the orchestra pit. Luckily it only grazed the surface, and Lestrade was not a heavy bleeder.

'One of the orchestra. I was on my way home from the theatre when he ran into the street screaming for a doctor.'

'So you weren't in the house?'

'No,' said Watson with some distaste. 'Most certainly not. I'm glad to say this is my first visit to such a cesspool. And I don't care to return.'

Lestrade studied the corpse, the angle of the body, the curious hilt of the knife.

'No point in asking the cause of death,' he murmured.

'Straightforward,' said Watson. 'One clean thrust to the heart.

Delivered downwards, I'd say. And with force.'

'Downwards?' Lestrade quizzed him.

'I'd say so.'

'Was he in this position when you found him?'

'Er . . . no. I moved him.'

Lestrade's eyebrow served as a slap to Watson's wrists. 'That is unfortunate, Doctor. Perhaps you would be so good as to move him back as he was.'

'I'd love to, Sergeant. But the fact of it is I'm not a well man. I've quite exhausted myself getting him to that position.'

'Indeed?' Lestrade's eyebrows expressed his doubts. Dr Watson stood squarely before him, a man of his own age, thirty or so, of florid complexion and clear eye.

'Indeed,' the medical practitioner asserted. 'I've recently served Her Majesty in Afghanistan, Lestrade. Have you ever been hit by a jezail?'

'No, but I've been severely bruised by a Methodist,' Lestrade assured him. 'We all have our cross to bear. What time were you summoned?'

'About midnight, I think.' Watson checked his half-hunter. 'God, it's nearly one. Mrs Hudson will worry.'

'Mrs Hudson?' Lestrade began to haul the corpse into a sitting position.

'Er . . . nothing. My housekeeper. The fretful type, you know. Then, there's Holmes. . . .'

'Your man?' Lestrade took the strain as the bulk of the deceased landed on him.

'Good Lord, no. My companion. If you'll leave things as they were, I'm sure he could help you. He has the most brilliant deductive mind I've met.'

'Very interesting, sir, but had you left things as they were I would not now be risking a hernia. Is this how you found him?'

'Not quite. His right arm was raised, as though. . . .'

'As though?'

'As though he were pointing to the gallery.'

Lestrade tried to move the limb, but it was useless.

'Trapped in the rigours of mortis, eh?' A voice behind them made them turn.

'Who are you?' Watson asked.

'Inspector Abberline, Scotland Yard. Now, then, Lestrade, what's afoot?'

'Twelve inches,' Lestrade muttered under his breath.

'The game, I sincerely hope!' roared Watson.

'Who might you be?' Abberline paused to sniff his buttonhole.

'I might be Spring-Heeled Jack.' Watson knew a hostile copper when he met one. 'In the event I am Doctor Watson. I was called to the scene when—'

'Yes, yes,' Abberline cut him short. 'Lestrade here can deal with this – can't you, Lestrade?'

The sergeant nodded – in the circumstances the politest gesture he could manage.

'I only came in, Lestrade, to remind you not to put in for your rest day this month. Sergeant Gregson's down with his trouble again.'

'Thank you, sir,' said Lestrade. 'Very thoughtful, sir.'

'Not at all,' Abberline beamed. 'I'm a thoughtful sort of chap. Saw your wagon and constable outside. Thought I'd just call in.'

'Taking Mrs Abberline home, sir?' Lestrade asked.

The inspector twitched his moustache and jerked back his shoulders. 'Absolutely,' he said. 'By the way, Lestrade' – he took his sergeant by the arm – 'cause of death a knifing. All right?' – and he pointed to the deceased.

'Thank you, sir. What would we do without you?'

Abberline straightened. 'Any more of that lip, lad, and you'll find out. You may have been Howard Vincent's blue-eyed boy, but you're not mine.'

Abberline glared at Watson and spun on his heel. Before he disappeared into the dark of the foyer, his step lightened. 'I shall expect your report on all this, Lestrade, on my desk bright and early.'

'Very good, sir,' Lestrade responded.

Abberline swaggered along the carpeted passageway, tapping his fingers on the seats as he went and he began singing quietly to himself, 'All together now'. No sooner had his bulk filled the doorway than another silhouette joined it, then another. 'Come on, Freddie, darlin',' a raucous female voice called out, 'I'm goin' off the boil 'ere.'

'Me, too,' another shouted.

Abberline seized them both and hurried from the theatre.

'Goodnight, Mrs Abberline,' chuckled Lestrade.

By morning Lestrade had the cast of the Mogul Theatre assembled. Some of them fumed at the inconvenience of the situation, of the outrage of being woken up at such a godless hour by flat-footed policemen. Mostly, they gossiped in their dressing rooms about recent events, and to men and women – troupers all – who never worked together and whose sole purpose for existing was to outshine the others even this conversation was unusual.

In order of their importance, they appeared before Sergeant Lestrade, who had commandeered the deceased's office and sat toying with the deceased's gavel.

'Mr Joseph Saunders?' Lestrade read out the name as the first witness entered. He was a strikingly handsome man, well over six foot, wearing a loud striped suit, hair carefully parted in the middle. He carried a pewter tankard and a bag of whelks.

'George Leybourne,' he corrected the sergeant.

'It says here Joseph Saunders, occupation hammerman, Westminster Bridge Road.'

'One of my older notices,' Leybourne sneered. 'To my following, especially the ladies, I am George Leybourne.'

'How long have you played at the Mogul, Mr Leybourne?' Lestrade asked.

'I have never played at the Mogul.' Leybourne sat down, careful not to spill his whelks, nor indeed crush his cockles. 'But I have worked the Old Mo for four weeks this season.'

'In what capacity?' Lestrade asked.

Leybourne looked astonished. No problem topping this particular Bill, he thought to himself. 'Are you unfamiliar with the halls, Sergeant?' he asked.

'Well, I. . . .'

'I have been packing them in of a night – *every* night, mark you – with a little number what I wrote – "The Daring Young Man on the Flying Trapeze". Do you know it?'

'Er. . . .'

'Yes, of course you do. All together now' – and he broke into song, a deep rich baritone voice that shook the lights around the deceased's mirrors. Lestrade growled something along with him but, as Inspector Palmer had pointed out some years before, he was not a natural for the Glee Club.

'No, no,' Leybourne broke off. 'You're humming "He Did It before My Eyes" – or was it "The Friar's Candle"?'

'Either way, Mr Leybourne, I did not come here to audition. A man is dead.'

'So he is, damn his eyes.'

'You didn't like Mr King?'

'If you are unfamiliar with the halls, Mr Lestrade,' Leybourne swigged from his tankard, 'let me enlighten you. Jonas King was an impresario, a chairman of the first water. What he could do with a gavel would bring tears to your eyes. And like all chairmen he was a proper bastard.'

'You mean. . . .?'

'I mean, Mr Lestrade, I am the foremost among the *lions comiques* in the Metropolis – nay, in the country. What's this?' He thrust his tankard under Lestrade's nose.

'Cider?'

'Champagne, sir. Moët and Chandon itself. I drink it by the pint.' He leaned forward. 'How do you get yourself to work, Sergeant?'

'I walk some of the way,' said Lestrade, a little confused by the reversal of roles. 'If the weather is bad, I take a bus.'

'I have my own carriage, pulled by four grey horses. What do you earn a week?'

'With respect, Mr Leybourne. . . .'

'All right,' said the lion. 'You needn't answer that. I earn a hundred and twenty pounds a week, Lestrade. Think of it. A hundred and twenty. That would keep you in skittles and beer for a long time, eh?'

'Mr Leybourne. . . .'

'The point I am making, Sergeant, is that I, even I, the great *lion comique*, am entirely – entirely, Lestrade – at the mercy of that man's gavel. Every word, every gesture, every look. One flick of his hammer, and my career could lie in ruins.'

'I thought *you* were the hammerman, Mr Leybourne?' Lestrade said.

'If you're trying to find a murderer, Lestrade, you'll have a full house here. King had his cronies, like they all do, grovellers who bought his supper and his cigars, but they all hated him secretly. Any of them would have garrotted him just to pass the time.'

'And you, Mr Leybourne?'

'Oh, yes, I include myself in that. Fortunately, if you seek out the Misses Keeler and Davis of Harrington Mansions, The Minories, you will find that I have what you police fellahs call an alibi for last night.'

For a moment, Lestrade wondered if Leybourne knew Inspector Abberline, but he let the moment pass.

'When did you last see your chairman?' he asked.

'Shortly before the curtain. He came backstage with his usual clique of cronies.'

'How did he seem?'

'Insufferable, as usual. Sergeant' – Leybourne adopted a more confidential manner – 'I am not one given to malicious gossip, but if I were you I would talk to one Alfred Peck Stevens, currently on the bill here and posing as the Great Vance. The only thing that's truly great about him, of course, is the bare-faced cheek he has to appear on stage in the first place.'

'I believe Mr Vance is waiting outside, Mr Leybourne. Thank you. That will be all for now. But you won't be going far, will you?'

Leybourne surveyed his tankard. 'Just to the tap room,' he said. 'I appear to be empty.'

A shorter man responded to Lestrade's barked order to come in. He was impeccably dressed in cravat, waistcoat and trousers which appeared to have been poured over his legs.

'Draughty in here,' he commented. 'I just felt a great gust of wind go out.'

'You must be Mr Vance,' Lestrade said.

'Great.' The second of the *lions comiques* sat down by arranging his feet just so and lowering himself as though on to a bed of nails.

'It's nothing really,' said Lestrade. 'You are in reality Alfred Peck Stevens, solicitor's clerk.'

Vance recoiled for a moment, then read Lestrade's notes on Leybourne, upside down, one of the many little tricks he had picked up in the trade.

'Rather superior to a hammerman, though, isn't it?'

'Which chambers?' Lestrade asked.

'A few,' Vance answered, placing his shiny beaver topper on the desk as though it were made of glass. 'Latterly of Hesketh and Hesketh.'

'Robert Uriah Hesketh?'

'The junior partner, yes. Why do you ask?'

'Nothing,' said Lestrade. 'It doesn't matter. What were your relations with Mr King?'

'Cordial,' said Vance. 'Nothing more. I did my turn. He had his. Of course, Leybourne was different.'

'In what way?'

Vance leaned forward, sweeping aside his magnificent waxed moustaches. 'You've met him. You've seen how he drinks. The champagne. He's on his way down. You mark my words. He'll be dead himself in two years.'

'What has he to do with Mr King?'

'Everything, my dear chap. King was carrying him. Lauding him at every turn. You see' – Vance became patronising – 'George has never really been able to carry a tune. You saw how he dressed this morning.' He shot his cuffs forward. 'Not quite the ticket, is he? Oh, he's average enough, had a bit of luck, but now . . . well, it's over.'

'I still don't follow. . . .'

'I knew a fellah once. Name of Ginger. Had a dog; miserable beaten old thing he was. He found it starving and brought it home. Fed it, tended it, cared for it. You'd think that dog would have loved him, wouldn't you?'

Never a lover or even understander of the canine breed, Lestrade said: 'Yes.'

'Not a bit of it,' Vance corrected him. 'One day the bloody thing bit Ginger's fingers off.'

'Why?'

Vance shrugged. 'Pique?' he suggested.

'Is that a particularly dangerous breed?' Lestrade asked.

Vance gave him an old-fashioned look. 'The point is, Officer, that George Leybourne is like that battered old dog. Jonas King was giving him every chance. Leybourne knew it. And he hated him for it. So he killed him.' Vance folded his arms and lolled back, the case, for him, closed.

'When did you last see Jonas King alive?' Lestrade remained unimpressed.

'Ah, let me see. Just before the final curtain last night. He came backstage to see Leybourne.'

'What about?'

'My dear fellah, I haven't the faintest idea. We *lions comiques* have our own dressing rooms, you know.'

'Do you own a knife, Mr Vance?' Lestrade asked.

'I have a clasp knife, yes. You can never be too careful with the riff-raff in the stalls. Mind you, it's tamer than it used to be. The music-hall is really quite respectable these days.'

'May I see it?'

Vance stood up, braced himself on one leg, settling his back against the desk, and proceeded to withdraw a knife from his boot. Lestrade looked at it. The murder weapon itself lay on the desk under Lestrade's bowler. 'Is that yours, too?'

'My dear fellah, I wouldn't be seen dead in a bowler like that.'

'The knife,' said Lestrade.

'Never seen it before.'

'Thank you, Mr Vance. You won't go too far, will you?'

'Just to my tailor's,' scowled Vance. 'I sense a rend in my kicksies' – and he collided with a tall angular man in the doorway.

'Vesta Tilley?' Lestrade was unsure of his ground.

'How dare you?' the tall man said. 'I am Sherlock Holmes of Baker Street.'

Lestrade riffled through his papers. 'I don't appear to have you down,' he said. 'You're not the Frisky Vocalist, are you?'

Holmes fumed to himself for a moment, then slid elegantly into a chair. 'You are . . .?'

'Sergeant Lestrade,' he said.

Holmes looked at him, the lights flickering over the long pale face. 'Lestrade. Yes. Watson mentioned you.'

'Watson? Ah, yes, of course, the good doctor.'

'I think "average" is a better description.'

'How can I help you?' Lestrade answered.

'No, no.' Holmes allowed himself a brittle smile and lit an ornate meerschaum. 'How can *I* help *you*?'

Lestrade looked at him. 'I really don't know. Unless . . . unless you knew or murdered Jonas King.'

Holmes mused for a while. 'Neither, I'm afraid.'

'Then, good morning, Mr Holmes.'

'Watson tells me the man was stabbed.' Holmes ignored the farewell.

'Mr Holmes, may I remind you that this is an official police matter now?'

'Well, then, as we are all amateurs, you'd appreciate a little help.'

'No, thank you, sir.' Lestrade tried to keep calm in the face of this madman. 'There is a constable outside to show you out.'

Holmes laughed. 'Very well, Sergeant. But let me at least tell you this. Your murderer is a heavy man, with only one arm. He may or may not be asthmatic, wears a cholera belt, which you'll agree is a trifle *passé* and out of place, and has at one time or another worn female attire.'

Lestrade sat there open-mouthed.

'Ah,' Holmes beamed between puffs on his pipe, 'I see you have such a man in mind. Well, strike, Sergeant, strike. While the iron is hot, eh? And, please' – he raised his cadaverous hand – 'no thanks. It's enough for me to know I am of service. The game is afoot!' – and he hurtled through the door.

'Constable,' called Lestrade, 'next time I want to see a certifiable maniac, I shall ask for one.'

'Very good, sir,' the constable saluted. 'Mr Bertie . . . from Burlington.'

'Well,' said the little man who entered in topper and tails, 'I've had some introductions in my time. Don't ever give that man a gavel, will you?'

'Mr Bertie?' Lestrade was ransacking his notes again.

Mr Bertie chuckled, then swept off the topper and let the light brown hair cascade over her shoulders. 'Don't none of you coppers do the halls?' she asked. 'I'm Vesta Tilley.'

And in the event she was no help at all.

Lestrade worked his way doggedly through the troupers and the day. He broke off at mid-afternoon to write out in triplicate the report Inspector Abberline had wanted that morning and sent the constable on his way with it.

By the time he had finished, the hall was filling with customers, the lights had dimmed and the band struck up.

'Why 'aven't yer asked me?' A Northern voice caused Lestrade to spring upright from the pillar against which he was leaning.

'Who are you?' the sergeant asked.

'I'm Ben Battle, Champion Clog Dancer o' North of England.'

'Champion what?' said Lestrade.

'Clog Dancer.' Battle lifted first one foot then the other to show the sergeant his heavy wooden boots. 'And I know summat.'

'Well,' mused Lestrade, following the wiry young man to a table, 'perhaps the game is afoot, after all.'

For once in a long and checkered career, drinks were on Sergeant Lestrade. In the swirl and shout from the high-kicking girls, the air was laden with the fumes of champagne and cheap cigars. As the sergeant plied the clog dancer with drinks, it transpired he was not all he claimed to be.

''Course, y'know, ah'm not really from t'North at all.'

'Oh?'

'Nay.' Battle's eyes sparkled mischievously, and he lapsed into pure Cockney. 'Unless you wanta call Somers Town Norf o' course.'

'Somers Town?'

'Right underneaf platform six St Pancras Station as now is.'

'What's your real name, just for the record?' Lestrade asked.

'Spong,' Battle replied. 'George Spong.'

'And you're a dancer?'

'Among uvver fings.' Battle suddenly swung his arm up round his neck. 'I also walks the Bloody Tower,' he groaned. 'Talkin' of which. . . .' He put his neck back in place and closed over his ale. 'I saw it again last night.'

Lestrade raised an eyebrow. 'It?' he said, echoing posturally.

'The ghost.'

Lestrade sat back. 'It's been fun, Mr Battle.'

'Nah, straight up, guv'nor.' Battle gripped Lestrade's sleeve. 'It was up there, in the gallery.'

'The gallery?' Lestrade sat down again.

'As I live and breave. Will you watch wiv me tonight?'

'Are you saying this . . . ghost . . . killed Jonas King?'

Battle shrugged. 'There's one way to find out.'

The theatre was silent now. The rows of seats empty. The curtain hung heavy in the stillness of the summer night. Only in the wings the ropes creaked and swung. Lestrade sat on the chairman's throne, one leg slung casually over one of its arms – less of a contortion than Mr Battle could manage. Then he heard it, a swishing sound, distant at first, then nearer. It was regular, rhythmic almost. He checked his half-hunter, the new one he had saved for, in the gloom of the dwindling limelight. Nearly three. It would be dawn soon. The swishing sound got nearer, and he made out through the darkness a shape, female, quick, darting from row to row, crouching, leaping now and then with long strides. Lestrade sat upright in the chair, hardly daring to breathe. He pulled the brass knuckles free from his jacket. All his life he had doubted the supernatural, the very existence of the spirit world. Was that doubt to be shattered? He wondered what effect his knuckles would have on thin air.

'Ah ha, ever been had, Mr Lestrade!' a maniacal voice cackled.

Lestrade subsided in the chair as though his heart had been in its usual place all along. 'You're late, Mr Battle,' he said.

'Do you like me Widow Twankey?' Battle bobbed into the light wearing a preposterous white wig and voluminous skirts above striped stockings.

'Not just now,' Lestrade muttered. 'I'm on a case. And don't call me Widow Twankey.'

'Nah, I'm sorry I'm late. Rushin' over to the Gaiety like that, I was bushed. I 'ad to get some shuteye, and when I woke up I remembered I should be 'ere. 'Adn't time to change when—'

A hollow moan stopped him in his tracks, and he spun round. 'Wassat?' he hissed.

Lestrade stood up. 'The doorman?' he suggested.

Battle whipped off his wig and shook free his thin macassared hair. 'Gone 'ome.'

Lestrade looked down at him. 'How did you get in?'

'Got a key, ain't I? There's only you and me in the place, Mr Lestrade.'

The sergeant dropped to one knee on the stage. 'What were you doing here at this time last night? You never told me.'

'Kippin'. I only do me Widow Twankey at Christmas usually, only tonight and tomorrow it's a charity do in aid of orphans.

More do-gooders and bloody chokers – oops, beggin' your pardon – vicars.' He looked up to the rafters and froze. 'Jesus!' he screeched and dived under the nearest table.

Lestrade looked up. In the darkness overhead, another shape seemed to hover among the ropes. It appeared to be draped in a cloak and it moved slowly from right to left, without noise.

'Who's there?' Lestrade cursed the fact that he had not brought a bull's-eye. 'Battle, get out of there.' He dragged the dame upright. 'You know who works this theatre. Look at it, man. Tell me who it is.'

'Old Mo 'isself!' Battle was as white as a sheet, even under the make-up.

'Who?' Lestrade shook him by the shoulders. 'That's the name of the theatre. Who is Old Mo?'

Battle pulled Lestrade across the room, kicking over tables in his anxiety to get to the door. 'For God's sake, let's get out of 'ere!' He struggled, but Lestrade was too big for him.

'Look.' He slapped the clog dancer around the head a few times. 'This was your idea. If you're so afraid and you saw this thing last night, why did you come back tonight?'

'All right.' Battle dropped his hands and stood quivering in his skirt. 'We was going to roll you, Mr Lestrade. Me and Bert who works the curtains. When times is hard and you're makin' your way . . . well, we do a bit of buzzin'.'

'You could have picked my pockets at the tables. Why wait until tonight?'

'That's where you're wrong, guv. I tried my best, honest. But you've bin around, aintcha? There's always stories about . . . things in theatres. I thought if I told you about it you'd come back, and it would give us a second chance.'

'So that's Bert up there?' Lestrade pointed to the ropes.

'No, it bloody ain't.' Battle made to bolt for the door again, until Lestrade stopped him. 'I just fell over Bert in the alley outside this gaff, dead bleeding drunk.'

'So who's Old Mo?' Lestrade could feel the hairs on his neck crawling.

'Nobody knows. Folks have seen him now and again over the

years. Some say he's a toff wot fell from the gallery when this was a penny gaff. Others say he's the Cock Lane Ghost. Still others. . . .'

'Yes?'

'When they built this place, they found bones, human bones. 'Undreds of 'em. They reckoned they was plague victims. Think of it, Mr Lestrade, 'undreds of corpses, rottin', stinkin'.'

'You've been at the gin, Battle.' Lestrade relaxed his grip on the ill-fitting corset.

Battle shrank to his side, folding like a pack of cards, covering his head with his arms.

Lestrade spun as he felt an all-pervading sense of cold. In the gallery, gliding as though above the ground, a figure swathed in black moved between the rows. Lestrade was rooted to the spot. A rasping sound, like tortured breathing, accompanied it, echoing, hollow.

'Stop!' Lestrade broke free from the fear that held him and he leaped up on to the stage. As he reached King's chair, his arm pointing at the shadow, he realised he was adopting the attitude of King himself, in the position in which Dr Watson had found him. The dead man had been pointing to the gallery and had died on the spot.

'Stop!' he shouted again, his word ricocheting around the theatre, his breath hanging on the air, although it was mid-July. The figure half-turned, its face white and deadly, with hollows where the eyes had been. It was a face which would haunt Lestrade to his dying day. He looked away, his blood racing, his throat dust-dry. When he looked again, the figure had gone.

'It went through the wall,' a small voice below the stage said. Battle knelt there still, visibly trembling. 'It went right through the bloody wall' – and he screamed, rushing wildly into the sleeping streets that criss-crossed Drury Lane.

'What was it, Sholto?' Harry Bandicoot found himself reaching for his brandy again.

Superintendent Lestrade sighed, jerking himself back from the old Mogul Theatre, Drury Lane. Back from the Year of His Lord 1882.

'It's funny. That day I fell off the *Titanic*,' he said. 'The day you fished me out. I saw it again then, that face. And I hadn't, not for years.'

'Was it a ghost, Sholto?'

Lestrade chuckled. 'I don't believe in such things,' he said. 'When it was light, I went up there, to the gallery. Battle had been right. There was no door in that wall. No trap. No false panel. No visible means by which . . . whoever it was could have left at all. . . .'

'Even so, Sholto' – Bandicoot's feet remained stoically planted in the earth of reason – 'they were music-hall people. Sleight of hand, eh?'

'Oh, quite, Harry, quite,' Lestrade mused. 'That must have been it. That's what I kept telling myself. That must have been it.'

'So who killed King?' Bandicoot asked.

Lestrade shrugged. 'Now only God knows.'

'You never caught anyone?'

'No. Jonas King was one of the most detested men I ever nearly met. It might have been any one of the stars at the Mogul. It might have been any one of his audience, as Miss Tilley suggested. As it was, Abberline took over the case, arrested a dozen or so stagehands and bill-bottomers. He had to let them all go, of course.'

'What happened to Battle?'

'Dead. A few years back. They say he became deranged at times. Had to be put in a straitjacket.'

'The hectic lifestyle, I suppose?'

Lestrade shuddered momentarily at the memory of that night in the theatre. 'I suppose,' he said.

'What has all this to do with Tom Berkeley?' Bandicoot drained the brandy into Lestrade's glass.

'Ah, well' – Lestrade shook off the mood – 'the week after Jonas King died, give or take a few months – my memory isn't what it was – I received another letter.'

'The numbers?'

'Full marks, Harry. You get even sharper at two o'clock in the morning. It said: "Seven for the Seven Stars in the Sky". Nothing more.'

'Seven Stars? The Pleiades!' Bandicoot exploded.

'What?'

'The Seven Stars, Sholto. The Greeks called them the Pleiades, the Seven Sisters.'

'What a wonderful thing a classical education is,' beamed Lestrade.

'Does it help?'

'I don't know, Harry. But looking back . . . the Mogul was full of stars – Leybourne, the Great Vance, Vesta Tilley, even Ben Battle, though he was just starting out then; and at the time the biggest star of them all was Jonas King.'

Bandicoot threw himself back in the chair. 'What did you mean the other night, Sholto, when you said the pattern had been broken?'

'The letter said: "Three, Three the Rivals." I worked that out as being Gordon Ushant, Edward Henry and Tom Berkeley – all up for the commissioner's job.'

'And?'

'And when Gordon Ushant died I assumed that was it, that Henry and Tom were in the clear. That's why I thought he was safe with Stalker. My God, Harry' – realisation dawned – 'I could have prevented this.'

The next day, Lestrade allowed Harry to talk him into going with him to Bandicoot Hall to spend Christmas. Fanny sat smiling. His Hornbyised Bath chair strapped to the back of Harry's motor, Lestrade accepted Mrs M'Traver's Cornish pasties with as much grace as he could muster and lashed the goggles around his head. He braced himself against the jolting of the Ghost, cradling Fanny in his arms, cursing Messrs Rolls and Royce every mile of the way until they snarled through the winter afternoon into the village of Huish Episcopi, where Peace and Love dwelt in the warm fires of Letitia and Harry Bandicoot.

'Daddy!' Emma held the goggled superintendent to her and helped Harry to bundle Lestrade into the house. Letitia and Emma hugged Fanny, and she began to cry quietly, the tears running down the cheeks of all three of Lestrade's women. The superintendent hugged Letitia and Ivo, Harry's wife and son, and they placed him in the drawing room. Here, Emma brought her young man.

'Daddy, I'd like you to meet Paul. Sholto Lestrade. This is Paul Dacres.'

The men shook hands. Was this the one? Lestrade wondered. Mr Right for his Emma? Time would tell.

'What is the time, Mr Dacres?' he asked.

'It's ten to three, sir.' Dacres glanced through the windows. 'At least by the church clock.'

'Come on, everyone,' Letitia announced. 'Honey for tea.'

The Cottage

'There is a gentleman to see Mr Lestrade, mum,' Letitia's man announced.

'Oh, how tiresome,' Letitia muttered. 'I did so want Sholto to have a real rest. After all he's been through, poor dear. Very well, Marjoribanks, show him in.'

The butler disappeared while Letitia finished putting the final touches to the Christmas tree.

'Sergeant Blevvins, mum.' Marjoribanks bobbed in and out, taking the new arrival's coat and hat with some distaste.

'Sergeant.' Letitia adopted the frozen smile of midwinter and raised her hand for Blevvins to kiss. It was a forlorn gesture. He merely admired the rocks that glittered on her fingers and once again regretted that he had been born the wrong side of the blanket. Men like Blevvins were in fact born the wrong side of the bed.

'Compliments of the season, Mrs Bandicoot,' he at least had the grace to say. 'Is the guv'nor in?'

'How did you know he was here?' Letitia countered one question with another.

'They told me at Mr Berkeley's house. I got that lunatic on the blower. That maniac obsessed with flies.'

'Is it vital you see him?' she asked.

Blevvins straightened to loom over her. Not a bad bit of skirt, he thought. In a poor light and with a tail wind. 'I *have* come rather a long way, missus,' he said.

'Well, let's hope you enjoy the journey back.' Lestrade hurtled through the door, which luckily was open, gripping the controls of the Bath chair for all he was worth and cursing the name of Frank Hornby. He brought with him a table-lamp, trailing by its flex from his spokes, and what was left of Letitia's rubber plant. Blevvins assumed it was some sort of disguise and shook the superintendent's hand.

'How's the leg, sir?'

'Excruciating, Sergeant. Thank you for asking. Now, what brings you this far west at Yuletide?'

'Mr Dew sent me, sir. Developments.' Blevvins jerked his head in the direction of Letitia.

'I'm sure Mrs Bandicoot wouldn't. . . .'

'Now, now, Sholto.' She crossed to him and planted a kiss on his forehead, taking the opportunity to defoliate him as she did so. 'I know the rules. You forget, my husband was on the Force once. Besides, it's time for Fanny's walk.' It had become a daily routine to fill the time of the daughter of the dead chief constable. Slowly, Letitia and Emma were bringing her out of herself, but it was an uphill struggle. Lestrade felt useless. Until he caught Tom's murderer, he couldn't help. Couldn't reach the woman he loved. Letitia went on: 'Sergeant, you must be exhausted. And famished. I'll get you some refreshment. Will you be staying the night?'

'No,' Lestrade answered for him. Blevvins shrugged and accepted the proffered seat. 'All right, Sergeant, what are Chief Inspector Dew's developments?' He was relieved to see the man go for his notebook. Walter Dew had come a long way from Miller's Court in the Autumn of Terror. He knew better than to trust a man like Blevvins with nothing but memory.

The sergeant cleared his throat. '"Miss Lola Atkins." . . . Oh, I'm sorry, sir.' He tore the page hastily from the book and stuffed it into his pocket. 'That's another matter entirely. Er . . . we have an eyewitness in the death of Dr Edmund Lucas, sir.'

'A witness?' Lestrade swung his chair round, shattering a vase.

'Ah, well,' sighed Letitia. 'The best-laid plans of Meissen men' – and she left the room.

'Go on,' urged Lestrade.

'A window-cleaner. One Albert Joiner.'

'He saw the murder?'

'No, but he probably saw the murderer. He was on the building opposite, the shady side of Harley Street.'

'I always thought both sides were. What did he see?'

'Well, I think he's a Tom, sir. Seems to make a speciality of doing bedroom windows at peculiar hours. Says he's an insom – imson – can't sleep, so he works at night.'

'I don't care about his habits, Blevvins. What did he see in Harley Street?'

'Well' – Blevvins became confidential – 'There was this woman with enormous—'

'The Lucas case!' Lestrade roared.

'Oh, yes, sir. Quite, sir.' Blevvins sat up straight. 'A woman, sir. Mid-thirties. Tall, comely. Dark hair.'

Lestrade waited. 'Is that it?'

'Yes, sir.' Blevvins looked like a man about to receive a medal from the commissioner.

'You risked the sandwiches of the Great Western line to tell me that?'

'It was on the day in question, sir. Probably within minutes of the murder.' He could see his guv'nor was not impressed. 'It's better than nothing, isn't it, sir?'

Lestrade sighed, long and hard. 'Yes, Blevvins. And nothing is precisely what we've got so far. Anything else?'

'This.' It was Blevvins's trump card, and he held it up, a diamond earring that caught the light as it twirled in the sergeant's hand.

'Very nice,' said Lestrade. 'Goes with your eyes. Paste, of course.'

'Oh, yes, sir, but it was found in the study of Chief Constable Ushant, late of Rutland.'

'Was it?' Lestrade looked at the thing more closely. 'Not one of his, I suppose?'

'Well,' sniggered Blevvins, 'you know what chief constables are. . . .' He lapsed into silence at the look which darkened Lestrade's features.

'Letitia.' The superintendent hailed his hostess, who had come in to supervise the pouring of the tea. 'What sort of person would wear this, in your opinion?'

She took the earring. 'A woman, Sholto,' she said.

Blevvins and Lestrade looked skywards.

'It's paste, of course,' she said. 'Belonging to someone youngish. Perhaps early thirties.'

The men waited.

'Well, really, Sholto, what did you expect me to tell you? Her bust measurement?'

'I'm sorry, Letitia,' he smiled. 'It was a long shot.'

'It certainly was. Milk, Sergeant?'

'Just a tincture, missus.'

'Apart from the obvious fact that the lady patronises Bodley's, I can't really help.'

'What?' Lestrade and Blevvins chorused.

'I'll ask the questions, Sergeant,' Lestrade reminded him. 'What, Letitia?'

'Bodley's, the jewellers. In Austria Street, Lambeth. You know, near the asylum.'

'You should know, Blevvins,' Lestrade commented. 'But how can you be so certain, Letitia?'

'Men!' Letitia fumed. 'Look at this, Sholto.' She flipped over the earring. 'It's a Fabergé design. Quite the rage in Paris last season. But a fake. Mr Bodley makes no bones about it. See these leaves on the back? What do they look like?'

Lestrade fought down the urge to say 'Leaves', and as the light of the tree-candles caught it he suddenly said: 'It's a face. Well, I'll be a chief superintendent, it's a face.'

'The Bodley head,' Letitia explained. 'I thought that was quite a witty idea. Don't you?'

'Oh, yes,' Lestrade smiled, as much in the dark as Blevvins now the winter afternoon was beginning to descend. 'Right, Blevvins. Any more developments?'

'None, sir.'

'Right. Get back to Town. Knock up this bloke Bodley in Austria Street. Comb his books. With a bit of luck, we'll turn up the name of the lady who dropped this at Chief Constable Ushant's.'

'Oh, let the poor man have some tea first, Sholto.' Letitia observed the rules of common humanity. And humanity did not come more common than Sergeant Blevvins.

'All right. One cup. Then you're on your Raleigh.'

'Sholto,' Letitia chuckled, 'it's nearly dark. I don't think the sergeant will find another train at this time. It *is* nearly Christmas, you know.'

'All right,' fumed Lestrade. 'One night. *Then* you're on your Raleigh.'

Afternoon ticked into early evening. Lestrade sat in Harry's study with its yards of unread books, trying to cope with the jigsaw of death which lay before him. It was an uneven struggle. He didn't even have all the outside pieces, and the size of the green leather that stared up at him from the gap in the middle was embarrassing. He excused himself from dinner early, largely because it was no fun watching Blevvins tuck the tablecloth into his collar and proceed to see how many peas he could balance on his knife. It didn't help at all that Emma and her young poet found it all hysterical and giggled over the syllabub. Fanny seemed brighter in the day, but night with its shadows brought old terrors and she retired early with Letitia for company.

It was nearly ten by Harry's grandfather when Blevvins knocked on Lestrade's door.

'I was wondering if I could help, sir?' Blevvins said.

'Like a dose of flu, Sergeant, thank you.' Lestrade did not look up from his pieces of paper. But conscience – or something – made him change his mind. 'How old are you, Blevvins?'

'Thirty-four, sir.'

'How long on the Force, now?'

'At the Yard, sir, two years. With the Mets, fourteen years, sir, man and boy.'

'Right, and it's boys I'm interested in at the moment.'

Blevvins closed the door as discreetly as an animal can and looked at his guv'nor under the light. He'd heard age could do funny things to people. Even so, this was rather a turn up for the books. He edged his way to the sofa, careful to keep his back to the furniture.

'What do you know about Cleveland Street?' Lestrade asked him, well aware he was not in the encyclopaedic presence of Dickens or Jones.

'Er. . . .' Blevvins was dredging what passed for a brain. 'Off Fitzroy Square, isn't it? Tottenham Court Road.'

'Very good, Sergeant,' Lestrade humoured him. 'Now, get your notebook out, and stay awake. I shall be asking questions later. Let me take you back a few years – to 1889 to be exact.'

Chief Inspector Frederick Abberline was in no mood to be kept waiting. His befuddled brain was already reeling with the aftermath of the Whitechapel Murders and he was convinced that Inspector Tobias Gregson, of the newly formed Special Irish Branch, was trying to subvert justice by appearing even more nattily dressed than he was. Sartorial splendour was Abberline's department, along with the old F Division, and he intended no one else to muscle in on it. When Inspector Lestrade arrived that morning, well over an hour late, it prompted Abberline into precipitate action.

'Well, Lestrade?'

'Well, Chief Inspector?' Never a man to mince words was Lestrade.

'What's your report on number nineteen?'

'It's essentially Constable Hanks's report, sir.'

'Don't beat about the bush, Lestrade. What have you got?'

A sweeter temperament than you this morning, Lestrade mused. 'Over the past week, sir, thirty-eight gentlemen have been seen entering the premises. Constable Hanks reports thirty-nine coming out.'

'Thirty-nine? I didn't know buggery produced offspring. Well, that's what you get for trusting a Post Office copper. Anybody known? Any of these Mary-Annes have a face?'

'Twelve of the thirty-nine are errand boys, sir, most of them Post Office employees. Of the others, we can be sure of only two.'

'Yes? Yes?' Abberline reached for little liver pills, in the grim realisation that his liver was probably too far gone for anything Carter could throw at it.

'One is Lord Arthur Somerset, Master of the Horse to His Highness the Prince of Wales.'

' "Podge," ' said Abberline.

'Constable Hanks assures me it's correct, sir.'

'No, Lestrade.' Abberline was as acidic as his stomach. ' "Podge" is Somerset's nickname. Do your homework. Who's the other one?'

'Captain Wesley Willoughby, Coldstream Guards. Hanks describes him as a constant visitor.'

'Coldstream Guards, eh?'

Lestrade nodded.

'Does he have a club?'

'Army and Navy.'

'Feel his collar.'

'Sir?'

'His collar, Lestrade, his collar. Arrest the sod.'

'On what charge, sir?'

'The abominable crime of buggery, Lestrade. We're men of the world. Need I say more?'

'With respect, Mr Abberline, to make a charge like that stick, I'll need to catch the good captain red . . . handed, as it were.'

'Well, that's your problem, Lestrade. Good morning.'

'Sir, I don't really think. . . .'

'I am aware of that, Lestrade. But I have a master, as you have. He in turn has a master, and that master, none other than the Home Secretary himself, wants results. This is London, Lestrade, not the backstreets of Cairo. It's got so a decent man can't walk down the road. It's a cesspool, Lestrade, a cesspool created by Mary-Annes like Willoughby. And it's up to the likes of you and me to clean it up.'

'You and me, sir?' Lestrade checked that he had heard Abberline properly.

'Get out!' Abberline threw his gardenia at the inspector. In the circumstances, it was an apposite gesture.

Police Constable Luke Hanks, Post Office Division, stood to attention as Lestrade reached the bottom of the stairs. He was a large, comfortably built man, devoted, obedient and hard-working. Even in '89, coppers like him were a dying breed.

'It's Tuesday, Hanks.' Lestrade always thought it wise to inform junior policemen what day it was. It gave them the edge over the average criminal.

'Indeed, sir.' Hanks had been around – and, judging by the style of his Dundrearies, for rather a long time.

'Who'll be there at this time?' The inspector checked his half-hunter. 'Nearly eleven-thirty?'

The dogged meticulous Hanks computed as he hailed a hansom for his newly acquired guv'nor. 'Thickbroom, sir. And probably Swinscow. Are you going in, sir?'

Lestrade paused at the cab door. 'Mr Abberline will have it so, Constable. Who are we to disagree? Are you armed?'

'Sir?'

'One thing I have learned about the love that dare not speak its name, Constable, is that its practitioners, contrary to their feminine nicknames, are among the nastiest bastards in the business. Watch yourself.'

'I'm a Post Office employee, sir,' Hanks was explaining.

'Yes, I'm a social worker.' Lestrade whipped free his brass knuckles and checked the switchblade to see it was oiled. 'Driver, number nineteen Cleveland Street and step on it.' Over-zealous in his efforts to please, the growler applied the whip, and Lestrade scraped the skin off his knuckles as he ran with the hack for a hundred yards or so before he managed to leap in. He reminded Hanks not to give a tip.

Cleveland Street, off Fitzroy Square, near the Tottenham Court Road, was a fashionable thoroughfare, averagely long as London streets go. Number 19 had a Regency portico and a highly polished handbell. As Hanks was in uniform, it fell to Lestrade to effect entry, in the nicest sense of the term.

'Yes?' A lad of perhaps seventeen opened the door.

'Mr Smith,' said Lestrade, pouting his lips a little in what he assumed was the right degree of femininity.

'Who did you wish to see?'

'Sally,' he said, remembering the details Hanks had given him.

'Not here,' said the lad, closing the door behind them. 'Nancy's available.'

'Good.'

The lad stopped him. 'Just a minute. Who recommended you, Mr . . . Smith?'

'Mr Brown,' Lestrade answered.

The lad smiled. 'That's all right, then. Can't be too careful.' He gave the inspector a peck on the cheek. 'Upstairs, lovey, room four.'

Lestrade smiled and made for the banisters. The walls were hung – very well, it had to be said – with portraits of young men in tights and tutus. At the door marked 'four' he knocked and waited. Another lad, perhaps a year older than the first, stood there in pink combinations. His lips were crimson and his cheeks dusky with rouge.

'Hello, I'm Nancy,' he lisped.

'So I see,' said Lestrade.

'Well, come in. Coffee?'

'Is it Camp?' Lestrade asked.

'Saucy.' Nancy flipped him with a teacloth. 'Who sent you?'

'Mr Brown.' Lestrade kept up the pretence.

'Ooh, 'e's a one, innee, that Lord George? Can't get enough of it.' The lad's smile vanished as business reared its ugly head. 'What'll it be?'

Lestrade had not relished this question at all. 'The same as Lord George,' he said.

The lad smiled. 'That'll be a quid,' he said. 'For now. Later, of course, it'll be a fiver.'

Before Lestrade could move, Nancy's deft sorting-office fingers had entwined themselves in his netherwear. His eyes widened with disbelief at what he felt.

'Sorry about that.' Lestrade moved the brass knuckles aside. 'You're under arrest, Nancy.'

'What?' the lad gasped, springing away. 'On what charge?'

'Obstructing a policeman in pursuance of his duty. Soliciting for immoral purposes. Importuning to commit an act of indecency – just how gross we'll never know, will we?'

'You bent bastard!' Nancy flew at Lestrade, as the inspector had warned Hanks, not with his nails and his handbag but with a brass bar from the bedstead. Lestrade stepped sideways and hauled the young man down to the floor.

'Tut, tut,' he said. 'We'll have to add striking a police officer to that, Swinscow.'

'Y-you know who I am?'

'I do.' Lestrade wrenched the bar from the boy's hand and threw him on to the bed.

Alarmed by the noise, the first lad crashed into the room. He took in the scene at once. 'Everything all right, Charlie?'

'Is it, buggery!' Charlie-called-Nancy fumed. 'This 'ere's a pig.'

Lestrade spun round and caught the boy by the ear, jerking him down beside the other one.

'Well,' he said, 'Babes in the Wood. Are you Newlove?'

'No,' pouted the first boy, 'I've been here for months.'

Lestrade leaned over as near as he dared. 'I'll do the jokes, laddie,' he said. 'Now, where's Captain Willoughby?'

Blank.

'Lord George?'

'I don't know what you're talking about, copper,' Nancy spat.

'Henry Newlove and Charles Swinscow, you are both under

arrest. You are under no obligation to say anything, but anything you do say will be taken down and may be used in evidence.'

Lestrade threw open the window to let in some fresh air and to summon the handcuffs of Constable Hanks.

Constable Walter Dew visibly paled the next day when he learned the identity of Lestrade's visitors.

'You'd better walk this way,' he said. 'Inspector Lestrade, gentlemen.' Dew opened the door on the converted latrine that served as his guv'nor's office. Surely, Norman Shaw wouldn't be *much* longer building the new premises on the Embankment, would he?

'Thank you, Constable.' Lestrade hauled his feet off his desk, 'You'd better look after Sir Dighton's horse.'

'We walked,' said the bearded man. 'Do you know me, sir?'

'Who doesn't know the Hero of the Mutiny?' Lestrade bowed. 'I can only offer you tea, gentlemen.'

'Thank you, no. If you know Dighton Probyn,' said Probyn, 'you will surely know Sir Francis Knollys.'

'No,' said Lestrade, but offered his hand anyway.

Knollys sat down heavily. 'I'll come to the point, Lestrade. I understand that you have been assigned to a case involving a certain house in Cleveland Street.'

Lestrade checked his visitors' eyes – the deep impenetrable brown of Probyn, the impeccable cold grey of Knollys.

'That is correct,' he said.

'Stop it,' said Knollys flatly.

'I beg your pardon?' Lestrade said.

'It's over, Lestrade. Done with. I've had a word with the chief inspector. The commissioner understands entirely.'

'Sir Francis, whatever Messrs Monro and Abberline understand, and however many words you may have had with them, an inquiry is under way. Wild orchids couldn't stop it now.'

'What are you, Lestrade?' Probyn asked. 'Some Juggernaut without breaks?'

Lestrade stared across his desk at the Hero of the Mutiny. 'I am a policeman, sir, doing my job.'

Knollys looked at Probyn and began to rummage in his pocket. He flipped out a chequebook. 'All right, Lestrade. One thousand? Two?'

The inspector felt the red mist rising but he contented himself with a curt, 'Good morning, gentlemen. You must have many duties.'

'Three thousand, then,' Knollys continued. 'Messrs Coutts can stand it.'

'Let it be, Francis,' growled Probyn. 'That is patently not the way forward. Lestrade, please forgive us. We are on the same side you are, believe me. There are. . . .' He began to pace the floor, but his turning circle was so tight he soon gave up. 'There are matters of the utmost gravity here.'

'Oh?' said Lestrade.

'A certain individual is involved – on the fringes, you understand – an individual who, should his involvement be known, could cause embarrassment to the Highest in the Land. Need I say more?'

'I think you'll have to, Sir Dighton, for the sake of clarity.'

Knollys fumed. Lestrade could almost see the steam whistling from his ears. 'I'll be frank,' he hissed. 'Lord Arthur Somerset is the individual to whom we are referring. He is not to be touched.'

'My information is that he has been touched several times already. It is a little late, gentlemen.'

'Damn it, Lestrade,' Knollys roared, on his feet by this time. 'You meddle in this and you'll be sorry. It is our duty and yours to—'

'Duty, Sir Francis?' Lestrade was on his feet, too. 'Let me tell you about duty, sir. Not many hundreds of yards from this office there is a group of individuals who make the laws of this country. One of them is Henry Labouchere. Mr Labouchere has recently had enacted an Amendment to the Criminal Law which demands that anyone who procures minors for acts of a homosexual nature shall serve a minimum of two years' hard labour and a maximum of life imprisonment. It is my duty, sir, whether I agree with Mr Labouchere or not, to enforce the law.'

There was a silence. Lestrade hadn't strung so many words together for days. In the vestibule Walter Dew, who had ambitions he could see floating away on the hot air, died a thousand deaths. Knollys, the master of the art, saw his opening. 'Whether you agree with Mr Labouchere or not? Is it possible that *you* are a visitor to the house in Cleveland Street?'

'Is it possible,' Lestrade countered, 'that it is still a hanging offence to strike an officer of the Crown? It may actually be worth it.'

'How dare you!' snarled Knollys, snatching up his hat.

'Gentlemen,' Probyn interrupted. 'Please. This is getting us nowhere. We must discuss this rationally. . . .'

'This is intolerable!' Knollys howled, disapproving of Probyn's gentler tactics.

'As intolerable as an officer of the Crown named Knollys hushing up the private affairs of the heir to the throne. Royal peccadilloes with the incontinent Mrs Mordaunt.'

Knollys lashed out in his fury, but Lestrade blocked the blow with his arm and slapped the confidential secretary so hard his nose bled.

'My nose,' mumbled Knollys.

'Best keep it out, then,' Probyn snapped. 'Sorry to have wasted your time, Lestrade' – and they vanished through the door.

'Dew!' Lestrade roared. 'Get me Hanks. At the double.'

The Post Office policeman was at that moment crossing the yard below. He was minding his own business when Dew grabbed his arm and whisked him into the basement. From there it was but three stairs' worth to Lestrade's office.

'Hanks,' Lestrade said.

'Morning, sir.'

'Who else have we got at the cottage in Cleveland Street,

besides Willoughby and Lord Arthur Somerset?'

'Quite a few, sir.'

'Anybody of note?'

'Sir?'

'A large man, for instance, full beard, poppy eyes, greying beard, Homberg hat?'

'The Postmaster-General?' Hanks was nonplussed.

'No, dammit, the Prince of Wales.'

'Prince of Wales?' Disbelief knitted the constable's brow. 'From what I've heard of him, Cleveland Street is the last place he'd be.'

'Yes, I suppose you're right.' Lestrade slumped into his chair. 'Show me your book again.'

He thumbed casually through the list of callers at number 19, then stopped. 'Who's this? Tall, poppy eyes, military moustache, long neck?'

Hanks shrugged. 'Couldn't fix him, sir. Most of the client – cleeon – callers are anonymous, sir. He did give his name as Mr Victor.'

A positive light shone from Lestrade's eyes. 'Did he now? Dew, is Abberline in?'

'I don't believe so, sir.'

'Not another bloody rest day?' the inspector muttered. 'Hanks, Dew. Come with me. We've got some society calls to make. I trust you've polished your boots this morning.'

Three policemen, albeit two in plain clothes, were not a common sight in the portals of the Army and Navy Club in Pall Mall. A uniformed lackey had gone in search of Captain Willoughby, and the policemen were shown into a smoke-laden billiards room. A bevy of fashionable young men of military cut lounged around the walls, vying with each other with their expensive mess dress and the length of their Havanas.

'Captain Willoughby?' Lestrade moved into the light.

'Not now, I'm trying not to kiss the cush,' the fair-haired man said.

'Would that be Hindu, sir?' Dew was poised with his notebook.

Willoughby paused from his shot. 'Who is this idiot?' he asked Lestrade.

'This idiot is Constable Dew of Scotland Yard. I am Inspector Lestrade and this is Constable Hanks of the Post Office.'

Willoughby chuckled. 'Don't tell me I've been caught for swindling the mail again. What you chaps don't seem to realise is the damnable cost of living nowadays. What with the cigars and the fizz, one has to cut corners somewhere. I do it by not buying stamps. Sorry!' – and he crouched for his shot.

'May we talk in private?' Lestrade asked, passing his bowler to Hanks.

'Oh, come now – your shot, Ardens-Grafton – I am among my brother officers here. Whatever you have to say, say it, man. I'm trailing three one.'

'Cleveland Street,' was Lestrade's calling card.

Captain Willoughby stood up as though he had been electrocuted. He threw down his cue and snatched up the scarlet mess-jacket. 'One moment, Ardens-Grafton,' he said, clenching his cigar more tightly than usual. 'I shan't be a moment' – and he stalked into an anteroom, checking that it was empty first. Lestrade saw him slip a coin into the palm of an orderly, who was told that they weren't to be disturbed.

'Well?' Willoughby tugged on the immaculate jacket.

'You are a regular visitor to number nineteen Cleveland Street?'

Willoughby decided to brazen it out. 'What if I am?'

'What do you do there?' Lestrade asked.

'Why, play cards, man. It's a baccarat school.'

'And I'm a fiddler's bitch,' said Lestrade. 'Number nineteen is a cottage, Captain Willoughby, a male brothel, run by one Charles Hammond, who is conveniently out of the country at the moment.'

'What?' Willoughby flustered. 'Whatever goes on elsewhere in that house is no concern of mine,' he said. 'I go there to play baccarat.'

Lestrade produced a paper from his pocket. ' "Captain Wesley Willoughby, Coldstream Guards, also known as Mr Green. This gentleman called on Wednesday last and was entertained by me, Charles Swinscow, in the following manner. Captain Willoughby removed my chemise and proceeded to—" '

Willoughby snatched the paper from Lestrade and tore it up.

'What a pity.' Lestrade shook his head. 'The time it took you to make that copy, Walter.' He looked levelly at Willoughby. 'The original is in my safe at Scotland Yard. And in cells nearby are Charles Swinscow, Henry Newlove and sundry others. . . .'

'What are Post Office boys to me?' Willoughby stubbed out the cigar in the nearest ashtray.

'I'm sure the court would like to know that, sir,' Lestrade told him.

'The court? God, Lestrade, you can't. The scandal. My family. The regiment.' Willoughby positively gibbered.

Lestrade held up his hand. 'Dew, Hanks. Leave us, will you?'

The constables exited.

'I'm after bigger fish, Captain. I want names. I know about Arthur Somerset already. Who else? Who else frequents Cleveland Street?'

Willoughby straightened. 'You're asking me to peach on my friends, Lestrade, brother officers. . . . What do you take me for?'

'A sodomite, Captain Willoughby. Or, conversely, two years' hard. Take your pick.'

Willoughby crossed to the window. He toyed momentarily with jumping through it. 'Let me understand you,' he said, his back to Lestrade. 'You'll see to it that my name is left out of things if I give you . . . names?'

'One name,' said Lestrade. 'The real identity of the man calling himself Mr Victor.'

Willoughby turned to him. 'That's blackmail, Lestrade. A dirty word.'

Lestrade crossed to him, nodding. 'It's a dirty world, Captain Willoughby. I am offering you immunity from arrest for twenty-four hours, that's all. You can leave the country, go on

the Grand Tour, retire if you like. But after twenty-four hours
I'm coming for you. And I can just imagine what certain
journalists will do with the name of Willoughby.'

The captain shuddered and closed his eyes. 'Very well,' he
whispered, 'Mr Victor is the Duke of Clarence – the heir
presumptive.'

Lestrade sighed with relief and complacency. He'd got him at
last. None of the boys from the Post Office would implicate
Eddy, old Collars-and-Cuffs, but Willoughby's evidence might
be enough to shake them. Especially if Lestrade could get to
Lord Arthur and Charles Hammond, the 'Madame' whose
cottage number 19 was.

'Thank you, Captain,' he said. 'Remember, twenty-four
hours. I'll see myself out.'

Inspector Lestrade had left it too late to question Lord Arthur
Somerset. 'Podge' of the Blues had run, no doubt to a brothel on
the Continent. 'Lord Gomorrah' as the Press christened him,
had vanished without trace, beyond the long arm of Lestrade, at
least until the fuss died down. And it was the next day that the
inspector was called to rooms in Berkeley Square. Sprawled
across a desk, wearing his immaculate full dress uniform and
with his bearskin hackled beside him, lay Captain Wesley
Willoughby, late of the Coldstream Guards, a bloody mess
where his head had once been. Lestrade picked up the Tranter
that lay near his hand and sniffed the muzzle. The chamber held
one bullet, and the one that had been recently fired was
embedded somewhere in the wall above the door. No one had
heard the shot. The captain's body had been discovered by his
batman that morning. Near the body were two letters, each in a
different writing. The Cleveland Street Scandal had claimed its
last victim.

Sergeant Blevvins finished the jottings in his notebook.

'*Two* letters, sir?'

'Ah, you've been following me, Blevvins,' said Lestrade.
'Well done. One of them, in what I ascertained was Willoughby's writing, was a letter of explanation. The classic suicide

note, written while the balance of the mind, et cetera, et cetera. It gave little away, in fact. Cryptic comments about not being able to go on.'

'Couldn't he have got out of the country, then?' Blevvins asked.

'I don't see why not,' said Lestrade. 'I gave him all the rope I could.'

'And he goes and shoots himself. Still, the dirty bastard. You did the world a favour, sir. I'd have loaded his pistol for him.'

'I'm sure you would, Blevvins. But that's not the point. It wasn't my threat which led to his death, not directly. It was the second note.'

'Oh, what was it?'

'A letter to Willoughby, dated the previous day and postmarked the Army and Navy. It told him the gaff was blown, though not precisely in those terms, that the captain's name was already with the Director of Public Prosecutions and that arrest was imminent.'

'And was it?'

'No. I checked with Abberline. I've never seen a man so frightened. Knollys and Probyn had leaned on him. He was just going through the motions so as not to lose face at the Yard. Willoughby's name appears nowhere except in Hanks's notebook, and I wouldn't be at all surprised to find that that didn't mysteriously disappear fairly soon after that.'

'What about the evidence of the Messenger Boys' – Blevvins consulted his notebook – 'er . . . Swinscow and Newlove?'

'Ah.' Lestrade tapped his tipless nose with his finger. 'The old incontrovertible-evidence ploy. I made it up. Dictated it to Walter Dew on the way to the Army and Navy Club that morning. I'm surprised Willoughby didn't notice the spidery writing – Dew was never a great writer, but in a Maria he was positively illiterate.'

'So who wrote the letter, the one which sent Willoughby over the edge?'

'It was signed by one Norbert Parker, chaplain to the Coldstreams.'

'Did you talk to him?'

'He'd gone. Done a bunk. The regiment couldn't explain it. I traced him to a private address in the Walworth Road, but he'd gone from there, too.'

'Well, the case of the churlish chaplain.'

'Very amusing, Blevvins. Then I got the letter.'

'The chaplain's letter?'

'Perhaps.'

'What did it say?'

'It said: "Six for the Six Proud Walkers."'

'Blimey.'

'In case you were wondering, the walkers – I assume, anyway – refer to the Coldstreamers, one of the oldest – and proudest – regiments in the British Army.'

'Does all this tie in with the recent murders, sir? Mr Berkeley, for instance?'

Lestrade nodded. 'I'm sure it does, Blevvins, but at the moment I'm damned if I know how.'

The Hidden People

That Christmas the snow held off until the twenty-fourth, and then it came, silently across the Devon Moors and across Somerset, blocking the lanes around Huish Episcopi. The Bandicoots dispensed largesse around a blazing log fire, Emma and Letitia more radiant than ever, their cheeks glowing as they gave presents to all the children of the estate. Even Fanny was cheerier, fussing in her own quiet way with the children, but in Lestrade's presence she was silent. He accepted it, because he had no choice. Half of Fanny Berkeley was better than none at all. Harry talked harvesters and cattle over hot rum punch. When the tenants had gone and the embers died in the grate, the talk turned to ghosts as it did traditionally on such a still and starry night at the Midwinter Solstice. Mr Dacres told one first, but admitted he had read it in the pages of M. R. James and could not claim any credit for it.

'Sholto,' said Letitia. 'One from you now.'

Lestrade guffawed. 'I'm not much of a storyteller,' he said amid howls of protest. 'All right, all right. But it's not exactly a ghost story and I'm not sure it's suitable for ladies' ears.'

'Nonsense, Daddy!' Emma cuddled into Paul's arms. 'It's nearly 1913.'

'Which reminds me,' chirped Ivo. 'Who's been at my cigarettes?'

She stuck her tongue out at him.

'Please, Mr Lestrade,' said Paul Dacres. 'Your story.'

He smiled, as though far away in another place, another time.

'It's a true story, isn't it, Sholto?' Fanny asked quietly. They all looked at her.

Harry filled the glasses glittering in the light of fire and candle.

'If you mean by that it really happened, yes, Fanny, it did. As to what is true' – he smiled ruefully – 'I'm not sure I know any more. Emma, Ivo, you were both five at the time. I was a hundred and three. . . .'

The vicar of Great Tew stood on the platform at Banbury station. It was a long glorious summer, that one of 1898; and, although the papers were full of the Sudanese campaign and the exploits of the Sirdar, events locally had driven all else from the vicar's mind.

'Inspector Lestrade? I am the Reverend Dunstan.'

'Sir.' Lestrade tipped his boater and extended his hand.

'I have a trap waiting.'

'For whom?' asked Lestrade, suspicious as ever. 'Ah, I see. Thank you.'

The Reverend Dunstan was a dab hand with whip and reins, and the miles flew by through the dumb heat of the Oxfordshire fields. Lestrade lit his cigar and, wedging his foot on his battered Gladstone, turned to his ecclesiastical driver.

'Well, Mr Dunstan, what do you have for me?'

'My local constable suggested I contact Scotland Yard, Inspector.'

'He sounds a good man. He'll go far. What's his name?'

'Anderton.'

Lestrade shrugged. 'Go on.'

'The deceased's name is – was – Charlie Reader. He had been a shepherd.'

'How old was he?'

'About sixty, I think.'

'A churchgoer?'

'On and off. I sometimes despair of the world, Mr Lestrade. My flock are wayward, I fear. It is a sign of the times. I suppose crooks are something we have in common, Mr Lestrade, you as a policeman, I as a shepherd.'

'Was Reader employed?'

'Yes, as a hedger and ditcher. He also gardened for me and for my opposite number in a neighbouring parish.'

'What happened to him?'

'He died, Mr Lestrade. Violently.'

'When was this?' Lestrade fanned his defunct cigar into life again with the boater.

'The day before yesterday, shortly before noon. Are you all right?'

'Yes, yes. It's just that my boater's on fire. Oh, and a lock of my hair, but it's . . . ouch . . . it's out now. Please go on.'

'Miss Trenchard found him. A dreadful experience for her and for the children.'

'Miss Trenchard's children?' Lestrade had heard about these goings-on in rural backwaters.

'Her charges, Inspector. Miss Trenchard is the schoolmistress. Church of England, of course.'

'Of course.' Lestrade tossed his smouldering boater into a passing pond. 'What did she find?'

Dunstan's face darkened. 'I'd better leave that part of the story to her,' he said.

'Ever been on the Force, sir?' Lestrade asked, impressed.

'I beg your pardon.'

'Never mind.' Lestrade chuckled and exchanged pleasantries until they rattled into the churchyard of Great Tew.

'Shall I come with you, Inspector?'

'No, thank you, sir. Is there any light in the crypt?'

'No. You'll find candles on your left, by the font.'

'Thank you.'

'You'll stay at the vicarage, of course?'

'Thank you again' – and the Reverend Dunstan led off his vehicle to have the horse watered. Lestrade entered the church, blissfully cool after the heat of the journey. Grass got up his nose, and he had punctuated his trap ride with sneezes of a violence which left him weak. He lit a taper and slid back the bolts on the heavy oak door. The uneven steps wound down in a tight spiral as they had done since the masons of Tew had hammered them out of the mellow Cotswold stone. It was dank down here, cold with the mildew of death. Above him, rough Norman arches supported the church floor. Cobwebs hung clinging and grey in the silence. A sudden scampering told Lestrade that St Michael and All Angels had rats.

He lifted the candle to face height. Old coffins mouldered on stone ledges. Spiders grew fat in the darkness on a glut of summer's flies. They droned around the gnarled old head of Charlie Reader, lying like a knight of old on a marble slab erected for a worthier occupant. On the old brass beneath his matted hair Lestrade read the Latin inscription – the only phrase he knew – 'Ora Pro Nobis': 'Pray for Our Soul.' Wherever Charlie Reader's soul was now, it was past praying for. His eyes were closed. That, Lestrade imagined, the Reverend Dunstan had done for him. His smock was draped around him like a shroud. His heavy labourer's boots were caked with the mud of the Cotswold Hills, and his leather gaiters and corduroy trousers had been scratched where the body had been dragged through rough country. It was the throat that held Lestrade's attention. Two large holes had punctured it, one on each side of the neck. Between them, half-hidden by dark congealed blood, but distinctive none the less, was a cross, carved deep into the flesh, shattering windpipe and cartilage. Lestrade stepped back from the corpse, crouched beside it, circled it once and left Charlie Reader alone with the spiders and the rats. If they had ever bothered him, they weren't likely to now.

Lestrade set up two headquarters in the village, one for the respectable and centred on the vicarage; the other for the tenants, centred on the Maiden's Lap. He installed the long-suffering Constable Dew in the pub, convinced as he was that the answer lay with the better sort. Besides, he couldn't stand to be with the constable and have to listen to interminable observations as to how Walter Dew's family must have come from 'they parts' originally on account of the similarity of his name.

Miss Trenchard came first, a frowsty spinster of the old school, with dowdy hat and hair strained into a barbed-wire bun. She had more wrinkles than a prune and shifty grey eyes which took in the Yard man in an instant. She didn't like his yellow scarred face, his taste in ties or shirts. In short, she didn't like him and was of the opinion, along with most of the village, that the corpulent constable at Lestrade's elbow, full of beard and girth, could easily have handled the matter.

'Our Miss Trenchard is something of an amateur sleuth,' Anderton informed him.

'There's no other sort,' Lestrade informed him. 'Miss Trenchard, I understand you found the body?'

'I did.' Her voice could shatter glass at forty paces.

'Would you like to tell me about it? Constable Anderton will take notes.'

She smiled at him. 'How is Mrs Anderton, Constable?'

'Well, thank you, mum, thanks to your herb tea. The scabs have nearly gone.'

Lestrade cleared his throat purposefully, and Anderton straightened, holding his notebook to attention.

'The body?' Lestrade reminded the schoolmistress.

'Poor Mr Reader was lying on his back. His arms were at his sides. There was a ... pitchfork through his throat. Most distasteful. The children were terrified.'

'Why were you and they there, at that place and time, Miss Trenchard?'

'It was the annual school outing, Inspector. Miss Newington was with me. We usually go to Skegness but, frankly, it's too bracing.'

'Quite. So this was a picnic?'

'It was. We had cress sandwiches. Little Billy Buggin had the runs.'

'A day to remember, then?'

'I hope you aren't being flippant, young man?'

Lestrade had not been referred to as a young man for a long time. It quite perked him up.

'So you're an amateur sleuth, Miss Trenchard?' Lestrade lolled back on the vicar's chair.

'I have on occasion proved of assistance to the local constabulary.' She beamed at Anderton, then closed on Lestrade tête-à-tête over Dunstan's desk. 'It's intelligence, you see. Policemen lack it.'

'Quite so,' smiled Lestrade, believing it best to humour the old biddy. 'Do you have any theories on this case, madam?'

'Well, it wasn't a sexual murder.' Lestrade and Anderton both whitened. 'Mr Reader was fully clothed. Besides, he was past sixty. The blood thins. The sap fails.'

'I'll take your word for it, madam.'

'My guess would be inheritance.'

'Inheritance?' Lestrade looked at Anderton.

'Mr Reader had a little put by for a rainy day.'

'He was a wealthy man?'

'Oh, not by the standards of the world, Inspector. But for a retired hedger and ditcher who did odd gardening jobs he flashed a largish number of gold sovereigns.'

'Did he now?'

'Miss Palmer saw him counting them one day in her garden.'

'Miss Palmer?'

'The sister of the vicar in the neighbouring parish. Reader did odd jobs for both vicars.'

'And he had left a will?'

'Doesn't everyone?' Miss Trenchard asked.

'No,' Lestrade informed her. It clearly came as a surprise to the amateur sleuth. 'Does Mr Reader have a large family?'

'One son,' Anderton informed them.

'He frequents the Maiden's Lap?'

'From what I have heard' – Miss Trenchard rose in splendour – 'he frequents many maidens' laps.'

'Thank you, Miss Trenchard.' Lestrade rose to her shoulder. 'You've been most helpful.'

She tapped him with her parasol. 'Mark my words, young Thomas Reader is your man. He was perfectly disgusting, even as a boy. Do you know, I once caught him with his head up a girl's frock?'

'No!' Lestrade was shocked.

'It didn't fit him at all. But in those days the Readers were a poor family. It's only recently they've become well heeled' – and Constable Anderton saw her out.

'Who's next?' Lestrade sipped Mrs Dunstan's appalling home-made lemonade. She'd been reading her parish temperance magazine again.

'Miss Newington, the pupil teacher,' Anderton told him.

The lady in question entered, a petite demure young lady of seventeen or so, who did not look him in the face. Essentially, she told Lestrade the same story as her revered headmistress, but she had no theories at all.

'You know what she needs?' Anderton grunted to Lestrade when she had gone.

'Promotion?' Lestrade beamed up at the constable.

The constable's brows knitted. 'Er . . . yes, sir, that would be it.'

The door burst open. 'Richard Ferrers,' the newcomer announced. 'Magistrate for this area.' He was dressed for the chase, in hunting pinks, and swished his way around the room with a riding crop.

'Local squire,' Anderton whispered out of the corner of his mouth.

'Are you Lestrade?'

'I am.'

'You're wasting your time. None of my people has anything to do with this ghastly business.'

'Your people?' Lestrade's eyes narrowed. He didn't care for the fiery squire.

'My tenants, man. My villagers. Go out of this house, look left, right, before and behind, and all you'll see is Ferrers land.'

'Did the deceased work for you?'

'Work? That shiftless old reprobate?' Ferrers threw himself into the chair. 'He didn't know the meaning of the word. The most work he did was hiding behind hedges spying on people.'

'Why should he do that?'

Ferrers sat upright. 'Because he was a filthy old pervert, Inspector. One doesn't want to speak ill of the dead, but if ever a man deserved to die. . . .'

'So this was a crime of revenge, then, Mr Ferrers?'

'Sir Richard,' the squire corrected him. 'I don't know what sort of crime it was. Reader was a Peeping Tom, a miser and a poacher. Three of the worst crimes known to man.'

'And murder?'

'What?'

'I thought murder was one of the worst crimes known to man.'

'It may be where you come from, Lestrade, but there is such a thing as justifiable homicide.'

'Is that a matter of law, sir, or of opinion?'

'I tell you,' Ferrers shouted, threatening Lestrade with his crop, 'whoever killed Reader, he wasn't from around here. If he was, I'd give him a medal' – and he left.

'I'm sorry, sir,' said Anderton, 'I should have warned you about the squire. Dressed me down something proper, he did, when he heard I'd gone along with the vicar in calling in the Yard. Dressed the vicar down, too.'

'The vicar?' Lestrade was incredulous.

'Well, squire holds the advowson, see. It's always been that way. Got Mr Dunstan in his pocket, so to speak.'

'Has he?' Lestrade mused. 'Well, don't worry, Constable. I don't think Sir Richard's pockets are big enough for Scotland Yard.'

It was late afternoon when Lestrade took the lane to Lower Ludgates, the field where Reader's body had been discovered by Miss Trenchard's children. The sky was blue and cloudless, the air perfectly still. The inspector picked his way through the low crumbling walls which had once been the Perpendicular grandeur of a Cluniac priory. Barns and farmhouses dotted here and there still carried the same mellow yellow granite. The very silence was eerie. He sat on a truncated column, once the support of a nave, and lit a cigar. To his left and to his right, the fields of Sir Richard Ferrers, heavy with their golden harvest. What was it? He had stood on murder spots before. Why did this one chill him? Was it the stillness? The silence? His eyes darted to the shadows under the spreading boughs of the elms that formed a spinney below the jut of the hill. Was it a movement? A sudden sigh in the wind? The wind that had not been there a second ago. He walked on, shaking himself free of the feeling that gripped him. He sensed there were watchers in the woods, sentinels in the stalks of corn. Even the cow parsley seemed suspect, privy to some terrible secret. He longed for the London pavements beneath his feet.

'Sir!'

He froze as the alien intrusion of a human voice shattered the moment. Then he relaxed. It wasn't a human voice.

'Over here, Dew.'

The constable of that name, sweating profusely in his thick serge, scrambled over the foundations of the reredorter with a working man in tow, complete with flat cap, scarf tied loosely and rolled shirt-sleeves.

'This is Thomas Reader, son of the deceased, sir.'

'You timed it nicely, Walter,' Lestrade said. 'Mr Reader, do you know the exact spot where the . . . your father was found?'

'I do.' Reader seemed proud of the fact.

'Could you show me?' Lestrade asked slowly, assuming he was addressing the village idiot.

'There.' Reader pointed to a piece of red cloth hanging limply in a hedgerow. 'Bill Anderton put it there.'

'Not exactly a cordon,' Lestrade muttered to Dew, and he stood on the depression in the grass. 'He was dragged that way.' He pointed to the track in the corn.

'Could be a fox,' said Reader. 'Or a dog. Could always be a

dog. Take my word for it, there's lots of 'em round here. Her who keeps the Maiden for one – right dog's lady she is.'

'I've heard everybody else's theory on your father's death, Mr Reader. Would you like to enlighten me?'

'No, thanks,' said the yokel with some distaste, 'but I'll tell you what I thinks.'

Lestrade looked at Dew. 'That's good enough,' he sighed.

'He stuck his nose in where it weren't wanted.'

'Anywhere in particular?'

Reader shrugged. 'Who knows? He were a meddler, my dad. A peeper, so they say.'

'What do you say?' Lestrade asked.

'Who am I to disagree?' Reader shrugged again. 'Look, Hinspector or whatever you are, I didn't get on with my old man. Ask anybody.'

'I have. Did you not get on well enough for you to kill him?'

'What?' Reader was outraged. 'What are you tryin' to pull? Blood's thicker than water, y'know.'

'I know. I saw a great deal of your father's. And, in answer to your question, what I'm probably trying to do is pull a rabbit from a hat. All right, Dew. You've taken the depositions?'

'Twenty-three of them, sir.' The constable looked a little dazed.

'You didn't have to have a pint with each one, though, did you?'

'Sir.' Dew stood upright, his pride hurt.

'Just a joke, Constable. I'm the one who does them, remember? Keep yourself available, Mr Reader. I may want to talk to you again.'

'Not joining us, then, sir?' Dew asked.

'No,' said Lestrade. 'I've got a trail to follow.'

'You'll only find a foxhole,' Reader assured him.

When the heads of the constable and the labourer were dots among the leafy glades that ringed the village, Lestrade pulled off his jacket, rolled up his sleeves and followed the track through the corn. After a hundred yards or so, he found a button, made of bone, of the type he had seen on the dead man's bloodied shirt. His assumption had been right. And if this was a fox trail, too, Lestrade couldn't smell it. Instead, he could smell his own fear.

At the angle of the hill, the hedge cut off his path. He now faced a choice: to follow the hedge back down towards the cluster of Cotswold cottages known as Little Tew or scramble through a sizeable bramble patch and to emerge on what he took to be sheep paths on the other side, where the grass was cropped short by the Ferrers flock of Jacobs. In the event, he chose the brambles and instantly regretted it because of the damage done to his forearms and face. At least it confirmed his theory. The late Charles Reader had come this way; the shattered brambles and twigs proved it. Whoever dragged him must have scratches, too, but he didn't see how in all conscience he could strip the entire village.

Beyond the brambles the air was even stiller and the view across the patchwork fields of Warwickshire spectacular as the evening sun caught them. Lestrade heard a rustling in the gorse bushes to his right and, picking up a stone from the chalky upland, hurled it into the centre of the thicket, expecting to see a pheasant start up, or a sheep break cover. Nothing happened. The rustling noise continued for a while, then stopped. The brow of the hill loomed ugly and bare above him. What was it in the bushes, unafraid of a whistling stone or a passing man? Lestrade felt the hairs on his neck crawl, and he felt for the brass knuckles in his pocket.

'Impressive, aren't they?' a voice said.

Lestrade shrieked and leaped backwards, losing his footing and rolling in an undignified heap in the brambles again.

'Oh, my dear man. Are you all right? I appear to have startled you.'

Lestrade looked up to see a diminutive lady of an indeterminate age reaching out to help him. She wore plus-fours and carried a stout walking-stick.

'What the devil were you doing hiding in the bushes?' he

snarled, annoyed at the loss of dignity.

'I beg your pardon?' The little lady looked at him. 'I was doing no such thing.'

'I heard you,' Lestrade insisted. 'I'm surprised my stone didn't get you.'

'My dear sir' – the lady squatted on the branching end of her stick – 'I repeat, I was not in the bushes. Neither did you throw a stone at me. I have just crossed from Nether Worton. Which means I came from that direction over the hill. I merely came to see the Rollrights. I'm sorry to have startled you. Good evening.' She tipped her hat and began to stride into the sunset.

'Madam,' he called after her. 'Please forgive me. I did not intend to be rude.' She bridled for a while as he went on: 'The Rollrights? Is that a local family?'

The little lady stopped in mid-stride. 'But surely that's why you're up here?' she said in astonishment.

'I am up here, madam,' Lestrade informed her, 'in pursuance of a murder inquiry.'

'Murder?' The little lady clutched her neck.

'I'm afraid so.'

'So you are a policeman?'

'Inspector Lestrade, Scotland Yard.'

'Goodness, how thrilling. Tell me, was the body found here?'

'Not far away,' Lestrade said. 'On the lower slopes.'

'May I ask who?'

'It's in this morning's papers, madam.'

'Tsk.' The lady stamped her foot. 'I never read newspapers. Drivel put together by inferior people too idle to work, don't you agree, Inspector?'

'Well, I—'

'You're avoiding *all* my questions, aren't you?'

Lestrade smiled and hauled on his jacket. Clever women bothered him, especially when they only reached his chest.

'It's just that I think I can help you.'

Lestrade's eyes rolled upwards. 'Don't tell me, you're an amateur sleuth.'

'I didn't know there was any other kind,' she said. 'And you are a very rude man.'

'I'm sorry, ma'am,' he said, 'but I haven't come to see friends. I've come to catch a murderer. Good evening.'

'The "friends" I've come to see are over there, Inspector.' She pointed to the hazy distance. 'The Rollrights.'

Lestrade followed her gaze to a circle of cold grey stones on a bare hillside on a level with their own position. Something ancient, primeval, reached out to Lestrade as he saw them, and they clutched his heart.

'The Rollright Stones,' the lady murmured. 'As I said a moment ago, impressive, aren't they?'

'What are they?'

The lady suddenly sat down cross-legged on the grass. 'Who knows?' she said, patting the area near her for Lestrade to sit down. Reluctantly, he did so. 'What is Stonehenge? The Avebury Circle? There are many such standing stones in this country. Whatever they are, they are not natural.'

'Not placed there by God, then?'

'That depends which God you mean,' she said.

'I didn't know there was a choice.' He lit another cigar.

'Ah, what a sheltered life you've led, Inspector.' She smiled. 'You are sitting in the heart of witch country, Mr Lestrade. Can't you feel it, in the very ground?'

Lestrade shifted uneasily, his nether regions suddenly very vulnerable.

'Legend says that the Rollrights were once a king and his knights and that a witch turned them all to stone to prevent his taking power in the land.'

'Legends don't catch murderers,' said Lestrade.

'Don't they?' She pointed to the north-west. 'Over there is the ridge of Long Compton, where, it is said, there are enough witches to draw a load of hay up Long Compton Hill. Dear old St Augustine is supposed to have preached there, on the spot that is now the church. He commanded that no excommunicated person could attend mass, and a dead man tore himself free of his coffin and left the place.'

'It's hard to keep a bad man down,' Lestrade commented.

'Over there' – she threw an arm in the opposite direction – 'is the site of Lawford Hall, haunted by the ghost of a one-armed man.'

Lestrade nodded, clearly unimpressed.

'You are clearly unimpressed, Mr Lestrade,' she said. 'All right, enough of local colour. Your corpse – male or female?'

Lestrade was content for the moment to play the game. 'Male,' he said.

'Age?'

'Sixty, give or take.'

'Local?'

'Not born and bred, but lived here most of his adult life.'

'Labourer?'

Lestrade nodded.

'Cause of death?'

Lestrade leaned nearer. 'I thought you'd tell me.' He smiled archly.

She looked him squarely in the eye. 'Very well. He was pinned to the ground with a pitchfork and his throat had been cut.'

Lestrade stood up suddenly.

'Ah ha.' She stood up with him. 'A palpable hit.'

'So you do read the papers,' he said, unable to take his eyes off the lengthening shadows of the Rollright Stones.

'If you're worth your salt as a policeman, you won't have allowed those vultures of the Press to obtain such detail. You won't, I'm sure, have mentioned the cross.'

'The cross?' He felt his archness draining away.

'There was a cross cut into your victim's throat?'

Lestrade nodded. He had not leaked that to the Press. Nor did the papers carry any mention of the pitchfork.

'Tell me,' the little lady said. 'Think carefully. Was the cross upside down?'

'Upside down?'

'Yes. Was the longer shaft pointing towards his chin or his chest?'

'His chin,' Lestrade told her.

'Oh dear,' she said. 'Oh dear, oh dear.'

'Madam, you have an uncanny aptitude for making the hairs on the back of my neck stand on end. May I ask your name?'

'Oh, how remiss of me,' she tittered. 'I am Margaret Murray, Professor of Archaeology at London University.'

'Professor?' Lestrade repeated in disbelief.

'Yes. Oh, I know, professors are supposed to be dotty old men. Well, I'm afraid you'll have to put up with a dotty old woman.'

'Mrs Murray—'

'Professor,' she reminded him coyly. 'I'm sorry, Inspector, but a female has too hard a path to such laurels to see them cast aside, even unintentionally.'

'Of course.' Lestrade smiled. 'Professor, please forgive me. Do you have a theory, then, about my "victim" as you put it?'

'I thought you didn't trust amateur sleuths,' she teased him.

'I don't, Professor. But, if I may say so, you are no amateur.'

She tapped his chest with her stick, nearly breaking his sternum. 'I'm afraid I think it was a sacrifice.'

'A sacrifice?' Lestrade squinted at her in the sunset.

'It's older than recorded history, Mr Lestrade. Your ancestors and mine were timid beings, afraid of their own shadow. When they emerged from the primeval swamp, they believed the only way to please their myriad gods, the only way to survive, was to give those gods presents, offerings. The Egyptians did it, the Greeks, the Romans. And in country churches, all over England, we do it still. We call it Harvest Festival.'

'Precisely,' said Lestrade. 'I thought the Church of England made do with a loaf of bread and a few apples. I didn't think they went in for murder.'

'Church of England,' scoffed Professor Murray. 'Johnnies-Come-Lately. Look at that.' She held out her right hand.

'It's your right hand,' said Lestrade. Twenty-three years on the Force had left their mark.

'And a few years ago it shook hands with an embalmed mummy, a young man who ruled over all the world, as he thought, five thousand years ago. He was Pharaoh of Upper and Lower Egypt, the great Tutankhamun. And what I'm talking about makes him look as though he were born yesterday, Inspector. There are older forces by far than the Church of England. Darker, wilder forces. And I think they're with us yet. Here, now, on this summer evening. Do you feel it? Do you hear it? It has to do with those stones.' She pointed again, then turned from side to side. 'Your body may have been found on the lower slopes,' she said, 'but he died up here, in sight of the stones.'

A shiver darkened the land.

The Maiden's Lap that night was less convivial than usual. After all, some copper had been there all day, regardless of opening hours, asking damn fool questions. It was obvious nobody knew anything. Whoever had put a pitchfork through Charlie Reader's throat, it was none of they. Lestrade and Dew sat in a corner of the tap room, the few locals who had arrived resolutely at the other end. Mine Host served them the warm flat beer in which Ansells excelled, without cheer, without a smile. It was only his profit margins that made him serve them at all. But one old man did not sit with the others. Neither did he sit with the Yard men. Instead, he slumped near the cellar door. It was obviously his habitual position.

'I haven't seen him before, sir.' Dew nodded in his direction.

'Buy him a drink, Walter. Bring him over here.'

Dew looked at his guv'nor. 'Expenses, sir?'

'Ah, we're all out of pocket, Constable. That's the way of it.'

Dew did as he was bid and dragged the resisting yokel to Lestrade's table. The sight of frothing pints made his step a little lighter.

'I am Inspector Lestrade,' reverberated around his ear-trumpet.

'Eh?'

'Lestrade. Inspector Lestrade. Scotland Yard,' he repeated.

'Oh, yesh. Lunnun,' croaked the old boy, his lips clamping on to the rim of the glass. 'I've forgotten me teeth again.'

'Never mind,' said Lestrade. That was the least of his problems.

'It'sh all right. I've got 'em 'ere' – and he fished a pair of brown dentures from his pocket and rammed them into his mouth. 'Now, wadyya want to know?'

'Who killed Charles Reader?'

'Eh?' The ear-trumpet caught Lestrade a smart one around the temple.

'Charles Reader,' Lestrade repeated.

'Oh, 'e's dead, y'know.'

'Yes, I did know.' Lestrade felt his knuckles whiten. 'I'm trying to find out how he died.'

The old boy thought for a moment, sucking the juice from his dentures as he did so. 'Well, I don't suppose the pitchfork helped.' He took a hefty swig from the tankard and wiped his lips with his sleeve. ''Course, it was the 'Idden People what did it, y'know.'

Dew closed to him. Lestrade circled back to the table.

'What?' asked the inspector.

'The Hidden People.' A voice made them turn.

The Yard men stood up. 'Professor Murray,' said Lestrade. 'I thought we'd said our farewells.'

'Yes, we had, but something occurred to me.'

The locals had paused from their beer. Mine Host dropped a glass.

'They're not used to seeing unaccompanied ladies in public houses,' Dew informed her.

'Oh, nonsense. I gave up worrying about social conventions years ago.'

'Oh, Professor Murray,' Lestrade introduced them, 'Constable Dew.'

'Charmed.' She shook his hand heartily. 'My man' – she

tapped the yokel, who appeared to be snoozing, on the chest with her stick – 'where did you see these Hidden People?'

'Well . . .,' he said.

'Dew.' Lestrade snapped his fingers, and the constable sloped off to buy another pint.

'At the Stones,' he said after the froth had passed his lips.

'The Rollrights?' the professor checked.

'Yes'm,' the yokel belched loudly.

'I thought so,' she said.

'What can it mean?' Lestrade asked her.

'That he's had too much for one night,' Dew informed the company.

'I'm not so sure, Constable.' Professor Murray was thinking. 'You there' – she prodded the yokel again – 'were the Hidden People dancing?'

'Ar.'

'In a circle?'

'Ar.'

'Which way round?'

The yokel looked perplexed.

'T'other way round from the clock.'

'Widdershins,' said the professor.

'Bless you,' said Dew.

'He may have to bless us all before this is over. When did you see these people?'

'T'other night.'

'The night Reader died?' Lestrade asked.

'Eh?' The ear-trumpet came into play again. What was it, Lestrade wondered, that made his words inaudible?

'Was it the night poor Mr Reader died?' Professor Murray prompted him.

'Ar.'

'The first of August,' she said.

'Does that have any significance?' Lestrade asked.

She looked at him. 'It does, Inspector. The first of August is

Lammas, the Feast of the Great Sabbat. It is the Night of the Witches.'

A silence fell again on the little room.

Lestrade whispered to the professor: 'Are you telling me this old idiot witnessed a witches' meeting?'

'He thinks they were fairies,' she whispered in reply. 'The Hidden People. Well, I'll keep an open mind about that. There is no doubt, so far as I am concerned, you have stumbled on a witch coven, Mr Lestrade.'

Lestrade signalled to Dew to guard their exit and led the professor to the door. 'Goodnight, gentlemen,' he said to the assembled drinkers, 'and thank you for your help.'

In the stillness of the warm summer's night, Professor Murray continued: 'That's why I came back. The date suddenly occurred to me.'

'So Tom Reader was right,' mused Lestrade.

'In what way?' she asked.

'He said his father had a long nose and was always poking it into other people's business. He witnessed the Sabbat, too, like the old boy in there.'

'Yes, but he must have been closer or perhaps he had a looking-glass. He may have recognised someone.'

'What does "widdershins" mean?' Lestrade asked.

'Anticlockwise,' the professor told him. 'It is the traditional circular dance of the witches. In direct opposition to the natural, you see, to the forces of light. At most Sabbats you would find twelve witches and a thirteenth – the God. He will probably wear a horned mask to symbolise his position as head of the cult. He will also copulate with as many of the women as he can, and they will kiss his posterior as an open act of blasphemy.'

Walter Dew turned away. 'You must forgive my constable,' chuckled Lestrade. 'He's a married man.'

Dew was grateful that the night hid his blushes.

'I think I know how you can catch them,' the professor said.

'Oh?'

'Go away. Leave the village. Announce that your enquiries are closed.'

'But. . . .'

'Then come back. With two or three plain-clothes men. I'll come, too, if I may.'

'When?'

'All-Hallows Eve, Inspector. The next Grand Sabbat. The next time the witches ride. I'd like to see who's under the goat's head.'

'So would I, Professor. So would I.'

'Is that it, Sholto?' Harry asked.

'There isn't much more,' Lestrade smiled.

'Oh, come on, Daddy. You can't stop there.' Emma rushed over to her father, hammering his chest with her fists.

'Did you go back, sir, at Hallowe'en?' Paul Dacres asked.

Lestrade chuckled. 'As a matter of fact, we did. It's about the only time I've taken the advice of a' – he caught the feminist glances of Emma and Letitia – 'civilian. But the professor was right.'

'Were they really naked, Daddy?' Emma giggled.

'Emma!' Harry's prudery was showing.

'Apart from the one with the goat mask, yes,' Lestrade said.

'And did he actually . . .?' Emma began.

'The point is', Harry jumped in, 'did you catch your murderer?'

'No, Harry.' Lestrade gazed into the dying embers of the fire. 'I didn't. You'd be amazed at what we saw among those old stones that night – and don't press me, Emma,' he forestalled her question. 'There are some things better left to the night. Miss Newington, Miss Trenchard, Tom Reader, the landlord of the Maiden's Lap, to mention but a few.'

'Who was the coven leader?' Letitia asked. 'Who wore the goat mask?'

'Sir Richard Ferrers, of course,' said Lestrade. 'No wonder he had been so keen to insist his people were not involved.'

'So who killed Charlie Reader?' Emma asked.

Lestrade shrugged. 'For all I know, they all did. I think Professor Murray was right. Reader was not one of the circle. But he was a Peeping Tom. He'd have blown the gaff on their secret doings.' He remembered without relish Miss Trenchard's secret doings. It almost made his plaster curl. 'But of course I had no proof. Certainly Miss Newington seemed genuinely shocked to have stumbled across the body. . . .'

'But that didn't mean she didn't have a hand in it, merely that she didn't know where the body had been left,' Emma said.

Lestrade winked at her. 'That's my girl,' he said.

'What happened to the witches?' Letitia asked.

'I thought witchcraft was still a hanging offence,' said Ivo.

'So it is, in theory,' said Lestrade. 'But up there, on that bleak hillside, what harm were they doing? All we could get them on was behaving in a lewd and lascivious manner likely to lead to a breach of the peace. Then the letter came.'

'Letter?' Harry repeated. 'Sholto, you mean this was another in the series . . .?'

'Which ended with Tom Berkeley's death?' Lestrade looked at Fanny. Her eyes widened for a moment, then she glided from the room. Letitia motioned everyone to stay where they were, and followed her. 'Yes, Harry,' Lestrade went on after a while, 'I believe it was. It just said: "Five for the Symbols at your Door."'

'And you've no inkling who sent it?' Emma asked.

'For a time, I supposed it was Professor Murray. There were times we could have done with her at the Yard. She denied sending it – and people like Margaret Murray are not known to lie – but she did explain it to me. The hill where we met, where Charlie Reader probably died, Long Compton Hill, and three others in the area form a five-pointed star, what the witches call a pentagram – a magic symbol. In the centre of the pentagram are the Rollright Stones.'

'But why should anybody want to point that out to you if it wasn't Professor Murray?' Emma asked.

'Why, indeed?' Lestrade whispered.

There was a silence.

The clock struck twelve. 'It's Christmas, everybody,' Ivo announced.

'Ho ho ho,' said Lestrade.

Hell's Bells

The rooks flapped westwards on that first day of 1913. Sholto Lestrade watched them go, shrieking and wheeling above the naked elms. He brought his eyes down to the dark silhouette of Tom Berkeley's house, its sad windows glimmering here and there with light.

Mrs M'Travers curtsied as Stalker helped him out of the taxi and across the hall.

'Happy New Year,' he said to them both, though there was nothing to cheer the moment. Stalker installed him in the study and brought the papers he asked for and left the decanter. Lestrade was alone with his thoughts, the labyrinthine twists in a tale he could not follow. He looked at the daunting pile of the dead chief constable's papers and his own reflection in the cut glass and the firelight. He turned up the lamp and tackled the mail first. Letters of condolence, addressed to Fanny. These he left on one side. Perhaps she'd be able to read them one day. Christmas cards, addressed cruelly to Tom Berkeley by those who had not heard the news. And there was one letter addressed to Lestrade. It said simply: 'Two, Two, the Lilywhite Boys.' He sat back, jarring his leg again, and swigged from the glass to dull the pain. Who were the two? And boys? Lilywhite? What new senseless twist was this? What incomprehensible pointless taunt?

'Happy New Year, Sholto,' a soft voice floated from the door.

He turned to see a silhouette.

'Fanny.' He held out his hand to her, as he had that day at the lake when Tom Berkeley had died. She crossed to him, with faltering steps at first, then threw herself into his lap and cried and cried. He ran his fingers over the golden hair and the sobbing body.

'I thought you were staying at Harry and Letitia's,' he said.

'I was.' She sat up, wiping away the tears. 'After you left, I couldn't bear it. I'd lost one of the men I loved more than anything else in the world, and as you went I thought I'd lost the other. I've been cruel, Sholto. Silent and cruel.'

'No.' He stroked her hair. 'I understood. We all did.'

'The last few weeks. . . .'

'I know, I know.'

She produced a handkerchief and blew her nose until the windows rattled. She looked at the red-eyed policeman in front of her. 'So, Superintendent Lestrade, who killed my father?'

'Happy New Year,' he said. 'Welcome home, Fanny' – and he kissed her.

Lestrade was on show that Saturday. The banns were about to be read. The superintendent was the toast of the village. People had heard of dark doings at the chief constable's residence, but it was a new year. A new start. Fanny Berkeley had come home, radiant as ever, and life could go on.

The church of St Anselm was about to celebrate its fifth century, a record the MCC would no doubt envy. Norman Penhaligon had polished his head and had had his collars starched. The church was a veritable bed of flowers, and Fanny had promised to join the choir in a celebration of music, religious and festive, to mark the occasion. Horatius Rivers, the well-known conductor, had been persuaded by the vicar to arrange, and the organist had been told he'd have to accept it or he'd end up relegated to blowing up his own bellows.

It was a glorious morning when Fanny pushed Sholto along the gravel path to the church. At the lychgate, Jane Penhaligon stopped them.

'Fanny. I heard you were back. It's good to see you.'

Fanny smiled. 'Thank you, Jane. Are you singing this morning?'

'I wouldn't miss it for the world,' she said. 'Sholto, how are you?'

'Well, Jane, thank you. Fanny, would you go on, dearest? I'd like a word with Jane.'

'Of course,' Fanny smiled. If she was at all put out by the request, it didn't show. 'I'll be inside. Stalker's there to help you with the steps, Sholto.'

They watched her swing with a lighter step than Lestrade had ever hoped to see again up the path to the mellow grey Perpendicular arch of St Anselm's.

'Jane,' said Lestrade.

She held her fingers to his lips. 'Don't,' she said. 'It doesn't matter.'

'But it does,' he told her, fidgeting with the bowler on his lap. 'What happened between us. . . .'

She leaned over him, the feathers of her hat tickling his nose. 'Was the most natural thing in the world,' she said. 'Now you have your Fanny and I have . . . I have Norman.'

'But that's not enough for you, is it, Jane?'

She looked at him, and a darkness swept over her face he had not seen before. 'After today, Sholto, it won't matter.'

He raised a hand to ask her what she meant, but she had gone, swaying her hips as she flounced into the porch. Long-suffering Constable Stalker came out to wheel Lestrade the rest of the way.

'I'm putting your intended here,' Jane Penhaligon said to Fanny. 'Out of the way.' She patted the Donegal. 'It's the warmest part of the church, Sholto. The sun catches the font beautifully, don't you think?'

He had to admit that it did. The nave swept before him, full now of milling choristers in their crimson and white. 'Two, Two, the Lilywhite Boys,' flitted like a ghost in his mind.

'We'd better take our places,' said Jane to Fanny. 'Mr Rivers does not like to be kept waiting. Enjoy the practice, Sholto. Just think,' she said, looking up to the wooden ceiling above him, 'the bells up there were struck when Henry V was King, the year the Dauphin sent him those tennis balls.'

Fanny kissed his cheek and went with Jane towards the choir-stalls. He saw them pause halfway down, the sunlight falling on them, the golden hair and the black. Fanny turned and smiled. 'Look, Jane,' she said. 'You wouldn't think that man was a bulwark against crime, would you?'

Jane looked sad. 'There is so much crime,' she said, 'so much evil. I wonder if Sholto is enough.'

The mighty organ of St Anselm's struck up, causing the very foundations of the building to rattle. Mr Rivers, elegant in frock-coat, cut away much after the manner of aficionados of the opera, took his place on the dais below the altar. He tapped with his stick on the lectern, and the choir burst into hymn. Lestrade sat, warm and for the first time in a long time happy, letting the harmonies wash over him – 'All People That on Earth Do Dwell'.

'I've put something new in,' he heard Mr Rivers tell the choir when the organ stopped. 'It's called the Dilly Song. I expect one or two of you will know it. For those who don't, it's on your song-sheets, page three. And . . . one, two, three, four. . . .'

The organ struck up again. This time, the roof above Lestrade visibly creaked and a small flake of plaster landed on his shoulder. He brushed it off, tapping his good foot in time to the jaunty air wafting through the church. St Anselm's hadn't heard such a rollock in years. The older eyebrows among the choir lifted a little.

'Wait, stop!' It was Mrs Penhaligon who was shouting out. The music died away, with much muttering and exhalation from the pipes and the screen that fronted them.

'Mr Rivers,' Lestrade heard Jane say, 'this is not on the original programme. I'm not sure the vicar would approve.'

Rivers ignored the chorused 'Hear hears' from the stalls and silenced them with a tap of his baton.

'Your husband gave me *carte blanche,* Mrs Penhaligon,' he said
tartly. 'May I remind you that *I* am musical director here.
A-n-d, one, two, three, four. . . .'

Jane Penhaligon resumed her place in the choir. Lestrade could
not see it, but Fanny could. The flashing eyes in the dark face,
suddenly sharp and wild. They frightened her.

'I'll sing you one-o,' burst forth the left-hand stalls of the
choir.

'Green grow the rushes-o,' burst forth the other.

The plaster dropped again on to Lestrade's shoulder. One,
two, several pieces. He glanced up. The planks seemed not to be
too secure. He shifted in his Bath chair. Perhaps it might be
wiser to move a little. He was getting as dusty as the tombs in
the crypt.

'What is your one-o?' demanded the left-hand choir.

'One is one and all alone and evermore shall be so.'

Lestrade found he could not move. The medieval tiles at his
feet were uneven, and the wheels of the chair were jammed
behind them. The plaster falling was now landing with audible
crashes. One or two of the choir had noticed and were distracted
by it.

'I'll sing you two-o,' they sang.

'What are your two-o?' the other stalls challenged them.

Lestrade was too busy wrestling with his controls to hear the
answer.

'Two, two, the lilywhite boys, clothèd all in green, oh, ho.
One is one and all alone and evermore shall be so.'

Fanny had not noticed Lestrade's predicament. She was too
close to the organ to hear the groaning timbers. Neither had she
read ahead in her music. Only Jane's smouldering eyes and
heaving breasts fascinated her. Surely Mr Rivers's alteration of
the arrangements couldn't have upset her so much?

'I'll sing you three-o,' the choir went on relentlessly. 'Green
grow the rushes-o.'

'What are your three-o?' Lestrade now began to feel the rising
sense of panic. The bells above the flimsy ceiling were groaning

and clanging like some demented blacksmith's shop.

'Three, three, the rivals,' he heard the choir shrill, and the shock made him stop struggling.

'Two, two, the lilywhite boys, clothèd all in green, oh ho. One is one and all alone and evermore shall be so.'

Lestrade was staring straight ahead at the choir, his mouth hanging open and plaster, lath and timbers crashing all around him.

'I'll sing you four-o,' the choir went on, but their concentration was wavering. Fanny had *heard* the words now, for the first time. Surely, they were the same words that Sholto had been talking about. The words in the meaningless notes he had been receiving for years. She looked at Jane Penhaligon. Her face was a mask of evil, contorted, shining, and she was looking down the nave towards Sholto. Sholto! When Fanny saw him, he was disappearing under masonry. The choir began to scream in a variety of sharps and flats. Fanny broke out of her stall and rushed headlong down the polished nave, calling his name.

Lestrade swung both hands across to release the brake. Mr Rivers, alone to hold his place, still had his back to the pandemonium and was now singing a solo, at a loss to understand the sudden exodus.

'Four for the Gospel-Makers,' he called out and lost the top note as he realised the situation.

With a squeal, Lestrade's Bath chair bucked forward, and he whizzed the length of the nave, bowling over Fanny and sundry choristers as though they were ninepins. He himself somersaulted on to Mr Rivers and ended up with the conductor's baton up his left nostril. Such was the impact of his collision and the shock that accompanied it that he had not heard the Great St Anselm Bell of 1413 drop with a last groan on to the font, shattering it and the floor below. In the tangle of ropes and splintered wood, but for the grace and ingenuity of Frank Hornby, would have lain Sholto Lestrade.

Rivers pointed weakly to the debris in the rising dust and whispered in Lestrade's ear: 'Ask not for whom the bell tolls. It may fall on thee.'

Fanny was with him in seconds, lifting him upright. Stalker was there, too, resurrecting fallen bodies, scrambling over the wreckage.

'Fanny, are you all right?' Lestrade asked.

'Yes, Sholto. The song. Did you hear the song?'

'I did, Fanny. I did. Stalker. Get me to that bell.'

'Be careful, Sholto,' Fanny held his arm.

'Keep back, all of you,' he growled at the quivering choir. 'Stalker, the rope.'

The constable braced the superintendent against a pillar and took the frayed end.

'Cut,' said Lestrade levelly. 'Stalker, get me up those steps. Put me in my chair. Then do what you can here. Look after Miss Berkeley.'

'Very good, sir.'

'Sholto' – Fanny held him upright – 'where are you going?'

'Where I should have gone a long time ago, Fanny,' he said, and wiped the tears from her cheeks. 'I shan't be long.'

'Wherever it is, I'm going with you. You can't manage.'

'No,' he snapped, then gentler: 'This is my kind of game, Fanny. I know how to play it. It's always played alone.'

She held his hands until Stalker lifted Lestrade to the saddle of his machine. Like a knight errant, Donegal in tatters, white with plaster, Sir Sholto Lestrade rode out of the church to do battle with dragons.

'Mr Rivers,' he called back to the dazed conductor stumbling into the sunlight. 'Tell me, what does the Dilly Song say about Number Eleven?'

'Eleven?' Rivers looked confused. 'Er. . . .' He tried to focus his scrambled brain. 'Eleven for the eleven who went to heaven,' he said.

Lestrade smiled grimly. 'Of course,' he said and steered south.

The Reverend Penhaligon was inspecting his rosebeds in the way vicars do when Superintendent Lestrade came calling.

'Dear me, Sholto. You're somewhat . . . somewhat dishevelled,' he said.

'Is your wife in, Norman?' Lestrade asked.

Penhaligon registered that this was not a social call.

'Why, no, Sholto. Jane is at the church.'

'She was,' said Lestrade. 'You didn't hear the noise of falling bells?'

'Falling bells? An accident! Dear God.' He suddenly paled. 'Is she all right?'

'I don't know,' he said. 'She wasn't to be found in the church when I left.'

'Sholto. . . .' Penhaligon was lost for words.

'Are you looking for me?' The voice made the vicar turn. Jane Penhaligon stood motionless on the steps beside the rockery.

'I have a few questions to ask you, Jane.'

'Jane?' Penhaligon looked anxiously at her.

'You'd better come inside,' she said.

Lestrade negotiated the drive admirably, but he was at a loss at the steps. 'I have a stick here, Sholto,' Penhaligon said. 'That can be one crutch and I shall be the other' – and he helped him into the drawing room. They all sat down.

'How long had you known Gordon Ushant?' Lestrade asked her.

'Who?' Jane remained cool and arch.

'I hadn't realised that you habitually wore black, Mrs Penhaligon. Gordon Ushant was until recently the chief constable of Rutland. He was killed – his throat was cut, to be precise – by an attractive woman wearing black.'

'Sholto!' Penhaligon stood up in shock and outrage.

'I'm sorry, Norman,' he said. 'There is no easy way to do this. I only wish there were. Tell me, Mrs Penhaligon, were you a genuine patient of Dr Edmund Lucas or was he another of your conquests?'

'Conquests?' Penhaligon was lost. 'Jane, what is he talking about?'

She stood up and walked to the window. 'You'd better ask the superintendent,' she said, staring blankly out across the frosty sun-kissed fields of the morning. 'He seems to have all the answers.'

'Tell me,' said Lestrade, 'when did you realise you'd lost the earring? And when did it dawn on you you'd left it in Ushant's study? And what sort of disguise did you use when you followed Tom Berkeley to the toy fair? Clever of you to design the Meccano crossbow, but somebody had to fire it, to release the catch at just the right moment.'

She turned to face him, smiling coldly. 'What made you realise it was me, Sholto?' she asked.

'Something hadn't sat well from the start. You were not what you claimed to be, Jane. A vicar's wife who is not the life and soul of the tea-party; who is unknown to most people in her husband's parish; the way you were' – he paused, reluctant – 'free with your favours.'

Norman Penhaligon dropped his head into his hands.

'I couldn't understand at first why you were so upset when Mr Rivers introduced the Dilly Song. When I heard the words I realised. By sheer chance the man was giving me the clues – all the letters you'd sent me over the years. It was your idea to place my chair under the bell-tower. Did you prise up the floor tiles yourself? They were a very effective obstacle for a moment. Ingenious, too, to cut the bell rope just so, so that with a little time and the resonance of the organ and choir, the lot would come down. But, then, you are a clever woman, aren't you? A brilliant touch to leave a cigar-stub burning in Dr Lucas's rooms. That threw me for a while.'

She walked towards him, between her silent husband and Lestrade. 'Yes, Sholto,' she purred, 'I am clever. How old would you say I am?'

He looked up at the curving figure, the long, sweet, dark hair. 'Thirty-one or -two,' he said.

'Flatterer!' she trilled. 'I am in fact thirty-six. How is your mental arithmetic?'

He looked blank under the plaster, both on his leg and all over his shoulders.

'When was I born?' She leaned over him.

He frowned. Mr Poulson's Academy had been a long time ago. His eyes widened.

'Let me do it for you,' she said. '1877. I was born in the year of the trial of the detectives. The year you received the letter which said: "Eight for the Eight Bold Rangers." I *was* forward, wasn't I? And as for the letters which spoke of twelve, ten and nine; well . . . they were nothing short of miraculous. . . .'

'For which', Penhaligon spoke for the first time, 'you need a man of God.'

Jane moved silently to one side to reveal Norman sitting there with a Webley Mark IV nestling in his hand.

Lestrade gulped. 'As I suspected,' he bluffed.

Penhaligon laughed. 'Suspected? Lestrade, you wouldn't suspect the entire inmate population of Wormwood Scrubs. You see, you really should leave it to the amateurs after all, shouldn't you? Father Brown would have you for breakfast.'

'It looks as though I shall have to arrest you both,' Lestrade said.

Both Penhaligons laughed this time. 'It won't really come to that, will it, Sholto?' Norman said, raising the gun. Lestrade raised his hand.

'May I at least know', he said, 'why? The Dilly Song? What was the point of it all?'

Norman looked at Jane. 'Go on,' she said. 'A dying man's last request after all.'

'Ashes to ashes,' Norman smiled gravely. 'Very well, Lestrade. To put what tiny mind you may possess at ease. I wouldn't want you to meet your Maker unprepared.'

Lestrade checked his situation. He had a stick and a switchblade. And he had a broken leg. Against him were two strong people, perfectly mobile. Perfectly homicidal. Probably mad. And one of them had a gun. There was about to be a Murder at the Vicarage.

'So Jane made love to you?' Penhaligon transferred the revolver to his other hand and poured brandies, one for himself, one for Jane.

'Well . . . er. . . .'

'Oh, come, Lestrade,' Penhaligon scoffed. 'No call to be coy, man. Especially now.'

'She's still your wife,' said Lestrade.

'Not exactly,' chuckled Norman. Jane took the brandy and sat on the arm of the sofa cradling her arm around him. 'Jane is my little sister. I rather liked her line to you that night at Tom Berkeley's. . . . What was it, Jane?'

She leaned forward in that soft way she had. 'He never touches me, Sholto.'

'Quite so,' Penhaligon smiled. 'Well, it wouldn't be right, would it? Something else you'd missed, Lestrade,' he beamed. 'We've met before, you know.'

'Oh?'

'It was a hot day in the summer of 1875, at Victoria Station if my memory serves me correctly. Of course, I had a false beard on and you were in a hurry. I tackled a railway guard you were following and gave the name of Hugh N. Crigh. Not being a student of medieval criminology, you didn't understand that.'

Lestrade blinked. 'Hue and Cry,' he said.

'It's a little late now, Sholto,' Jane told him.

'I still don't see your motive. What of the letters?'

Penhaligon stood up. 'In the beginning,' he said, 'the word was Palmer.' He spun round on the crippled detective. 'Are you getting my drift?'

Lestrade's heart sank. 'Inspector Palmer?' he asked.

Penhaligon nodded. 'It all began as a joke, really. William was a good policeman, Lestrade. Better than you could ever be. He told us about a rookie constable who had joined his patch, back in seventy-three, a man of my own age, slightly older, by the name of Lestrade.'

'You were the younger brother, off to the University. Going in for the cloth?'

'I was. William told me about that old idiot Claverhouse. I was an idealist in those days, Lestrade. I thought it was shocking that you should have taken a bribe to cover things up. To hide the fact that he had been found dead in a brothel.'

'That's what William told you?'

Penhaligon nodded. 'So I remembered the Apostle Club and the last line of the Dilly Song we had learned as children: "Twelve for the Twelve Apostles." It fitted with unerring accuracy. I sent it to you, to prick your conscience, to see if you would admit your duplicity, salve your soul. . . . You didn't.'

'Go on.' Lestrade slid inexorably downwards. His one hope was to get that gun from Penhaligon.

'Then came Hesketh.' Penhaligon poured himself another drink while Jane sat in a chair behind Lestrade. The superintendent couldn't see what she was doing, and that bothered him. 'He was a tragedy, that man. A simple dupe. He loved his wife, and she played a cruel trick on him. A trick that became fatal, as it happened. Again, despite my letter – "Ten for the Ten Commandments" – you did nothing.'

'There was nothing to be done,' said Lestrade. 'Hesketh himself realised that.'

'You aren't listening, Lestrade.' Penhaligon suddenly slapped him savagely round the head. 'You weren't then and you aren't now. Oh, ye of little faith! So' – the venomous vicar straightened – 'I decided to make you take notice. You were the worst sort of scum, Lestrade. A crooked copper without a shred of remorse. You didn't know the meaning of the word *justice*.'

'So you engineered the downfall of Valentine Baker?' Lestrade asked. 'Do you call that justice?'

'Perhaps, perhaps not. I was testing you, man. Seeing what you'd do. How far you'd go.'

'I almost got myself killed,' Lestrade snapped.

Penhaligon rested with his back to the window. 'Yes, you did. I nearly relented there. I of course was the clergyman whose carriage Miss Dickinson took refuge in from the rapacious beast. Poor Baker! All he did was tip his hat to her. When the train reached Victoria I dashed off in search of a policeman. We already knew it was your beat and that you would be the nearest on hand when the train arrived. I just had time to put on my false beard and I couldn't resist introducing myself to you – call it a little conceit. Clever of you to realise that Miss Dickinson had other callings.' His face darkened. 'She was always such a wayward girl. . . .'

'And so the Bright Shiner was brought down?'

'Yes. Then, Lestrade' – Penhaligon crossed and placed the cold muzzle of the Webley beside the superintendent's ear – 'then you put William in the frame.'

'If you're talking about the Trial of the Detectives, he put himself there,' said Lestrade. 'He and Meiklejohn and Druscovich. They all did. Don't you realise, Penhaligon, Palmer, whatever your name is, all this has been based on a lie?'

'Shut up, Lestrade!' Jane hissed behind him, and he felt the other side of his head ringing with a slap.

'You,' Penhaligon roared. 'You should have been in that dock, not William. Do you know what it did to him? He was a good policeman, Lestrade, a great policeman. You broke him. You know what happened to him, Lestrade? To William?'

The superintendent did not dare risk a shrug, facing a hair trigger as he was.

'He died three months ago.' Tears ran down Penhaligon's face. 'Chained to a wall in the Bethlehem Hospital.'

'The Asylum, Lambeth,' echoed Lestrade. 'The postmark of the letters. You posted some from there?'

'I did,' said Jane. 'Poor William was my half-brother. I was the child of our father's second marriage. But I shared Norman's resolve.'

'His obsession, do you mean?' Lestrade asked.

Jane held Penhaligon's shaking arm. 'It got so bad that Norman could not bear to visit him. So I went. What those visits cost me, I cannot begin to describe.' She shuddered.

'And you stopped on one of them to buy earrings from Bodley the jeweller in Austria Street,' Lestrade guessed, though Bodley's books had not been helpful.

She looked at him. 'A pity you couldn't have put your information to better use.'

'From then on, Lestrade,' said Penhaligon, 'it was open season on you and your appalling lack of talent. It galled me I was not available always to goad and worry you. That's why the letters – and the cases – came erratically. For much of my career, I have served overseas.'

'In the Indian Ocean?' Lestrade asked.

'Yes,' Penhaligon smiled through the tears. 'Dear old Arnold. Fancies himself a criminologist. Jane didn't kill your Tom Berkeley. I did. I built the Meccano contraption. I realised it wouldn't look out of place at a toy fair. Arnold was inches from me when I released the catch. Of course, he saw nothing.'

'That's what comes of reading all that Conan Doyle,' Lestrade still had the wits to observe.

'Jonas King was next. I was playing it by the song, you see. "The Seven Stars in the Sky." The music-hall was full of stars. It was I who organised the charity performances Ben Battle was in.'

'You were one of the chokers?'

'Ah,' Penhaligon smiled. 'The working-class cant.'

'I wouldn't call Battle that,' said Lestrade.

'I could have chosen Battle, Vance, Leybourne, any of them. King was a bastard. Of all of them, he deserved to go.'

'You were the ghost in the gallery?' Lestrade asked.

Penhaligon looked up at Jane. 'I don't know what you're talking about.'

'Never mind,' said Lestrade. 'Let me see if I can fill in the rest. You were the Reverend Norbert Parker, chaplain to the Coldstreams, who sent that malicious note destined to drive Wesley Willoughby to his death?'

'I was. If you look up the pages of *Crockford's,* Lestrade, you will see I appear in several guises.'

'And you employed Charlie Reader as a gardener?'

'In the neighbouring parish of Long Compton, yes. I knew about Ferrers's pathetic little charade at the Rollright Stones. It was indecent, immoral. I wanted it stopped.'

'You could have reported it to the police,' Lestrade suggested.

'I did. I mentioned your name to old Dunstan. I knew he'd call you in. But you just smacked their wrists, didn't you, Lestrade?'

'Just as well, considering that you'd killed Charlie Reader.'

'No, Lestrade.' He grinned at Jane. 'That wasn't me.'

Lestrade felt a shiver at his back. It was Penhaligon who held the gun, but the female of the Palmer species at his shoulder-blade was decidedly more deadly than the male.

'And of course', Lestrade said, 'you unleashed your little sister here on Edmund Lucas and Gordon Ushant, both of them susceptible to female charms. Tell me, Jane.' He half-turned to her. 'Did you practise with Norman's gun here? And how does it feel to slit a man's throat?'

Jane shuddered. 'They got what they deserved,' she said.

'Tom Berkeley didn't deserve to die,' Lestrade told them both.

'Neither did my brother, not the way he did,' hissed Penhaligon, jamming the pistol against Lestrade's head for a second time. 'Whimpering like a kicked dog. I vowed vengeance,' he snarled. 'Vengeance on the head of Sholto Lestrade. Oh, it's taken me a while. But it's been worth it. You know, Lestrade, I've almost enjoyed it. Twelve for the twelve apostles, the disciples of Our Lord. Eleven, Lestrade, the letter I couldn't send – until now – for the eleven who went to heaven. Count them if you like. Ten for the Ten Commandments you broke with so little thought, abusing the trust society had placed in you. Nine for the nine angels, the mystic number of great power. It stands for journeys, Lestrade. Did you know that? A fatal train journey for Valentine Baker, eh? Eight, Lestrade,' he intoned as though reading a funeral ode. 'Eight is the number of Justice of which you understand so little. It is also the symbol of eternity to which you are going. Seven – ah, the most powerful of all numbers.' He paced the floor in a tightening circle, his voice rising in intensity. Lestrade sensed Jane quivering behind him. 'The planets – the Sun and the Moon.'

Good God, thought Lestrade, Bandicoot had been right after

all. He was pleased to have witnessed that before he died.

'Six' – the gun barrel whirled around his head – 'is a Dreamer of Dreams. The days Our Lord took to build the Earth. Five, the Senses you so clearly lack. A dangerous number, Lestrade. It vacillates from past to future, future to past. Four, four for the Gospel-Makers. Matthew, Mark, Luke and John, bless the bed that I lie on. And if I die before I wake I pray the Lord my soul to take.'

The gun clicked into position.

'Three?' Lestrade squawked, desperate to keep Penhaligon going for a few seconds more.

'Three the Trinity, the Cosmic Breath. Father, Son and Holy Ghost, world without end. Two, two the lilywhite boys,' he broke into hysterical song, 'clothèd all in green, oh ho. The Good Book, Lestrade – the Testaments Old and New – which I doubt you've ever opened.'

The gun came level with Lestrade's eyes. He heard no sound now but the thump of his own blood.

'One?' he shouted.

'One is one,' said Penhaligon, suddenly calm, 'and all alone and evermore shall be so. One is the Godhead, Lestrade, the root of all things. It is also you. Totally alone at last. Blasphemous, isn't it? But, then, your life has been one long blasphemy.'

He held the Webley rock-steady in his fist. 'Abyssinia,' he said and pulled the trigger.

Instinctively, Lestrade's arm jerked up, smashing into Penhaligon's pistol, so that the shot went wide. Lestrade threw himself forward, lunging upwards from the Donegal with the blade of his Apache knife. He felt the steel rip through cloth and flesh and grind against bone as his full weight brought Penhaligon down. He rolled back to face the murderous sister, but Jane Penhaligon was sliding down the wall behind him, blood trickling from her nose and mouth.

Lestrade crawled over to her as she reached the floor.

'Jane, I'll get a doctor,' he hissed, fighting for breath.

She shook her head, coughing blood from her ruptured lungs.

'Sholto, Norman . . . Norman didn't tell you everything,' she gasped.

He cradled her head. 'It doesn't matter, Jane. Try not to talk.'

'Sholto. . . .' She smiled. 'In a strange sort of way, I'm glad.' Her eyes widened. 'I haven't killed anybody,' she said. 'Not anybody.'

She slumped forward against his chest. There had indeed been Murder at the Vicarage.

That night, by the embers of the fire, Lestrade sat alone. His mind was racing. Exhausted, worn out beyond sleep, he had not eaten. Fanny, too, numbed by the events of the day and his narration of it, was lying silent, in the darkness of her room. At least, she told herself, it was over. If happiness could be salvaged from the whole tragic affair, then it lay with the man downstairs.

Lestrade lit a cigar, and to calm his mind he riffled vacantly through Tom Berkeley's papers, the great and daunting task he had put off for days. His eyes fell on a document in Tom's handwriting and pinned to another, typewritten and official. The curious thing about the letter was that it was unfinished. And so absorbed was he by the contents that he didn't hear the door click behind him or the faint rustle of a skirt. 'My God,' he murmured as the realisation of Tom's letter hit him.

There was a scream from the door in front. He looked up to see Fanny there, staring in horror at something behind Lestrade's head. Instinctively he rolled to the right, in time to see an axe blade whistle past his face and bury itself in the desk-top. He scrabbled upright behind the desk and brought his arm down with all the strength he had left on the crossbow Frank Hornby had made in eight minutes and three-quarters. The deadly bolt hissed across the darkened room and thudded into the solid bulk of Mrs M'Travers. The axe dropped from her hand, and her eyes crossed as she went down.

Fanny dashed to Lestrade and held him to her, crying uncontrollably.

'Sholto, Sholto. What's happening? I didn't realise poor Mrs M'Travers was dangerous.'

He helped her out of the room and bellowed for Stalker, who appeared dutifully at the double, nightshirt flapping.

'Perhaps she thought I was a fly,' said Lestrade. 'Stalker. In there.' He pointed to the study and sat down beside Fanny in the drawing room. 'It's all there,' he said, 'in your father's papers. And I hadn't checked them. What a perfect idiot! Perhaps Penhaligon was right when he talked of my appalling lack of talent.'

'Why, Sholto?' She choked back the tears. 'I don't understand.'

'Tom was going to have Mrs M'Travers committed. To do so he needed to find out details. She either wouldn't or couldn't tell him, so he went to Somerset House. That was what he found out the day he died. That was why he was going to London to see me. Look.' He held the paper up to the light.

'Her maiden name was Palmer,' Fanny said in astonishment.

Lestrade nodded. 'That's what Norman meant when he said: "We had learned the Dilly Song as children." But he wasn't a child when Jane was. He was in his twenties when she was born. He was talking about Mrs M'Travers, his other sister.'

'My God.'

'And that's what Jane meant when she said Norman hadn't told me everything. She said she didn't kill anybody. And I don't believe she did. Oh, she seduced Gordon Ushant all right, but on the night in question, I believe, it was Mrs M'Travers under the black veil. It needed a powerful woman to cut that man's throat. I doubt whether Jane could have done it.'

'And she who shot Dr Lucas?'

'Probably. We'll never know, I'm afraid. Come with me.' Fanny helped Lestrade back to the study. 'Stalker, get me more light here, will you?' Lestrade began to dab at the dead woman's face with a handkerchief. 'My God,' he said.

'What is it, Sholto?' Fanny asked.

'Meet Miss Hannah Dickinson,' he said.

Fanny looked perplexed. 'The girl on the train, with Valentine Baker?' she said.

'The years have not been kind,' Lestrade nodded. 'I would never have guessed. How long had the M'Traverses been with you?' he asked.

'About a year,' she said. 'Do you think M'Travers knew?'

'That she was a Palmer and mad as a hatter? I doubt it. I don't think the shotgun business was intentional. Mrs M'Travers meant that for Tom all right. Poor Tom. He couldn't have known he was only a pawn in the game they were playing for me.'

She helped him up and held him close, nuzzling her head into his chest. 'Is the game over now, Sholto? Is it?'

He patted her head. 'Yes,' he whispered. 'Yes.' And he turned to Stalker. 'Your name isn't Palmer, is it?' he asked.

On a spring morning in that year of 1913, Superintendent Sholto Lestrade alighted from the Clapham omnibus, along with the rest of mankind, and bounded up the steps into New Scotland Yard. Sergeant 'Buildings' Peabody stood to attention as he swept past.

'Nice to see you back, guv'nor,' he saluted.

'I prefer to see your back, too, Peabody,' Lestrade countered.

'I was just wondering, sir,' Sergeant Blevvins hailed him, 'when we'll be allowed to get down to some serious interrogation of witnesses.'

Lestrade paused and whipped a leather cosh from the sergeant's pocket. 'Not for a while yet, I'm afraid,' he said, and threw it in the wastepaper-basket. Sergeants Jones and Dickens straightened as he entered the outer portals of his office. Chief Inspector Dew took his feet off the desk, and a young constable brought them both steaming mugs.

'Thank you, Constable Dew,' Lestrade said. 'Nearly as good as your old man.'

'Thank you, son.' Walter winked at the boy.

'About the Lucas case.' Lestrade stopped the retreating

constable. Dews senior and junior froze. Lestrade fished in his inside pocket. 'Have a cigar,' he said.

'Excuse me, Superintendent.' Jones put his encyclopaedic head round the door. 'Sir Edward Henry would like a word.'

Lestrade stood up. 'His wish is my command, Sergeant' – and he bowed to Chief Inspector Dew before dashing for the stairs.

'Late again, Frank?' he threw at the puffing head of the Serious Crimes Squad, who was at that moment staggering up the stairs, too.

'You married types,' grunted Froest. 'You're all the same.'

Lestrade knocked on the frosted glass which said in bevelled letters: 'Assistant Commissioner's Office.'

'Come!' called Sir Edward Henry.

The superintendent did. He stood for a moment, rooted to the spot.

'I believe you know this young lady, my new personal secretary.'

'Hello, Daddy.' Emma bounded over and kissed his cheek. 'I'm. . . .'

'I know,' he said, holding up his hand. 'Helping the police with their enquiries.'

They both laughed.

'Right, Lestrade,' said Edward Henry, who had the sense of humour of an old sofa. 'Now you've had plenty of time to convalesce, how about getting down to some work?'